THE
LACE
WIDOW

THE
LACE
WIDOW

AN ELIZA HAMILTON
MYSTERY

Mollie Ann Cox

CROOKED
LANE

NEW YORK

Copyright © 2023 by Mollie Cox Bryan

Published in the United States by Crooked Lane Books, an imprint of The Quick Brown Fox & Company LLC.

Crooked Lane Books and its logo are trademarks of The Quick Brown Fox & Company LLC.

Library of Congress Catalog-in-Publication data available upon request.

ISBN (hardcover): 978-1-63910-528-1
ISBN (ebook): 978-1-63910-529-8

Cover design by Lynn Andreozzi

Printed in the United States.

www.crookedlanebooks.com

Crooked Lane Books
34 West 27th St., 10th Floor
New York, NY 10001

First Edition: December 2023

10 9 8 7 6 5 4 3 2 1

This book is dedicated in memory of Eliza Hamilton, wife of Alexander Hamilton, gatherer and keeper of stories, and one of the important Mothers of the United States of America.

"Best of wives and best of Women"
—Alexander Hamilton in his final letter to his wife

This book is also dedicated to the lacemakers, weavers, and craftswomen who found solace and a slice of freedom through their artisanship and hard work.

CHAPTER 1

New York City, 1804

Eliza Hamilton focused on the milky-gray pigeons circling Trinity Church's spire. She strained for a good view from the carriage window as her sons William and John slumped onto their sister, Angel, snoring lightly against her. Now, sweaty, spent, and rumpled, the children had behaved well through the entire ordeal of a day.

The birds flew downward to the graveyard. Eliza twisted around to watch the spire until it disappeared from her view, as if somehow she'd glimpse her husband—now dead for ten days. As if by her staring hard enough, he'd rise from the ground, wrap his arms around her with his familiar warmth and comfort, and tell her the duel and his murder were the worst kind of jest.

Eliza's throat tightened. She swallowed hard, but a sob escaped. Angel sat forward and patted her lap. Hot tears sprang and Eliza twisted her mouth, trying to hold it in.

Her bones ached with each bump the carriage wheels hit along Wall Street, heading toward Bloomingdale Road along the North River and their Harlem home, the Grange. Away from the noise, crowds, and smells of the city, Eliza and Hamilton had found respite at last at their uptown home. She'd hated to leave their little paradise, but her business was timely: justice for Aaron Burr must be swift.

Angel slid forward on the seat. "Mama, why did the lady talk about Papa like that?"

Why, indeed? Eliza shuddered. How could she explain this to her daughter? At just nineteen, Angel, named after her Aunt Angelica, was an innocent. Besides, with the death of her older brother Philip, two years ago, Angel had suffered a nervous collapse. She'd not recovered. Now, with the loss of her father, Eliza worried Angel would never live a normal life. Eliza had considered leaving her daughter at home for the day, but it unsettled her not to have Angel nearby. Only Eliza could calm her daughter's spells.

Eliza contemplated her words, trying to keep an even and optimistic tone. "I don't know. But we changed her position, and that's the important thing, my dear. We've done everything we can to see that New York society shuns Aaron Burr."

"But how could Lady Collins not have realized Burr murdered our father?" Angel wiped her brow with the back of her sleeve.

Murder. Eliza drew inward, crumpling into herself, almost as if she'd been punched. There she wanted to remain, but as she looked at her young sons asleep and her daughter's emphatic face, she searched her mind for the right words.

"I don't know, but we must make them all realize. We will find justice for his death. If it's the last thing I do. We'll continue to campaign against Burr. We can't trust our fledgling judicial system. If left to his own devices, he'll be a free man. We can't have that." If anybody was on the fence about Burr's guilt and what his act had wrought for the Hamilton family, they no longer would be by the end of Eliza's visits. But, despite the tableau they'd presented, Eliza in widow's weeds with her children hand in hand,

Lady Collins had nothing kind to say about their dear Hamilton. She'd gone on about the "nature of duels" and the "foolishness of him not firing," even though one should never speak ill of the dead. By the end of their visit, she'd agreed that Burr must go to prison and be taken out of polite society. She also agreed that as his widow, Eliza Hamilton could mourn as she wished.

"As to the women 'guardians' of mourning traditions with their tongues wagging, I've more important matters to tend. I don't like their prying natures. If anybody should dare to think you didn't love your husband because you're not observing the strictest of the traditions, then why should you care about them?" Lady Collins's voice had lifted.

Eliza agreed. She'd not wallow in her mourning when she had work to do. They cut her husband down, but they would not cut his legacy short. She promised him. After everything he'd done in helping to forge this new country—all the sleepless nights, the sore, callused, ink-stained fingers from his countless hours of writing, and much personal turmoil—she'd see he'd be remembered well. Her husband had not been perfect. This she grasped more than anyone. Certainly more so than the brash Lady Collins. But what man or woman could lay claim to perfection?

The carriage swayed back and forth, rattling, then yanked sideways. It came to a jolting halt, throwing them left. "What's going on?" Angel clutched little William and John, now awake. "Mama? Are we being robbed?"

The boys squealed and clung closer to the weathered leather seats.

Eliza righted herself and the children. "Hush. It'll be alright." There'd been a string of robberies along the North River, but none happened in broad daylight. The carriage lifted and creaked as Davey McNally, their driver, dismounted. He quieted the startled horses, then opened the door.

"I'm sorry, m'lady. Trouble up ahead. It'll resolve soon enough, I should think." He stood, thick and sturdy as an oak, his fiery red beard glowing in the sun.

"What is it?" She poked her head out the door, straining to see through the gathering crowd.

"Nothing that a fine lady should fret about." He held his hands up as if to stop her from exiting.

"Nonsense, man. I've dressed soldier's wounds, been at the bloody bedsides of both my son and husband—and birthed nine children." Her eyes met his as her jaw tightened. "Help me out of this carriage or step aside."

"I canna let ye." He veered more into his Irish homeland accent as he crossed his arms.

Eliza ignored him, kicked down the step, moved him aside, and made her way onto the dusty street. She swallowed a mouthful of dust and dirt, coughing then slipping her lavender-scented handkerchief out of her bodice to cover her mouth and nose. Several carriages sat askew and off to the side of the cobble street. A crowd of people gathered close to the banks of the river. Constables arrived, driving a carriage with a body wagon behind, horse clomping and wagon rattling.

"Step aside," one of the constables yelled as he dismounted. Throngs of people moved in all directions. Gray, brown, and blue skirts and jackets danced in front of Eliza.

Eliza tramped through the parting crowd, careful not to catch her boot heel on a cobblestone. A swollen body lay on the ground in front of them. Hair the color of Hamilton's plastered what must be a cheek. For a split second, Eliza's mind slipped back to her husband's deathbed a mere eleven days ago, and in her mind's eye she glimpsed Hamilton there instead of the body, swollen, blue, tangled in weeds and tattered clothes. The mind and memory were strange. Shaking, she squinted her eyes against the sun.

Eliza drew in the air as sick threatened to creep up her throat. She swallowed to avoid retching on the street. She tugged at the collar of her itchy mourning dress. Air. She needed more air. The sweltering heat offered nothing for her lungs.

Several men lifted the dripping body. Eliza shifted her gaze away. The man was pulled away from the riverbank. Quite dead. She gnawed the interior of her mouth to stop from gasping, clutching her stomach to ward away the sick. What a horrible end for him—whoever he was.

As the men carried the body by her, she glimpsed the face. A pulse of recognition tormented Eliza as she studied his bloated face. Yes—he was a friend of her husband's, who'd been with him during the duel. A man who'd tried to help him, who carried his body to the boat that sailed to Manhattan and stood vigil outside the house where he died. John Van Der Gloss. She tamped down the scream caught in her throat as she caught pieces of conversation from the crowd around her.

"That's no accident."

"Look at the gash across his neck. Good Lord."

"One of the duel witnesses."

Everybody understood which duel. It was the only duel on the minds of New Yorkers. Eliza froze, unable to move. Heat rushed through her. Was this related to the duel? Why were these men discussing the duel *now*?

"Mrs. General Hamilton," Davey said, loud enough for the noisy men in the crowd to turn their heads toward her. She glared at them as she lifted her chin. The men lowered their eyes and one slithered away.

Their words sent her pulse racing. John had witnessed the duel. He'd helped her husband. She searched her mind. She'd an inkling there was more to the duel than what she knew—what anybody knew. John understood the duel, probably more than

Eliza herself. Maybe someone killed him for that reason. If that was the case, other witnesses might be harmed as well. Waves of panic jabbed at her.

She recalled the day before the duel. Hamilton had paced in their bedroom. "If anything happens to me, I want you to take the children and go to your father."

"Why are you talking like this?" Eliza's hair had pricked up on her neck.

He turned to her and cupped her hands in his. His blue eyes filled with concern and fear. "Eliza, please!"

"This is our home. Why go to my father and leave this place?"

He brought her hands to his lips. "Eliza, you know I don't like to worry you. But there have been threats. Maybe nothing more than idle ones. We simply don't know."

"Threats?" Eliza pulled away from him. "What threats? Alexander?"

"I can't get into it right now and need to go. I'm late for a meeting. We'll talk about this later. I'll tell you everything, just not now."

"Don't walk out that door, Alexander Hamilton," she said.

He turned and grimaced. "Later, I promise, my love. We need to talk about this. Just please promise that if something happens to me, you will get our children to safety."

Now, as Eliza remembered the day, and Hamilton's demeanor, she chilled. She wondered if this incident was connected to what her husband had warned her of. Where her children were concerned, she couldn't take any chances. This blow struck too close to home. She'd ready the entire family for her father's home in Albany tomorrow.

In the meantime, the constables heaved the body into a wagon. The driver hitched himself to the driver's seat and drove off with the bloated body of John Van Der Gloss jiggling behind him.

"Mrs. General Hamilton." Davey held up his arm. "May I take you back to the carriage?"

"His poor wife." She willed away a tear, swallowed the creeping pain in her throat, and grabbed Davey's arm to steady herself. Light-headed, she pulled at the top of her dress. At only forty-seven, Eliza was ill-prepared to wear widow's weeds. It didn't suit her. And she was aware that Mrs. Rose Van Der Gloss was much younger than herself. Eliza's heart broke for her. Even though she didn't know her well, they'd both lost their husbands. Eliza would pray for her.

"What do you know of this?" she asked Davey as he prepared to shut the carriage door.

"Only as much as you. I just drove by."

She refrained from poking him in the chest. "That's not what I mean. I mean the same as what that man said. That it wasn't an accident, it may have had something to do with . . ."

"Rumors, my lady. Nothing more than flapping tongues." His eyes sparked with warmth.

But a knot formed in her stomach. It was an all-too-familiar knot. Being the wife of Alexander Hamilton meant ignoring rumors and gossip if she were to find any kind of contentment. Of course, being his wife meant many other things. Those things for which she now ached. Just to have him by her side. To fall asleep once more to the rhythm of his breath.

Eliza had assumed marriage to Hamilton would be an exciting prospect. No young bride could see into the future, but on Eliza's wedding day, surrounded by her family at their home, she felt the fear of uncertainty as much as excitement. He was a man of little means, but she, her father, and a bevy of countrymen believed in his political brilliance. To be the bride of such a bright and bold man was heady. She had often asked herself if she was up to the task. The only thing she didn't question was how much she loved him. She vowed to do her best as his wife and prayed it would suffice.

And in truth, it was the love between them that saved them time and time again. Through the cold and lonely nights during the war, the months of anguish forming a new government, the ever-constant rumors, infidelity, and the death of their son Philip. Even though she'd been a practical young woman, her ideas of love and romance were those of an innocent girl. She'd struggled to think clearly, her heart racing wildly with every glance from Hamilton. Eliza's view of their love had become tempered. Of course, there had still been moments of romance—but the relationship grew deeper, filled with ordinary quiet moments as well as countless quarrels. Through it all, she'd never doubted his love for her and for their children.

His loss pierced her soul. But each time she slipped into a dark, drifting state, her children pulled her back. They needed her.

"Traffic is moving. We best be going." Davey shut the creaky door and muttered to the horses. The carriage dipped with his weight as he lifted himself to the driver's seat.

Eliza turned back to the three of her children accompanying her. Had she done right in bringing them along? She and Hamilton both agreed that it was pointless to shield them from reality. But, oh, how she wished otherwise. Sometimes she longed to take them to a remote island or mountain, where they could run free and grow unhampered by people knowing their famous father. But she could not. Her jaw clenched. The best thing was arming them with knowledge. *Your father was a great man, but he was also a good man. He loved this country, and he loved you.* Preserving his legacy was not just important for the country, it was vital for their children.

Angel raised her head from her nail-biting. "Are you well, Mama? You are quite pale."

Foreboding swept through Eliza's body, and bone thick weariness threatened at her edges. A tug of fear. A premonition of danger. "I'm fine, my dear."

And she would be.

"That's no accident." "One of the duel's witnesses." Eliza balled her hands into fists, vowing that she would not sink into mourning and fade away, like a forgotten belle. She ignored the impulse to take to her bed, to follow her husband into the grave, or simply to sob until raw. She'd already done that last week. She was the wife of a great man, the daughter of another, and was determined to conduct herself in such a manner.

CHAPTER 2

After the two-hour carriage ride home, Eliza craved nothing more than to change out of her heavy clothes and sit in the garden. Since her oldest son's death in a duel two years ago, she and Hamilton had found refuge there among the tulips, hyacinths, and lilies. He often teased her about her farming roots and how much knowledge she had retained from her youth about planting, herbal remedies, and such.

"I thought I was marrying an astute general's daughter, not a farm girl," he'd said.

"Why can't a woman be both?"

He'd laughed. "A woman, especially Eliza Schuyler Hamilton, can be all that and more."

She *was* all that and more. Even though she left behind her barefoot childhood on the farm and in the woods for the city, as she grew into adulthood she sometimes longed for the days of freedom to explore a stream, climb a tree, or track deer through the woods.

She'd learned much through formal schooling, but excelled at gardening, brewing herbal remedies, and handcrafting—whether embroidery, lacemaking, or beading wampum, as she learned to do from the Iroquois. When Eliza was a child, the local tribe were more than her friends; they were family. One night, during a political trip with her father, Eliza's friend Two-Kettles-Together braided her hair in two plaits like the Iroquois girls wore and led her through an adoption ceremony. She was welcomed into the tribe as "One-of-Us."

She showed Two-Kettles-Together how to embroider, which she picked up quickly as it was so similar to the stitching of wampum beads. They busied themselves during rainy days with such activities. Both girls loved to ride horses and chase one another in the forest.

Eliza witnessed another way of living after taking part in ceremonies. She learned much from Two-Kettles-Together, but what she loved the most was dancing. Later, when she shared the dances with her sisters and mother, they squealed in reaction to the coarse movements. Eliza had merely shrugged and laughed.

But her childhood neighborhood friend, Maggie, loved the dances and the stories she brought home from her adventures with her father. The two girls fashioned drums from hatboxes and danced until they couldn't move.

"It's so much fun," Maggie had said, breathless. "So much easier than dancing with a partner."

Eliza agreed. At thirteen, both girls struggled to learn the formal dances they'd be required to do in a few years as part of New York society.

Dancing aside, Two-Kettles-Together had taught Eliza more useful things than any of her formal schoolteachers—things like using willow bark to help with pain, predicting an oncoming storm by watching cloud patterns, and identifying which animals were nearby from observing their scat.

Eliza didn't know what happened to Two-Kettles-Together, as the older she grew Eliza was discouraged from traveling with her father. Instead, she was sent to the city for another kind of education. But when she thought of Two-Kettles-Together, her heart warmed.

Eliza smiled, remembering, but as Davey pulled up to the front door, her smile faded. She had visitors.

"Shall I pull around back, m'lady?"

She'd been shirking her duty as the grieving widow of the great Alexander Hamilton. Throngs of people wanted to express their condolences and sense of loss. Exhausted from a day of visits, she wanted to retreat and rest, but guilt picked at her. She sighed. "I'll be fine here, but please take the children around to the back."

On entering her house, Eliza gasped to see her son, Alexander Jr., who'd only left to go back to school yesterday. As she walked farther into the parlor, he stood, as did the man next to him.

"Mother." Alexander Jr. greeted her with a stiff embrace and a kiss on her cheek. A tingle traveled up her spine. Something was wrong. What was he doing here?

"Madam, I'm truly sorry to bother you at a—" the man started to say when Angelica Schuyler Church, Eliza's sister, stepped into the room, placing herself between Eliza and the stranger. Angelica's jaw twitched and her complexion flushed the same as it had the time one of their brothers had teased Eliza until she cried.

Whatever was happening was not good. Eliza searched Alexander's face for answers.

"Please, let's sit down." Angelica led Eliza to the settee in the sitting room with the others. Angelica had been staying with Eliza since Hamilton died, taking care of countless details. Eliza sat on the side of the settee.

"What is it?" Her eyes scanned her son, her sister, and the strange man standing at the edge of the room, with his hands held behind his back, shifting his weight.

"Mother, I—"

Angelica held up her hand. "A young man escorted home by a constable needs to sit quietly." Alexander slumped over in his chair.

"Constable?" Eliza clutched her breast.

"Aye, he was in a brawl in the wee hours of the morning." Angelica patted Eliza's hand. "As if you don't have enough heart-ache, dear sister."

The constable stepped forward. "With all due respect, Mrs. Church, 'twas a good bit more than a brawl. And the gentleman he fought with turned up dead today."

Eliza gasped, searching for words.

"Of course he didn't take the man's life. This is absurd!" Angelica hissed.

Even though Eliza didn't think her son capable of killing a man, she appreciated that his temperament resembled his father's. And it also worried her. "What happened?"

Alexander lifted his chin, straightened his shoulders, and looked at his mother before glancing away. "I had a bit too much drink and overheard him talking. I asked him about what he said and he, uh, overreacted. Said he should whip me for my impertinence."

Eliza eyed the constable, then looked back at her son. Call it mother's intuition, or years of being the wife of Alexander Hamilton, but Eliza only half believed this story. There had to be more to this. "What did he say that upset you?"

"That's not important," the constable stated, his square jaw lifting as he pursed his lips. "What's important is the young man attacked him. Beat him to a pulp."

"I swear I didn't. I only hit him once, he went down, and I ran. That's the last I saw of him. I promise." Wisps of his red curls stuck to his sweaty forehead. Eliza refrained from reaching out to brush them away.

"But we have witnesses who claim otherwise," the constable said in a quiet voice, with one eyebrow lifted, as if waiting for a reaction.

"What witnesses? A bunch of drunks in a tavern?" Angelica crossed her arms and her dress sleeves twisted.

The constable straightened his coat as his face hardened.

Eliza swallowed. "I need to speak to my son alone. Constable? Angelica? If you will excuse us."

Angelica's jaw twitched again, but she stood gracefully and escorted the constable out of the room, the sound of her skirt swishing in the otherwise silent room. She shut the door behind her.

Alexander gazed at Eliza as if she offered an answer. Her son had been drunk last night. He admitted it, and he also admitted that he had hit the man. She tried to hide her disappointment. She had tried so hard to raise her children as good Christians who would walk away from trouble. If only her husband was beside her, holding her hand, advising with his wisdom. But he wasn't. This was up to her. She sat straighter. What would her husband do in this situation? She closed her eyes and remembered the few times their children needed to be punished: the boys wrestling around with one another until one got hurt, Angel stealing a necklace from her grandmother, Philip cheating on a test at school. Hamilton had been the disciplinarian.

"Don't make me pry the truth from you." She touched his shoulder. "And don't make me pull you away from your schooling, which, as God is my witness, I will do. If you continue to act in such an irresponsible manner, I'll have no choice."

He exhaled and looked her in the eye. "He was talking about Father."

She blinked back an unexpected, burning tear, as a sudden ache of grief moved through her.

"I'm sorry, Mother." Alexander rushed to her side. "I don't want to hurt you more."

"You say that and yet you behave in such a manner. Drinking in a tavern. Striking a man! Alexander! What has come over you?" She wiped a tear away with her finger and sniffled.

"The man said something about the duel and how nobody knew the truth of the matter. I merely asked him what that truth was." He said it without emotion, but his words stuck daggers into Eliza's chest.

Her mind swirled. It was the second time today the duel had been mentioned in the same light. "Are you certain? You'd had drink."

He nodded. "He said what he said, and I punched him. That is all, Mother, I promise."

Alexander had his father's temper, but he also had his passion for the truth. Her son was confused, grieving, and could be foolish at times. But he was no liar.

"What shall we do, Mother? They think I killed John Van Der Gloss."

The man she saw today! He was the man they accused her son of killing! The words of the strangers on the street rang in her head again: *That's no accident.* *One of the duel's witnesses.* What had her husband done? What were people hiding from her?

Her son, looking like a younger version of his father, sat in front of her, asking for answers. Her heart thudded against her ribs. "We will engage a lawyer to help us fight this accusation."

He shook his head and looked at his feet. He was eighteen years old, but he resembled the boy he used to be in this moment. His face softened. His eyes would not meet hers.

"What is it?" she prodded.

"I don't think there's enough money to engage a lawyer. The bursar at school called me into his office yesterday, seeking payment. I spoke with father's solicitor. He says we are lacking funds."

Eliza's heart sank to her feet. There must be a mistake. Alexander would not have gone to a duel without leaving them enough money to live on. Would he? She shuddered, but she tried to hide it from her son. They'd accused her son of murder, and she resolved to do her best for him. She believed in him. "He was mistaken, son. It will be fine."

If only she were as confident as she sounded!

A knock interrupted her reflections, and the door opened. Angelica slipped into the room. "I'm sorry. Constable Schultz needs to leave. It's getting late."

"Shall I see him out?" Eliza stood.

"No. He's taking Alexander with him. He'll be keeping him in custody tonight."

"What? Jail?" Eliza exclaimed, clutching her chest.

"John, my husband, will see to his release in the morning," Angelica said.

"Promise me, Angelica! Promise me that John can help!" Eliza reached for her sister. "Please."

"Eliza, calm yourself. John will do his very best. You know that." Angelica wrapped her arm around Eliza, who watched her son leave with the constable. She curled her hands into fists at her sides as stone-cold dread swept over her. What would jail be like? Would he be safe? She sensed it would not be easy for the son of Alexander Hamilton. Her planned escape to Albany grew further in the distance.

CHAPTER 3

After a fitful night of prayers and curses, and very little sleep fretting about Alexander, Eliza arose the next morning with a plan. In her heart, she believed the constable had exaggerated. But if what Alexander said was true, she needed to prepare. Did the family not have funds for his schooling?

Wasn't it just three weeks ago she and Hamilton hosted a ball in this house? A ball at which they'd spared no expense? A ball in which the guest list included Nabby Adams Smith, daughter of President Adams?

Before sunrise, with the rest of the household still sleeping, she dressed and went downstairs, candle in hand, to Hamilton's library. She'd been avoiding this room since his death. He worked from home often, even though he rented an office in lower Manhattan.

If any clues to financial insecurity existed in this house, they would be somewhere amid his papers. She stood outside the room for a moment and drew in air. The sun was cracking the sky and soft light streamed in the hall. Did he leave them with no means? Would she be forced to sell this home they'd been living in for only two years? After living in small rental quarters for years and moving frequently, they'd finally purchased their own home. He died before they'd even paid off the mortgage. Would she need to sell his dream of a home to feed their children? Or to defend his son in court?

Eliza rummaged through the papers strewn on his desk, trying to find answers. She sorted them into three stacks: personal correspondence, business, and accounts. She opened the desk drawers and reached in to find heaps of more unsorted papers. *Oh, Alexander.*

An hour later, the sun burned higher in the sky and she'd yet to find any clue about how much money he was owed. Client receipts? None. There were, however, many debts. They owed thousands on the house. Hamilton had assumed he'd have the rest of his life to pay it off.

But this was not a complete picture of the situation by any means. Alexander Jr. was studying at King's College—when not drinking in the pubs, evidently—and Eliza also needed to secure a position for James's schooling, who at sixteen was ready. And there were the other children: Angel, and the younger three, John, twelve; William, seven; Eliza, five; and little Philip had just turned two. Thank goodness their adopted child, Jenny, had married well and now managed her own household. Still, Eliza missed her and clung to every word of her letters.

Eliza's heart dropped. How would she manage? She hated imposing on her own father, who was aging and in ill health. She hoped she would not have to rely on him, as many widows in her position did. Before that happened, she needed to think about her options.

As Eliza straightened the piles, one square letter on blue-gray fine woven paper refused to stay in the stack.

She read the note:

You were right, though it pains me to say. There is evidence they set you up. With all due patience, we will find a way forward.

Yours, John Van Der Gloss.

Set up for what? Her heart raced. What evidence? She grabbed the sleeve of her dress and twisted it.

The door opened behind her. "There you are," Angelica said. "You gave me a start."

Eliza shoved the letter back into the stack. John Van Der Gloss, the man found in the North River yesterday. The man they accused her son of killing. Cold crept over her.

Angelica walked toward her. "Eliza?" She placed her hand on Eliza's shoulder. "What are you doing?"

She dared not face her sister. Eliza's trouble always showed on her face. She didn't wish to worry Angelica, who'd been fretting over her like a mother hen. She continued to gaze toward the desk. "I'm trying to sort his papers."

Angelica squatted beside Eliza. "You don't have to do this. There's plenty of time."

Eliza wasn't ready to speak further until she figured out these matters. Part of this puzzle would be solved when Alexander's executors came forth with their findings. She then could turn her attention to untangling the mysterious letter. She bit her lip, an untoward habit she'd had since a child. Eliza was not a good liar. But she needed to keep her own counsel. She couldn't even open up to her closest sister because of her shame. The words would not come from her aching, burning, breast. *Alexander may have left us next to destitute. But he still may have left us a way to tell his story—if I can figure this John Van Der Gloss note out.*

"Mrs. Cole has a delightful morning meal prepared. Let's get you something to eat." Angelica stood and reached for her arm. Even clad in mourning wear, Eliza deemed her sister more elegant than her. Her mourning dress fit her precisely, tucked where it should tuck, and cascading in harmony with her figure. The jet beads draped with perfection over her neck and breasts.

"I have no appetite." Even less so than she had an hour ago. Eliza allowed her to help her stand. *They've accused my son of murder. My husband is dead. And I may be penniless.*

"I know. But you must force yourself to eat a bite or two. You must keep up your strength. For the children, if nothing else."

Eliza's weakness was her children, and Angelica was not a woman to ignore anybody's weakness.

★ ★ ★

The note Eliza had discovered pricked at her mind during breakfast and throughout the day. She needed to find out what it meant. She had an inkling it concerned the unfounded accusation against Hamilton that he stole money from the government while he was serving as Secretary of the Treasury. Had he been working all these years trying to find the thief as well as the person who blamed it on him?

Eliza's heart raced. Proof that he did no wrong. The very thing that would help protect his legacy. If such evidence existed, she'd rest easier—and so would her Hamilton.

And if unraveling the mysterious letter led to helping her son, so much the better. If only she'd found the letter before John was killed, she could have asked him. But now the most she could hope for was that he'd mentioned the situation to his wife, Rose, who Eliza planned to visit as soon as she could manage.

"Mrs. General Hamilton," Mrs. Cole said as she came through the bedroom door. A woman Hamilton had insisted on hiring when they moved to the Grange two years ago, their housemaid was shorter than Eliza and rounder than two of her put together. She had a heart-shaped face, with cheeks that bloomed pink quickly. A woman who kept her personal life to herself, Mrs. Cole had the curious distinction of having one blue eye and one brown. "You have a visitor."

Eliza's stomach tightened. She'd promised to stay home to receive visitors today. But she was uncertain she had the wherewithal. Still, she managed to stand and open the door, marching forward. "Fine." It was better to try to keep her mind off of her son, still in jail. She would welcome mourners and drink tea and pretend everything was fine.

When she entered the light-filled parlor, Angelica cast aside her needlework to chat with a woman who Eliza struggled to recognize. But when she turned to face her, Eliza remembered. "Alice Rhodes!"

"Mrs. General Hamilton," Alice Rhodes said, standing and greeting Eliza with an embrace. "I was so sorry to learn of your husband's death."

"Thank you." Eliza batted away the creeping, burning sensation in her eyes.

They sat as Mrs. Cole brought tea and arranged the new mourning tea dishes, black with hand-painted white lilies, one of many mourning purchases Angelica had made for Eliza shortly after Hamilton's death.

"You're looking well, Alice," Eliza said, noticing the fine cut of her dress, along with the sturdy but pretty gray poplin. A far cry from the rags she had worn when first coming to the Widow Society, a group Eliza helped to create and where she volunteered as often as she could.

"Thank you." Alice straightened. "Widowhood has been good to me, thanks to you and the excellent ladies at the Widow Society."

When Eliza's friend, Isabella Graham, had asked for her help in forming the society, she could not say no. She'd known more than one woman whose life turned inside out when left widowed— even women in her own station, let alone poor women with small children to feed. If she could help, she had said, it would be an honor. They'd aided countless women, though not all turned out as well as Alice.

Eliza's spirit lifted, recalling how Alice had pitched in and helped with the chores at the home for widows and organized the other women there, as well as stayed with the children. Even though she was downtrodden, Alice remained useful and energetic. Qualities Eliza aspired to gain. "Wonderful. Are you faring well, then?"

"She's well turned out, indeed," Angelica said. "Mrs. Rhodes told me of her previous hardship and how you two met." She turned to Alice. "Have you remarried?"

Alice drank from her teacup, holding up half her pinky finger. She'd lost the other half in an accident. "Pshaw. No, indeed. I'm my own woman. And my daughter is gainfully employed as well." She placed her cup first in the saucer, then on the table. "In fact, she works for Lady Collins, who you visited with yesterday."

Eliza's face heated. "Oh! I'm uncertain if I spotted her. I'm not sure I'd recognize her."

"How could you? She's blossomed into a young woman. When you knew her, she was a half-starved waif." Alice fiddled with the small gold locket hanging around her neck. Once again, her half-pinky was prominent. "I've enough to be grateful for. My daughter wedded a fine lad, also in service with the Collins family, and I'll soon be a grandmother,"

"I'm so glad to see that life is treating you well." So many of the widows tried hard, but never could quite survive in any kind of pleasant, reliable manner. Eliza clasped her hands and rested them in her lap. *I am a widow now. A precarious and ironic situation.*

"What a fine lace." Alice tilted in close to Eliza.

Memories of Alice tatting lace sprang to Eliza's mind. She'd watched the woman's deft hands and wondered if Alice had married beneath her station, because they only taught gentle-women skills like tatting. Eliza fancied a romantic story in her mind where Alice left her good family behind to marry a handsome blacksmith. But it was only a guess—Alice never spoke about her past and never uttered a word about her husband.

"Thank you. My grandmother made it. We all have pieces of her handiwork." Eliza ran her fingers over it.

"Remarkable. There's a seller's market for lace." Alice smacked her lips together as if the mention of lace was a delicious tart or candy.

"It's all the rage in Paris," Angelica said. She'd lived in London and had made several trips to Paris. She fancied herself a fashionable, sophisticated woman. But Eliza's favorite memories of her sister involved running around barefoot with the local Iroquois when they were girls. She gestured. "But here?"

Alice nodded. "Yes, the fine ladies and gents will pay a price for it." She turned back to Eliza. "I know a fair man who purchases lace and other fine handiwork."

Eliza chewed the inside of her cheek. Was Alice aware of her situation?

"Not that you, Mrs. General Hamilton, would need funds." Alice sipped her tea, the corners of her mouth creasing as she drank. Her wrinkled, rough hands held the fine porcelain teacup with delicacy.

"Our grandmother made the lace. None of us would part with any of it." Angelica looked up from her embroidery, light playing over her face. The room was perfect for stitching, with its large windows overlooking the garden. She was one of the wealthiest women in New York—also one of the liveliest. If she were ever to be widowed, she would not face Eliza's financial dilemma.

"Of course not," Alice said. Her eyebrows lifted. "But life has its twists and turns. Look at poor John Van Der Gloss."

Eliza's stays tightened around her ribs. She opened her mouth but couldn't speak.

"What about him?" Angelica said, flush with the excitement of fresh gossip.

"They found his body yesterday afternoon along the banks of the river. Dreadful. The papers said he didn't simply drown. Sliced with a knife and thrown into the river, he was." Her eyes widened. "He was in a brawl and his body washed up along the river!"

Eliza twisted her sleeve. She and Angelica exchanged knowing glances. Alice was not one for idle gossip. She was as good a woman as she'd ever met. She spoke the truth, even when it was inconvenient.

Once again, Eliza wondered if the Van Der Gloss murder had anything to do with the note from him she'd just read this very morning. It was too coincidental. Eliza's stomach continued to turn as the hair pricked up on the back of her neck and a tingle traveled up her spine. What measure of mischief and evil was this?

Angelica tucked her embroidery away in her basket. "Have they found the culprit?"

Eliza hoped that Alice's sharp wit didn't suspect Angelica's fishing attempt.

Alice shook her head. "Not yet. They have a man in custody. But it's hush-hush. Nobody knows who it is."

Eliza exhaled, certain the man she talked about was her son. At least nobody knew.

"Just a rumor then?" Angelica prodded.

"Pardon me for saying, but I think it's more than that. The suspect must be from a wealthy family. 'Tis the only thing I can think that would stop tongues wagging. For the time being."

Angelica darted a look at Eliza, then glanced at Alice. "Surely being wealthy doesn't keep justice from turning its wheels."

Alice fingered her cross again. "Not always. But you must know Aaron Burr's money and influence is the only thing keeping him from hanging. I want to see him brought to justice. Burr!" She spat the word.

"Of course Burr should be punished," Eliza said, still hoping her campaign against the man would bring him down.

"Then, madam, you will agree—the killer of John Van Der Gloss should also see justice."

Eliza's hands twisted in her lap. "Of course!"

But that killer was not her son.

CHAPTER 4

Alice had been in other fine houses, of course. The modesty of the Hamilton home surprised her, for it was much smaller than many of New York City's wealthiest homes. Certainly Aaron Burr's.

But then again, the Hamiltons had always been different.

As she walked along toward the forest that sat between upper Manhattan and Harlem, a slight breeze blew across her skin. The scent of wild honeysuckle hung in the air. She only had a few miles to the cab stand, where she hoped to hire one to take her to her home on Pearl Street.

Something wasn't right with Eliza Hamilton.

Oh, of course she was grieving her husband. But it was more than that. Alice sensed an edginess, along with the heaviness she'd been prepared for. Eliza was not an edgy woman. Yet her dark eyes had darted back and forth as if she were hiding something. Her hands gripped one another in her lap. What else was happening?

Eliza Hamilton was no woman of secrets and shadows. Alice recognized it in other women, always. Eliza was normally open and full of light. Not a bright and sunny light, but the glowing light of a full moon—soft, steady, almost unnoticeable.

The first word Alice would use to describe her was *compassionate*. Years ago, when she herself had lost her husband and had nowhere to turn, it was Eliza and the good women at the Widow Society who helped her through. She had deliberated turning to her family in Europe, but thought again, as none of them had supported her marriage and her leaving for the New World. No. It had been better to turn to Eliza and her friends.

Eliza had stood out among them. She worked alongside them, cleaning, sewing, teaching. Many other women just gave their money. Alice grunted and smacked her lips. Money was good, too. For they all needed it to survive.

She stopped and rested. She pulled a light wrap over her head to shield her face from the sun. She couldn't remember a hotter summer. Nor could she remember a worse one. For she had been there for the worst of it.

On the day Hamilton died, she'd been on Jane Street, on her way back from selling embroidered silks at a fine home, when she stopped in her tracks. The crowd was unsettled and shouts pierced her ears. What was going on? A group of men carried someone in their arms. Alice refocused her eyes. The men carried Eliza's husband into a nearby house. Before he disappeared into the house, she locked eyes with the bloody Alexander Hamilton. She perceived little life in them, even as New York City held its breath as he fought for his life. A battle he ultimately lost.

Alice's thoughts turned to Eliza and their family. She didn't know what she, with her humble circumstances, could do for her. But she vowed to help.

At the moment when she and Hamilton had exchanged glances, it was as if they made an unspoken pledge. She would watch out for Eliza, whether he lived or died.

Most people would want to help Eliza. The entire city was bereft. Eliza and her husband were so much a part of the fabric of

New York City. The city they helped to build would go on; cities always did.

When he died, every New Yorker had taken to the streets for his funeral procession. Every New Yorker, save one: Eliza.

Alice clucked her tongue. Something wasn't right.

CHAPTER 5

Alice wasn't the only visitor that day. Once word got around that Mrs. General Hamilton was at home, many locals paraded into the house to express their condolences. Eliza appreciated the concern. But images of her son sitting in filth, surrounded by dangerous men in jail, taunted her.

"His uncle will see to his release. My husband knows his way around the system. Thank goodness." Angelica reached out and patted her hand. Her sister knew her so well. "You need rest. Mrs. Cole, please bring tea and no more visitors for the day. She is spent."

"Yes, mum," Mrs. Cole said and then left the room to fetch the tea.

Late afternoon shadows and streams of sunlight played against the butter-yellow walls of the parlor. Eliza rose and paced to the window and back, wringing her hands.

"Please sit down," Angelica said. "You're making me nervous, Betsey."

Eliza was only called Betsey by three people—Angelica, Hamilton, and her father. It took her straight back to her girlhood and the feeling of safety.

"I've been sitting most of the day." Eliza stopped at the window and gazed at a portion of the thirty-two acres of land that was the Grange. "Cooped up in this house."

The older she grew, the more she longed for her youthful days of running barefoot in the gardens and woods, and the more that indoor activities bored her.

"You've been all over this city the past few days. I should think you'd be happy to be home," Angelica quipped.

A pang of guilt tore at Eliza's breast. She should've stayed here, in her lovely home, taking in visitors. She was luckier than most widows, than most people. But she couldn't rest knowing that Burr was roaming about the city as a free man. Her compulsion for justice throbbed in her veins, almost like blood.

Mrs. Cole brought tea to them.

"Thank you," Eliza said, turning to face her.

The newspaper was lying on the tray alongside the tea. She almost sprang for it. But Angelica grabbed it first. "Do you need to worry yourself with this?"

"I like to stay informed. Give that to me!" Eliza tore the paper out of her sister's hands.

"Eliza!" Angelica squealed. "You're irascible."

"Indeed." She opened the paper and scanned it for news of John Van Der Gloss. She plopped on the floor and spread out the paper.

Angelica followed suit, her fingers skating the page. "There! Next to that odd little owl. That's what you're looking for!"

"'Man Held for Questioning in Van Der Gloss Murder,'" Eliza read aloud as she pointed to the headline. "'A young man seen brawling with Van Der Gloss the night before his death has been picked up by the local constable and is being held for questioning. Van Der Gloss, whose body was pulled from the river, had his throat slit before being pushed in the water, according to local authorities. They are searching for the blade that was used.'"

"They don't mention Alexander's name! Thank the heavens!" Angelica said.

"Not yet." Eliza stood, her chest tightened with what felt like a lack of air.

Angelica followed suit, with a cracking of her back. "Ach, my back. I don't know how you remain so lithe, sister."

"Are you alright?" Eliza asked.

"I'm fine." She stretched until her back cracked again. "I've never seen you so drawn to the paper, except when they were reporting about Hamilton's troubles with that woman."

That was most likely true. Eliza knew it wasn't good to read about her husband's dalliance, but she could not help herself.

"I don't wish to think about that now. I've got enough on my mind. I have an idea." She clapped her hands together. "We should go to the tavern."

"Tavern? What tavern?" Angelica's eyes widened. "We don't go to taverns and pubs." She waved her sister off as she sat down on the settee.

"I think we should ask questions about that night." Eliza paced between the table and the window again.

"Your mind is warped. You're not thinking clearly. Losing Hamilton has been harder on you than you realize. Eliza, you cannot be seen in a pub."

"But—"

"But nothing. Think about it. If people see you there, the widow of Alexander Hamilton, asking questions about the death of John Van Der Gloss, it will raise suspicions. People will assume we have a connection to the person in jail. You don't want that."

Eliza released the idea. Angelica was right. People recognized her. Tongues would wag as if on fire. "But we need to find out what happened in that pub. There must be other witnesses."

"We're certain Alexander didn't kill the man." Angelica picked up the teapot and poured. "Let my husband handle this."

Eliza sat on the corner of the settee. "Your husband will do his best to get Alexander out of jail. But we need to find out what happened."

"Why? As long as we get Alexander home and freed?"

"Because John Van Der Gloss was a friend of Hamilton's." Eliza took the teacup her sister offered her.

"And? Hamilton was a friend to half the men in this town."

Eliza hesitated. She sipped her tea, keeping her own counsel on the other half of men.

"What do you know?" Angelica asked.

"Nothing." Eliza shrugged. She didn't know whether or not to worry her sister. Angelica was an emotional woman and not one to shy from the dramatic. Meanwhile, Eliza had had enough drama to last her a lifetime.

Angelica set her tea down. "Are we sisters or not? You must tell me."

"There was a rumor yesterday that Van Der Gloss was killed because he witnessed the duel. Or at least, that was the allusion."

Angelica's face went stone still, which flummoxed Eliza. This reaction was not her usual. But Angelica was mourning Hamilton too and was not herself.

"Why can't they let the poor man rest?" She pressed her hands down on her lap. "Why, even after his death, do people persist in dragging his good name in the mud?" Her voice was barely a whisper.

Eliza shivered. "Why, indeed? And now his son. We must find out what happened in the tavern that night."

"You and I cannot enter such an establishment." Angelica narrowed her eyes.

Eliza agreed. "You're right. But we can send someone else. A trusted person."

"John is busy getting Alexander out of jail."

"Who else can we send?"

"One of your people?"

Eliza's brain raced. "Not a solicitor . . ." She couldn't fathom speaking with the solicitor yet. "Davey McNally was with me yesterday when I heard the rumor."

"He's quite devoted and trustworthy."

Eliza nodded. "He has been so far." She was not one to get others to do her work. But the times were such as they were. She was too well known to slip into an establishment and find out the truth. But McNally? He might just suit the job. Yes, indeed.

CHAPTER 6

Sometimes Eliza's grief almost swallowed her. After her discussion with McNally, she went to her room and lay in her bed alone. She closed her eyes, wanting to pray. She was a woman of prayer. But she'd not been able to find the heart to speak to God since her husband's death.

Nor had she been able to find any peace. From the moment her eyes shut to find sleep, images of her husband's bloody body taunted her. Her mind rolled with thoughts of when Burr's bullet entered his spine.

Eliza turned over on her side. Now this. This business with Alexander. Her son was in jail!

Sinking into the mattress, her weary bones found relief. But what of her spirit? She'd promised she would dine with the children that night, but instead she drifted into sleep.

A rapping at her bedroom door awakened her. As she fluttered her eyelids, she realized she'd been crying. She wiped the tears away and sat up. "Yes?"

Angel walked into the room. "Mama? Are you ill?"

"No, just tired." She stood, straightening her dress.

"Supper is ready. I suppose Philip won't be joining us. He has exams."

Sorrow, fear, and worry tangled and plucked at Eliza's chest. Philip had been dead for years, yet his sister still had to be reminded of it. His death had broken her. Eliza walked over to her daughter and cupped her face, then took her hand. "Darling, Angel. You know your brother has passed away. Have you forgotten?"

Angel's eyes lit with fright. "Forgotten? Are you certain, Mother? Are you certain he's gone? I just spoke with him yesterday."

Eliza's heart fluttered. She inhaled some air. "Yes, I'm certain." She forced a smile. "Let us eat. I'm famished. Aren't you?"

She and Hamilton had taken Angel to several physicians since Phil's death. There didn't seem to be anything to be done about Angel's mental wanderings. The best they could do was to redirect her mind when she had an incident like this one. Sometimes it worked. A few times it hadn't, and the child had to be medicated to calm her down.

Eliza's oldest daughter skated between sanity and insanity, though she was not a lost cause. Weeks would go by and she would not mention Phil. Then, out of nowhere, his name would come across her lips. Angel insisted she had conversations with him, claiming he wasn't dead, and sometimes, when Eliza would bring her back to reality, she'd fight it.

Angel and Phil had been very close. And Angel had always had a sensitive disposition. Eliza prayed her daughter would heal from the traumatic loss of her brother, but it would take time.

As they stepped into the dining room, Eliza surveyed her other children sitting at the table, waiting for her. As the years unfolded, how would the loss of their father affect them? Some of them were so young, he'd only be a dream in their minds. But the others . . . She resolved to be both mother and father as best she could.

"The fish smells lovely," Angelica said.

Eliza nodded and smiled even as her stomach heaved. Her appetite was nonexistent. But the sweet faces of her children gazing up at her forced her to eat.

A pea flew across the table and hit John. "Ow!"

"William!" Eliza scolded. "We do not fling food across the table. Do you understand?"

He flushed. "He kicked me!" William pointed at his brother, who had a falsely innocent look on this face.

"Boys," Angelica said. "Please be quiet and eat."

Her eyes caught Eliza's. Angelica's jaw tightened. She was trying not to laugh, no doubt remembering the food fights their parents had suffered from the two of them. The sisters glanced away from one another in an effort to avoid laughter.

After dinner, Eliza and Angelica were in the sitting room with needlepoint projects when Angelica's husband John Church burst in, holding Alexander Jr. by the arm.

"Alexander!" Eliza stood and rushed to him, wrapping her arms around him. He smelled of urine, beer, and something else she couldn't pinpoint. "You need a bath!" She pushed herself away.

He grinned.

"Eliza, you know I love you and I love this boy, but he needs more than that!" John said as he shoved him away.

"I didn't kill anyone!"

"Please take a bath. I can't stand the smell." Angelica covered her mouth.

He nodded. "May I?" he asked his uncle.

"Yes, and then to bed. No escaping through the windows. I will see you in the morning, lad." He sounded gruff, but when the boy left, he turned to Angelica and hugged her with tenderness.

"John, please sit and tell us what you've learned." Eliza gestured to the settee.

"I can't stay. I've got my business to attend to and have been in the courts all day." He smiled. "But thank you for the offer."

"Sit down, John," Angelica said, forcefully. "You may go once you've told us what happened."

He sat with a huff. "Everything Alexander has told us appears to be true. There are murky bits in his story. He was drinking so he doesn't remember a lot. But he remembers leaving the tavern after hitting John Van Der Gloss."

"Do you believe him?" Eliza asked after a moment of awkward silence.

"Of course I do."

"But?" Angelica said.

"It doesn't look good, and they've yet to find the weapon, which could help his case."

"But they've let him out!" Eliza said.

"Yes, under my good name. If he strays again . . ."

"John," Angelica said. "What are the terms?"

"He needs to behave, of course, but there will be an investigation and he is a suspect." He glanced at Eliza. "I'm sorry to say, he's not cleared yet. I'm doing my best to keep this out of the press. But Van Der Gloss was a well-respected man and people want answers."

Eliza clutched at her dress with damp hands. *I want answers as well.*

"But we'll prove his innocence, which shouldn't be too hard. Since he is innocent," Angelica said.

John crossed his hands over his protruding stomach. "How do you plan to do that?"

Eliza stood and walked to the window, where the sunset splayed across the sky. "We've got a man asking questions at the tavern."

"What?"

"Well, John, we couldn't go to the tavern ourselves, could we?" Angelica said.

"Still, you two stay out of this. It's man's business."

Eliza whirled around to face him. She gathered her composure before she spoke. "I love you like a brother, John. So I will speak to you as a sister."

Angelica stiffened.

"Alexander is my son. I will do whatever it takes to clear his name, just as I have done for my husband. I appreciate your help and would love more of it. But if you are going to throw around words like 'man's business,' I assume you don't want to help, and I'll do what I can alone."

John's face bloomed red. His jaw tightened as his eyes darted back and forth between the sisters. He finally stood and silently exited the room.

CHAPTER 7

After drinking Mrs. Cole's sleeping elixir, made of whiskey, lemon, ginger, and other herbs, Eliza laid her head on her pillow. Her mind swam with the brew's dreamy sensation. When she closed her eyes, her mind's eye spun visions of her with young Hamilton and the nights of passion they'd so often shared. She drifted with warm, honeyed memories.

The next day, Eliza awoke with one thing on her mind: Davey McNally. She hastily dressed and hurried to find him.

Mrs. Cole was startled to see Eliza as she entered the hallway in the servant's quarters.

"Madam, can I help you?" she said after she gathered her composure.

"Yes, I want to see McNally."

"He's in the stable this morning, ma'am. May I assist you?"

"No." Eliza kept moving toward the door at the end of the hallway. She opened it and stepped out into sweltering heat, even this early in the morning. The scent of fresh manure greeted her. Ah well, it wasn't the most offensive thing that had ever met her nose.

She found McNally brushing Hamilton's gray mare, which had been his pride and joy. Eliza stood in awe at the gentleness the rough, masculine man exhibited. Hamilton was right about him. She hadn't wanted to hire him as he seemed crude and rough. Hamilton said that was bluster, that a gentle nature lay beneath. She cleared her throat.

He turned to her. "Mrs. General Hamilton. Good morning."

"Good morning, Davey. Please continue with your grooming."

He nodded and continued his brushing. "Ah suppose you're wanting information about the tavern and your boy."

She stepped forward onto the dry ground. Did he have news already? This was more than she hoped for! "Do you have any news for me?"

He continued brushing. The horse might have been a purring cat beneath his large hands. "Several men saw your boy strike Van Der Gloss."

"I know he did that, McNally."

"But I only found one man who saw young Alexander leave."

Her heart nearly stopped as she moved closer to him, careful not to trip over her own feet. "And?"

He stopped brushing and turned toward her. "Odd so many of 'em had the same story. It was like, you know, somebody told 'em what to say, if ye get my meaning."

Eliza did. A flicker of hope ignited in her. "Yes, I do. Who is this man and why isn't he sticking to the same story?"

He shrugged. "Maybe he's got integrity? His name is Paul Jinkins."

"Paul Jinkins . . ." Eliza searched her mind, but the name was unfamiliar to her.

Davey wiped his brow with his sleeve. "He's British and is here on business. He's staying at the Mariner's Arms."

Eliza was familiar with the place. It was close to the docks. "Very well. I shall need you to ready the carriage." She turned to go.

"Wait," Davey said. "Maybe someone should else should accompany you."

"Like who?" Did he not wish to go with her? He was an odd sort.

"I was thinking maybe you could take the constable?"

"Davey! That's a brilliant idea. Can we get a message to him to meet me there?"

Davey beamed and nodded. "Leave it to me."

★ ★ ★

Two hours later, Eliza had eaten, kissed her children, and left the house in the carriage, heading for the hotel. Arrangements made, her heart lifted. She needed to clear her son's name. Why did men get themselves into the kind of trouble where their women had to clean up after them?

Eliza cared not to think about the many times her mother helped her father or brothers with numerous incidents, and she with Hamilton. At one point during their marriage, Eliza stopped. She herself was broken and had no ounce of compassion for Hamilton. It was a sin to feel a lack of compassion, especially toward one's husband. But thankfully God was forgiving. Eliza tried to embrace forgiveness as the Bible preached, even as her husband was enmeshed with Maria Reynolds. In every paper. On the lips of people on every street corner and in every pantry—or at least that's what it felt like. The humiliation was almost too much to bear. Finally, she came to a resolution within herself and was able to put it behind her and continue helping him and loving him—albeit not with the same wide-eyed love as before.

She peeked out the window of the carriage, the river in the distance, before they made the turn onto Bloomingdale Road. Trees, river. Dirt path. It was the same view as ever, but so much else had changed.

Constable Schultz met them outside the establishment. He seemed on edge and harried. "Mrs. General Hamilton, I'm happy to help. But I can't stay long. Let's get to it, shall we?"

When Eliza and the constable walked into the Mariner's Arms, the man behind the desk looked up from his writing. The place was dim and dusty and could use a thorough washing. Eliza drew her handkerchief to her nose as she sneezed. *No wonder women were discouraged from these places.*

The man looked up, startled. "Mrs. General Hamilton?"

Eliza nodded. Her image had been in the newspapers way too often. Not simply as the wife of Alexander Hamilton, but also through her charity work. Though she never thought the newspaper sketch artists did a good job capturing her likeness, it seemed they did.

The constable stepped forward. "We're here to see a boarder."

"Yes, sir. Who might that be?" His eyes were brownish, bloodshot, sagging orbs behind gold-rimmed spectacles. The dim light reflected in them.

"Paul Jinkins, please," Eliza stated.

The man groaned. "I'm sorry. He's no longer here."

Eliza's heart almost slammed out of her chest. "What? Where is he?"

The man's jaw firmed. "I'm sorry, madam. We don't ask our patrons about their comings and goings."

"Do you at least know if he was heading out of town?" the constable asked.

The innkeeper shrugged. "I assume he was heading back to London."

"Thank you. We shall go to the docks." The constable started to depart.

Eliza lifted her hand. "May I ask something?"

"Anything, Mrs. General Hamilton," the innkeeper said.

She leaned across the counter. "What is Jinkins's trade?"

"Importer of something . . . tea? Textiles?"

"And he was here from London? For business?"

"That I don't know. I'm sorry." The man looked genuine, as if he wished he could help.

Constable Schultz reached for Eliza's arm. "We must go if we are to catch that ship."

They turned to go. Eliza's heart pounded like thunder. Could they catch Jinkins before he boarded a ship to London?

"Mrs. General Hamilton?"

She turned back to the innkeeper.

"My condolences for the loss of your husband."

She raised her chin and met his sincere eyes. "Thank you."

★ ★ ★

Outside of the inn, back in the glorious fresh air, Constable Schultz took his leave. "I have an appointment in court. I'm sorry, madam. If you find him, please let me know." Before he left, he turned to McNally. "Are you sure of all this, McNally?"

"Aye." He nodded his head. "As certain as I am of my own mother."

"Very well. Good day then, sir."

Eliza and McNally rode off toward the docks. Eliza didn't even look out the window. She drew inward, slumped in the gig's corner. She was so close to finding a witness who could help Alexander. But what if they didn't find the man? What then?

There must be other witnesses who had not been bribed into falsifying their statements. She'd just have to find them.

The carriage came to a jolting halt. She found they were at the docks. McNally dismounted and peered at her. "Sit tight. I'll see what I can find."

She opened her mouth, but he pointed his meaty finger at her. "I mean it. The docks is no place for a lady."

She tamped down her anger, as he was right and she knew it. Besides, this was not a battle worth fighting. If anything, being a general's daughter had taught her to pick her battles. She sat in the carriage and waited, peering out at the passersby, wondering what far lands they might be traveling to. When she was a girl, she dreamed of a life full of travels to faraway lands with delightful new food and costumes. Her father made it seem possible. He made all things seem possible. Especially as he took her with him to meet the natives of this land. Eliza dreamed of adventure, the Far East with its spices and silks, or Spain with its matadors, or Africa with its wide-open spaces and wild animals. She sighed. She'd had a different adventure as Alexander Hamilton's wife. And it wasn't over yet.

McNally approached the window. "There are no ships leaving for London for days. A storm at sea."

"Which means our man is still in the city," Eliza said as she poked her head out of the window. "Where could he be?"

Davey jutted his chin. "We will find him."

Eliza wanted to feel as confident as McNally, but Manhattan was such a large place to find one man. Where to begin?

If he hadn't left to return to London, then why did he leave? Did someone talk him into it—the way they had swayed the other witnesses? Why couldn't people just tell the truth? Why was someone setting up her son?

As they drove along, she glanced out, hoping for a breeze to no avail. She caught a glance of a familiar figure. A woman carrying a basket. The woman lifted her hand to wave to someone on the other side of the street and Eliza realized the hand was missing part of a finger. Alice! What was she doing in this part of town? Wasn't it dangerous for a woman alone just outside the port? She pulled the bell, which notified Davey that she wanted to stop.

"Alice!" Eliza yelled out the window. "Alice!"

Alice walked over to the carriage. "Why, hello, Mrs. General Hamilton."

"Do you need a ride?"

Alice tilted her head and gathered her eyebrows in confusion. "I've got business here to attend to. But I thank you for the kind offer."

Eliza opened the door. "Please come in and let my driver take you."

Alice paused before saying, "If you insist." She hefted herself into the tiny gig. The carriage bobbed down and up with the added weight.

"Where to?" McNally asked with impatience.

"Six hundred Canal Street," Alice replied.

Davey whipped his head around. "Are you certain?"

"Yes."

Eliza knew better than to go anywhere on Canal Street alone. What was Alice thinking?

"Alice, I don't mean to pry," Eliza said as the carriage started moving again, rocking back and forth.

"You can ask me anything." Alice clutched her basket closely to her chest.

"I don't believe it's safe for a woman alone on Canal Street."

"What? What do you mean? I'm there several times a week selling lace and other textiles."

Eliza's breath nearly stopped. "I don't want any harm to befall you, my friend. Is there another way?"

Alice's confused face turned into a smile. "Aye. I know what's going on. I know where your mind is." She nodded. "It's unsafe for a *lady*. Especially a famous one. But for me? Nobody pays me any mind. I'm plain and I am only an old woman selling pretty lace."

"I don't understand." Eliza clutched the seat for fear of sliding across it as McNally made a sharp turn.

"It's one of the secret pleasures of my old age. I'm invisible." She smacked her lips together. "If you get my meaning."

Why hadn't Eliza recognized that? How freeing old age could be. "I believe I do. Even so, are you certain you're safe?"

Alice shrugged. "As certain as any person can be."

Eliza's imagination fluttered as she considered living her life undiscovered, unencumbered by her name and status. Notions that were as tangible for her as smoke.

"I go anywhere I like." Alice tucked something into her basket. She leaned closer. "Within reason. Of course, Mrs. General Hamilton, there are some establishments where I wouldn't have reason or need to darken their doorsteps."

"Very well." Eliza sat up straighter. "Do your travels take you to inns or hotels? I'm looking for a British gentleman who left the Mariner's Arms this morning."

"Sometimes I meet buyers at inns. What's his name? I'll keep an ear out."

"Wonderful. I will need your discretion, as it's a very sensitive matter."

Alice lingered, as if mulling it over. "I may not know how to do much, but one thing I know how to do is to keep my mouth shut."

CHAPTER 8

Alice exited the carriage, stood on the side of the road, and waved at Eliza.

She had known something was off about Eliza the day she visited with her. Alice wasn't certain she was quite at the bottom of it, but she was circling it.

She hefted herself to the side of the road. *Paul Jinkins.* Alice planned to ask around about the man. She'd go to as many hotels and inns as she could. And she'd set her friends out to do the same thing. Like her, they were women of a certain age and status, giving them more freedom than women like Eliza could ever dream of. Knowing what she knew now, would Alice change her station? Would she trade her freedom for her husband? If God in the heavens could give him back to her, would she take it?

"Alice!" A man approached her. Long and lean, with a face to match, he dipped his hat to her.

She smiled. "Yes, Mr. Harracker. How are you on this fine day?" He looked surprised that she remembered his name. Of course she did. He was a client. He owned a small but fine hotel and required lace-edged pillowcases and embroidered sheets from time to time.

"I'm so glad I ran into you." He fiddled with the hat on his small head. "I've expanded the establishment and need more linens. Just like the ones you brought me before."

Alice smiled. "Of course I can help you. When do you need them?"

"In a week."

"A week?" Alice now remembered how difficult he was to work with. He paid well, but often gave her hard conditions to maneuver. She hated to turn away the money though. She mulled it over. "I'm sorry. I don't think I can do it." She had several projects to finish up and needed to make deliveries over the next few days. She was certain she couldn't fit it in.

"I will double the money," he said.

Could she refuse that kind of money? The rent was due soon, and she'd spent more money on taxis over the past few days than she'd planned. The price of tea and flour had escalated. She'd work all day and night and maybe one of her friends could help. She'd get it done. Yes, she would. "I'm happy to help," she said.

They shook hands.

"Mr. Harracker? I wonder if you might know a British gentleman. A friend of mine is looking for him. Paul Jinkins." Alice chose her words with care, not mentioning who her friend was. That was none of his concern.

A group of loud, laughing men passed them. "I know the name. Is he in trade?"

Alice nodded.

"If I find him, I'll let you know."

"Thank you, Mr. Harracker."

Alice turned to go.

"Alice?"

She turned back. "Yes?"

"See you soon with those linens." He tipped his hat again.

She lifted a finger. "Double the price."

He smiled and nodded.

Alice turned toward her home on Pearl Street. It had been quite a day. Deliveries made. A new job. And Eliza Hamilton, a woman of more secrets and shadows than Alice had estimated.

CHAPTER 9

Even after downing a cup of Mrs. Cole's special elixir before bed, Eliza found it difficult to sleep that night. Either Alice or McNally would find the mysterious Brit. His testimony would surely help Alexander's case, which was the most urgent matter. But she faced a puzzle larger than this one piece.

Why would anyone kill Van Der Gloss? And why would they try to blame Alexander for it? And was this matter connected with Hamilton, as the rumor suggested? Then there was the note she found from Van Der Gloss alluding to someone scheming to make Hamilton look like he had committed the Treasury robbery.

How did all these elements fit together?

Her father used to accuse her of seeing things that didn't exist. Making connections between things that didn't, on the surface, appear linked. In a desperate effort to free her mind, body, and soul from her longing for her husband, was her mind tricking her into thinking there was a grand conspiracy surrounding her husband even after his death?

But the note she found on Hamilton's desk was real.

Van Der Gloss's death was real.

The mysterious British gentleman was real.

And the incident with her son was real.

These were not childish fantasies or intrigue.

The question was—how did they fit together?

Somehow, she slept and awakened to a summer storm's rain pelting the windows. For the first time in days, hunger pangs jabbed at her. She rose from the bed and wrapped herself in a morning robe to go downstairs and find breakfast.

She walked into the kitchen to find Mrs. Cole and the cook discussing oysters, one of New York's bounties. Mrs. Cole often helped the cook, when time allowed.

"Good morning." Eliza pulled her robe closer around her. "What's for breakfast? I'm famished."

"Breakfast? Mrs. General Hamilton, it's almost noon."

"What?" She clutched her hand to her chest.

"Mrs. Church said to let you sleep. She's with the children in the nursery. We'll have lunch in a few minutes. Alexander has taken William fishing."

"In this weather?"

Mrs. Cole smiled. "It only just rained. I lay odds they will be home soon. Wet sopping messes."

The image made Eliza smile. Hamilton always said getting caught in the rain was good for the children. They'd learn to be more watchful of the weather. She'd learned the signs from the Iroquois and her father. She'd tried to teach her children to watch for the cloud patterns and the breeze turning over leaves, but it was one thing to be told something, quite another to experience it.

Eliza excused herself to her room and dressed for the day. When she entered the dining room, the children encircled her in a group embrace. Ah yes. Her heart split open.

After a lunch of sliced cheese, biscuits, butter, and strawberry jam, made from strawberries grown in their garden, Eliza and

Angelica sat and watched the storm. Mrs. Cole brought them tea and the newspaper.

Eliza reached for the paper, looking over the back page first, but not having the patience to read it. She noted an "apprentice wanted" notice for a printer, next to a strange-looking owl with numbers, letters, and symbols. She unfolded it, turned it over, and read the headline: *Floyd Peabody Found Hanging in His Own Barn.* She gasped.

"What is it?" Angelica asked.

Eliza pointed to the headline. The newspaper shook in her hands.

Angelica read over the paper. "Dreadful! I know the family. This is . . . absolutely dreadful."

"It's not right." Eliza stood. "Something is off."

"What are you talking about?" Angelica asked.

"You know the Peabodys. Suicide?" Eliza replied.

"Wait," Angelica said, pointing to the article. "The writer used the word 'suspicious.' You're right. Something is off. But then again, sometimes the human condition makes no sense. Remember Harold?" How could Eliza forget? Harold was a man they'd known as girls. Wealthy, with a beautiful, healthy family. But he'd take to his bed, for days sometimes, just from "exhaustion," and one day he shot himself straight through the heart. His death shocked the entire community.

Much like this would.

Angelica's rosy cheeks went pale. "So much death . . . ," she muttered.

Eliza stood. "So much, indeed." Too much. That two of Hamilton's closest friends had died within a week of one another, on the heels of his own death, pricked at her.

"Poor Victoria." Angelica rubbed her hands on her dress. "How will they bury him in the church cemetery? Can you imagine?"

Eliza nodded, but her mind reeled with the strange possibilities this death could entail.

"They won't bury suicides in a churchyard. I'm sure of it." Angelica bit her lip. "Imagine spending eternity . . . I don't know where."

"Would you stop fretting about the man's burial?" Eliza snapped. Angelica's brows gathered. "He was a friend of Hamilton's. The second one to die within days. Something is not right."

Angelica's head tilted, the sun lighting her porcelain skin. "I'm not following. People die. Didn't Mother always say people died in threes?"

"That's a silly superstition, and you know that." Eliza paced between the window and the settee. "I need to speak with the widows." She couldn't shrug this potent feeling that these deaths were no coincidence, especially after the note she found in Hamilton's study.

Mrs. Cole joined them in the room. "Constable Schultz to see you, madam."

Eliza spun to face her. "To see me? Whatever for?"

"Said it was important."

Eliza nodded. "Please show him in."

The constable entered with a huff and coughed.

"Can I bring you a glass of water?" Angelica asked.

"Water would be grand," he replied.

After he sat and drank his water, he cleared his throat and looked at Angelica flitting about the room. All eyes often followed her, but Eliza was growing impatient. "How can we help you?"

"They have dispatched me to check in on young Alexander. Is he here?"

Eliza glanced at Angelica, then back to the constable. "He's taken his young brother fishing. I do not know when he'll return, or what part of the river they went to. You're welcome to wait, sir."

His face fell. "Aye, I'll have to."

"Why?" Angelica said. "What are you doing here?"

He hesitated. "Someone said they observed him leave the Peabody barn late last night."

"Impossible," Eliza said. "He was here. I can assure you."

His right eyebrow cocked. "And yet, you do not know where he is right now. Do you?"

Eliza crossed her arms. "Who said he was leaving the barn?"

"I cannot tell ye that, madam, and I think you know it."

"I think you'd know that if Alexander was involved with any shenanigans he'd be more careful. He's a smart young man," Eliza said.

"And it seems as if someone wants us to think ill of him, that he committed these crimes," Angelica said as she sidled up to the constable. "Maybe it's just my woman's intuition, but something seems off here."

The constable blushed but cocked his eyebrow. "Something is off, all right."

They were interrupted by a shuffling sound coming from the hallway. People giggled, and Mrs. Cole's voice ordered, "Get that mess into the kitchen!" She then entered the room. "The children are back, madam, sopping wet, but with enough fish to feed an army or two."

The constable cracked a reluctant smile.

"Please tell Alexander to clean up and come here immediately." Eliza's heart raced as she considered her son being wrongly accused. She wasn't certain the two deaths were linked—though it seemed likely—but she was certain Alexander had nothing to do with either.

CHAPTER 10

Alexander entered the sitting room in dry clothes but smelling slightly of river and fish, mixed with a hint of soap. Eliza refrained from rolling her eyes. He sized up the situation. "Constable, how can I help you?"

"Where were you last night?" Constable Schultz asked. Right to business.

"I was here, sir, as I was told to be. Either here or with my uncle, sir," Alexander replied.

"Have you any proof?"

"How absurd!" Angelica retorted. "Proof that he was in bed!"

"Aye, I do," Alexander said. "I slept in the same room as my younger brother last night. He was having a bad dream so he came to my room."

The constable's face softened. "I'm sorry, sir. But may I speak to the young lad?"

"Certainly—but what is this about?"

"Someone claimed they observed you leaving Peabody's barn late last night."

"It wasn't me, obviously. But why would it matter?"

Eliza handed him the newspaper.

He glanced over the paper and his cheeks twitched. "You're saying you don't think it's a suicide, that someone harmed him and made it look that way." He hesitated. "And you think it's me?"

"We are just looking at all the possibilities, sir. If you were there, maybe you saw something . . ."

"Was it a suicide or not?" Angelica asked.

"It looks like it, but we can't be sure. Without going into much detail."

"He was a godly man," Eliza said.

The constable nodded. "His family finds suicide hard to believe. But I've seen it . . . even with godly men."

The room quieted.

"It's awful. I'm so sorry to learn about his death. He and my father were friends." Alexander dropped the paper. "But I can assure you I had nothing to do with this. I was with my brother. I'll get him."

There was silence in the room. Then the constable held up his hand. "No need, sir, I believe you. I may be back, though. Good day."

After he left, Eliza sank to the settee with an exasperated sigh.

Alexander rushed to her. "Mother, are you alright?"

She waved him away. "I'm fine."

"Who would have said you were at the Peabodys'?" Angelica sat down next to her sister.

"I'm confused. What does that matter?"

"Alexander! Think! Someone said you killed Mr. Van Der Gloss, and now someone said they observed you coming from the Peabodys' barn." Angelica's words could have been Eliza's, for she was thinking the same.

Alexander looked as if he'd been struck. "I simply don't know. The only thing I know the two men had in common was their friendship with my father."

Eliza found the words she needed to say. But it wasn't easy for them to come across her lips. "Were they at the duel?" Her whispery voice extracted the words from deep in her chest.

Alexander bent down on his knees and took her hands in his. When did his hands become a man's hands? Large, with wiry red hair on the back of them? Eliza focused on him, taking in the man her son was becoming.

"Mother, you know that normally there are not supposed to be any witnesses to such a thing, except the seconds. I don't know this for sure, but I think there were several uninvited witnesses. So I can't say for certain if these two men were there." He spoke in a soft and measured tone. She almost found comfort in his words. But his face spoke otherwise. His face grew redder with each word, the scourge of being a redhead—it was very difficult to hide emotions, like embarrassment or anger. Was he hiding something or just upset?

She embraced him. "Thank you, Alexander."

Eliza glimpsed her Hamilton in Alexander. She wished she could find comfort in knowing pieces of him were in their children. So many told her she would. But she was far from finding any peace anywhere. Someone was trying to blame their son for one murder, and perhaps a second one. And both men most likely were witnesses to the duel that stole Hamilton from her. What was going on here?

What would Hamilton do? If only she could ask. If only they could discuss these matters, as they once did. She ached to hear his voice. Even if it was just to debate or argue with her. She sighed. Hamilton had been freer than she was to roam about the city, and his men would be pounding in the pubs and meeting houses now, seeking answers.

★ ★ ★

Sometimes Eliza wished she'd been born a man. But she had her own friends, didn't she? A circle of women, both wives and widows. She'd probably made a few enemies over the past few days with her campaign against Burr, and she was certain tongues were wagging. But she was still the wife of Alexander Hamilton. Most doors would be open to her.

Most.

"A note from Papa just arrived by messenger," Angelica said, handing Eliza a paper.

Eliza read the short note: *Please come home. Let us take care of you.* She squeezed back a burning tear. "I wish I could escape and rest at home."

The Pastures, her girlhood home, was a place of sweet memories and comfort, a place where her father's steady hand never wavered, and where her late mother's embrace seemed to still fill the air. It was also the place where Eliza and Hamilton had married. Where her hopes and dreams came together and soared as she looked into her new husband's eyes.

Philip Schuyler had always been Eliza's champion. He had loved Hamilton like a son but had expressed concerns for his Betsey in marrying him.

"This family has been blessed. You'll have no such blessing with Hamilton. Your life will be very different, I'm afraid," he had said to her the night before her wedding. "He's a bright young man and maybe he will surprise me and make a fortune, but, in the meantime, if you're in need of anything, please let us know."

At that moment Eliza couldn't have imagined needing anything but Hamilton. They'd faced life together hand in hand. Come what may. She blushed over the many times during her life with Hamilton and the children that she had needed her father's help. After Angel was born she had been so overwrought with her responsibilities that she accepted his offer of sending a maid to her. It had bothered her husband almost more than it bothered her.

Unfortunately, even as she clung to her pleasant memories, she hated that her father still kept enslaved people. When she allowed herself to think about it, it would sicken her spirits, as it often had, even as a child, struggling to make sense of it. Hamilton and her father had many rows over the matter. Still, she loved her father and hoped with time that his views would soften.

It remained a great mystery to Eliza, how you could love someone and still be angered by their actions and their lifestyle.

"I shall write to him for you, Betsey, letting him know you'll be there as soon as you can. There are matters for you to attend to."

"Thank you, Angelica." Her voiced belied the anger she felt. "And attend to them we will."

CHAPTER 11

Eliza longed to attend both John Van Der Gloss's and Floyd Peabody's funerals. But, as she considered her own status, she instead sent notes to both widows, expressing her heartfelt condolences. Showing up at either home now would take much-needed attention away from the grieving widows, as Eliza herself seemed to cause a stir everywhere she went, first as wife, now as widow, to Alexander Hamilton. But she hoped to pay them each a visit over the next few days. In the meantime, she also sent a notice to Alice, inviting her to come to the Grange with any word about the British gentleman. Why hadn't she received word from her? Where could he be? Was there another way to find him? She had two people searching for him. Who else could she enlist? Where would a British businessman stay in the burgeoning city? Why did he leave the place he was staying to begin with?

It would be a wealthy Brit who refused money to lie about an incident in an establishment. Brits moved about the city with a swagger and a confidence that Eliza did not admire. It was as if they hadn't lost the War of Independence. But Eliza recently read that sixty thousand people now lived in the city. It was a difficult number to fathom. When the Dutch handed it over to them, there were a mere nine thousand residents.

"My grandparents came to America to overcome our Dutchness and then found we will never overcome it. It's a part of our souls," Eliza's mother once told her.

Eliza folded her letter to Victoria Peabody and slipped it into an envelope. She recognized the searing loss the woman was feeling and longed to embrace her, but it would have to wait.

★   ★   ★

The next morning, several mourners visited Eliza. Most of them were strangers to her but knew her Hamilton and loved him. She tried to maintain good decorum as the widow of an important man, but she was hoping to see Alice or McNally for any word on the British man who witnessed the fight in the pub.

They needed to find him.

"Mrs. General Hamilton? Are you quite well?" the petite Cynthia Collins said, leaning forward on the settee.

"Oh, I am sorry. I'm so distracted." Eliza just wanted to be left alone to ruminate on the mystery before her. She felt the urge to jot down what she'd learned.

"It's quite alright." Cynthia's brown eyes oozed sympathy. She lowered her voice. "Have you heard about the Peabodys?"

Eliza nodded. Maybe she could pry more information from Cynthia. "A suicide, wasn't it?"

"Yes. But the latest news is the family packed and left town. They even took their animals."

Eliza's hands formed fists against her black dress. "What?"

She nodded. "I don't know if it was humiliation . . . or . . . heaven knows. But it devastated the family, of course. They want no formal funeral or mourning."

A flicker of respect moved through Eliza. Bucking the formal mourning traditions? She was all for it.

Angelica cleared her throat. "Maybe they have family elsewhere. Maybe he can be buried there."

Confusion played out on Cynthia's face. "I wish they'd stayed. We well loved them in the city. We could have petitioned the church for a proper burial. That family deserves it."

"It is odd that they left so quickly. I'd planned to leave town soon for respite with my father, but there is so much to attend to." Eliza didn't believe what she was hearing. The Peabodys would not leave so soon after Floyd's death. Especially since there was no clear ruling on whether it had truly been a suicide . . . or murder.

Why else would they run off?

Angelica glanced over at her and shrugged.

Eliza loved her home's distance from the heart of the city, but now she was feeling lost and as if she didn't know the latest news. She didn't realize until that moment how Hamilton was one of her principal methods of receiving the news not published in the papers. If not from him, then she'd learn things from their friends that they'd socialize with. She'd just sent a note to Mrs. Peabody and hoped with all her heart she'd received it.

"My husband remarked it seemed as if they were frightened." Cynthia lifted her teacup and sipped.

"Frightened of what? The worst has already happened, surely," Angelica said.

But fear struck into the center of Eliza. She'd been ready to take her children and go to Albany for fear a dark mischief was afoot. Was that what Mrs. Peabody was doing? Had her husband warned her the same as Hamilton had? Cold swept through her.

"Maybe not." Eliza wrung her hands.

Cynthia seemed to follow. "Maybe she feels she must protect her children from the social ramifications."

That wasn't what Eliza had meant, but she followed her train of thought. "Because he took his own life."

"Surely some would look down their noses."

"I think not," Angelica said. "Not the Peabodys. I feel sad for them."

"But I fear not all are as kind as you, dear sister." Eliza hesitated. "But isn't there a rumor he didn't take his life?"

Silence hung in the air.

"But what—" Cynthia began.

Angelica interrupted. "Just rumors."

"That he was murdered, and they made it to look like he wasn't?" Cynthia's fair skin mottled. "Why, that would be the third murder in two weeks! Van Der Gloss, Peabody, and . . . your dear Hamilton." She reached into her bodice, retrieved a black lace-trimmed handkerchief, and dabbed her forehead.

Eliza was glad to hear that Cynthia considered Hamilton's death a murder—as it was. Just as much as Van Der Gloss's. But Peabody? She needed to know more before jumping to conclusions. They all did, before Cynthia fainted. "Let's be careful with our imaginations. We are overwrought."

But Eliza remembered again the letter in Hamilton's study and now wondered if there might be one from Peabody—or anything else linking them besides their friendship. Perhaps his witnessing the duel.

She placed her hands in her lap and steadied her breath. She needed to see this visit through. Then she'd tell Mrs. Cole to close the doors to guests, other than Alice, of course, and Paul Jinkins.

"Yes," Cynthia said. "But my husband's comment would make so much more sense if it was a murder and not a suicide. That they acted as if they were frightened. So many times, men like to keep unpleasantness from us." She quieted and waved her hand as if to brush away invisible men standing in front of her. "Which I find odd since we bear the children. I suppose they don't realize how messy that business is."

Angelica lifted her teacup. "And let us hope they never do."

CHAPTER 12

Eliza slipped away after supper, feigning a headache so she could make her way to Hamilton's study. Maybe if people believed she had a headache they would also leave her alone. Even Angelica hovered over her like a mother, not a sister. Soon, Eliza would insist that Angelica return to her own family and life. At some point Eliza would need to stand on her own two feet.

She lit a candle and its beam of light circled her view. She sat in Hamilton's chair and closed her eyes. She inhaled so deeply that she dizzied as she took in the scent of him. He'd spent countless hours here. The stacks of paper were still in the same places as when she sorted them a few days ago. She set the candle down and began her search for anything from the Peabodys.

She found a note from President Washington that Hamilton had saved. A notice of payment due. Another payment that needed notice. There were more debt notices than anything else.

Finally, she found a personal letter from Peabody thanking Hamilton for the lunch they shared. Nothing of what she sought. She'd have to use other measures. Eliza hoped Mrs. Peabody would get back to her. She'd see to it. Where had they gone? And how to find out?

Eliza spread out all the notices of what Hamilton owed to people and hoped there was a cache of money somewhere that he'd failed to mention. They had yet to read his will. But she was uncertain if he even had one.

She shoved the papers away. She would not find answers here. Maybe his law office would hold more clues to their finances and his last few days of his life. His executors had anything in the office in hand already.

She sighed. Great men were often troublesome men. This she understood as truth, as she'd been surrounded by them since a child. But were *any* men easy? Eliza didn't know. She didn't care to know. She would be done with them and their treacherous business if it were not for her sons.

"Mama?"

Eliza jumped up from Hamilton's chair and turned to find Angel.

"I knew you'd be here. Papa said so." Angel's voice was whispery as it usually was when she claimed she'd been speaking with her dead brother. Now it was her father.

Eliza reached for her hands. "My sweet girl, your father died. Remember?" Her face fell and turned ghostly pale. "Let's get some warm milk and see if Mrs. Cole has cakes in the kitchen." In the past, at such a suggestion Angel would brighten, but instead a darkness came over her.

"Papa doesn't want you here in his room."

Eliza's heart sank, but she found her legs and stood up, even as a chill traveled up her spine. Perhaps Angel needed to see another physician. "Let's get that milk, my dear."

Her face softened. "Okay, Mama. Papa will be glad you've left his room alone."

Even if her husband had come back from the dead, Hamilton would know the folly of telling her to stay out of his study. Eliza had business to attend to. For their children. For her peace of mind. Not just concerning the finances, but she desired to ensure his story was told—the correct story. And then there was whatever intrigue was happening with Van Der Gloss and Peabody and why her son had been implicated. Eliza would not rest until Hamilton's legacy was secured.

Eliza led Angel into the kitchen, where Sally, the cook, was baking biscuits for the morning.

"Good evening," Eliza said. "Might we trouble you for warm milk and a slice of something sweet?"

Sally looked at Eliza and then Angel. "Yes. Should I bring it to your room?"

"Bring it to mine, please," Angel said.

The cook nodded.

"Thank you, Sally," Eliza said. "How is your mother?"

Sally shook her head. "She's having a hard time with her breathing. Thank you for asking after her."

"Of course. Did the doctor I sent help?"

"Yes, he did. Thank you." Sally poured white, frothy milk into a pot.

Eliza had been so distracted by her own trauma that she'd forgotten about the others in her life. "If she needs more medicine, please get it for her and tell the chemist to charge our household."

The woman brightened. "Thank you."

"Good night," Eliza said. "And thank you for helping Angel tonight."

"My pleasure."

Eliza and Angel exited the room and climbed the stairs to their bedrooms.

Eliza kissed Angel on the cheek and held her. "I hope the warm milk helps you sleep." She cupped Angel's chin in her hands and studied her daughter. She was a beauty with dark eyes and soft pale skin, but her eyes were not as they used to be—observant, bright, and filled with light. Now they were dull and watery and sometimes held a vacancy that scared Eliza. "Good night."

As she left her oldest daughter alone in her room, Eliza deliberated on a physician she could call on. For, even though admitting it seemed a loss, Angel's malady had seemed to worsen. Was losing her father going to prompt her daughter to finally slip away?

Eliza shuddered to think how the children were grieving their father. She tried to be there for them, but she was wrapped up in her own pain. Thank goodness for Angelica.

Once Alexander's name was cleared, and it was safe to do so, she'd take the children to The Pastures for respite, as planned.

In the meantime, she was tired of waiting on McNally and Alice. Tomorrow she'd endeavor to take matters into her own hands. If she must search in every inn in the city for the mysterious Brit, she would. Just as she'd gone to every necessary household to campaign against Burr.

Eliza's life had taught her she could not rely on others to take care of her business. She found that was the case once again. This matter was urgent. Didn't McNally and Alice see that? Her son's reputation and future could be at risk. It was of the utmost importance that Hamilton's children kept themselves above reproach. It was a burden they'd all learned to bear, especially since Phil's death.

CHAPTER 13

If Paul Jinkins was still in this city, Eliza would find him. She slipped on her boots and readied for the journey into lower Manhattan after breakfast. Angelica would stay with the children and McNally would drive her from hotel to hotel, searching for Jinkins. Or at least that was the plan. With the curious manner in which events were unfolding, Eliza checked her expectations. She'd deal with anything else that arose, if warranted.

After their journey, McNally stopped the carriage in front of the Bleecker Hotel, one of the newer establishments in the city. Close to the harbor, where another hotel was being built, its sign read "Welcome to all weary travelers."

McNally opened the carriage door and attempted to help Eliza as she exited. She didn't take his hand. He'd failed at finding Jinkins and he obviously didn't like the fact that she'd taken up her own cause.

"A fine lady, such as yourself—" he'd started to say earlier. Eliza stopped him. She didn't think of herself that way at all. Eliza Hamilton was more than that. First, she was a mother. Now she was a mother whose son was wrongly accused of murder.

She stepped out onto the cobblestone drive of the white-bricked hotel. She'd never stayed in a hotel. When she and

Hamilton had traveled, they'd always stayed with friends or family. Hotels were foreign to her. Angelica, however, had been to many fine hotels in Paris and filled Eliza's head with stories about fresh strawberries in the morning served on silver plates and silky bed linens.

She opened the heavy wood door to a large room, appointed with blue velvet furnishings and smelling of fresh roses. A gentleman stood behind a desk and welcomed her with a tight smile.

"Good day, Mrs. General Hamilton. How may I help you?"

How she longed for a little anonymity. How freeing it would be to not be recognized. But today, it might be useful.

"Good day." She girded her loins and approached the desk where the man stood. "I hope you can help me. I'm looking for a traveler."

He tilted his head and inclined toward her. "We have several guests staying with us." He placed his glasses on his face. "Name?"

"Paul Jinkins." She watched for a reaction from the balding clerk. A reddening of the skin. A quickening of the pulse in his neck. There was nothing. He continued to scan a large registry.

"I'm sorry," he said. "He's not a guest here. But the city now has many fine hotels. It seems as if they build a new one every day. I'm sure he must be in one of them. Do you know anything else about him?"

"He's a British man here on business." Hope caught in her chest.

"Ah, yes. There are several hotels where the Brits like to stay." He lowered his voice. "Most of our guests are from the lower states. Our owner is a Southern gentleman."

"Oh, I see." Eliza did not know why it mattered.

He reached for a paper and pen. "I'll write the names of the hotels the British and other foreigners frequent."

She beamed. "Thank you. That's very helpful."

He handed her the paper. "I'm honored you came to us, Mrs. General Hamilton. Please accept my condolences on the loss of your husband."

She lowered her eyes as a pang shot up through her. "Thank you." She took the paper from him and exited the hotel.

McNally's eyes met hers, as if to say, "I told you so." He was not supportive of this venture. Eliza ignored his obvious look of victory.

"We go to this one next." She pointed at the first hotel on the list.

He cocked an eyebrow. "Is it open?"

"New hotels are opening every day." She tried not to be short with him. She liked him. He was a loyal working man, but he just wasn't good at finding Jinkins. "According to the man inside, British people favor these places." Her finger skirted along the paper.

"Do they now?" McNally's face was full of incredulity.

It was almost as if he didn't want her to seek out Paul Jinkins. Eliza turned and opened the carriage door. "Let's go, McNally. We've no time to waste."

"Yes, Mrs. General Hamilton."

She plunked herself down in the carriage. Maybe she was getting somewhere. The hotel list was culled. If the gentleman was correct, she only had five hotels to visit. Only five.

McNally climbed onto his seat and readied the horses. They moved forward. Eliza slid to the window and gazed out at the sliver of sky within her sight. *Please, God. Let us find this man who could prove Alexander's innocence.*

The fifth hotel on the list was the Bevington, and after failure at the others Eliza held little hope she'd find her man. It was getting late in the day. Even though the hotels were not distant from one another, traffic on the dusty streets prevented a smooth journey. She'd mostly sat in the carriage and sweated while traveling to the hotels, where she'd say a few words, only to find that Jinkins was not a guest.

The Bevington was a tall building with a white façade, with urns of hyacinths edging the walkways. McNally insisted on coming with her. He was afraid people were not being forthright with her. As if he would be able to tell.

As she approached the desk with McNally on her heels, Eliza heard her name and turned to find a polished gentleman standing there. "Yes?"

"I understand you've been looking for me. I'm Paul Jinkins."

Eliza's heart fluttered. Here was the man in the flesh. The man who could prove Alexander's innocence and maybe more. McNally and Alice had been searching for Jinkins, as had the constable. As had Eliza. And now here he was. A balding man with piercing blue eyes and a paunch. And a kind smile.

"May I offer you a cool drink?" He led her to an area in the small lobby where there was a carafe of water.

She nodded, following him.

McNally stood nearby, as the two of them sat together on a settee. Passersby glanced and moved on. She in her widow's weeds in a fine hotel might give one pause. But she shoved those notions aside. She needed to get to the point.

"Mr. Jinkins, I come to offer my thanks."

"For what?"

"My son, Alexander, was in a fight a few nights back."

He stiffened. His warm smile vanished.

"I believe you were there?"

His eyes flitted back and forth, then came to rest on Eliza's face. He nodded. "I was." He lowered his voice. "And I noticed Alexander leave after he hit the man."

A tear stung at her eye as a knot in her stomach loosened. He wasn't lying. Relief swept through her. All she need do was to repeat to the constable what Jinkins had just said. But there was another matter at hand.

"I'm relieved to hear you say so, of course. I know my son didn't kill him."

"What can I help you with?" He edged forward.

"I wonder why you're the only witness to say Alexander left. The others claim he stayed and fought more."

He glanced at the tower of a man standing behind Eliza. McNally had no affection for the Brits and Eliza was certain the man sitting with her didn't like the Irish. He sized up McNally.

Eliza drank her water in an unladylike rush. She didn't realize how thirsty she was until that moment.

"I am a trader," Jinkins said as he brushed something from his trousers. "My business takes me all over the world. I'm a keen observer of men and their foibles."

McNally cleared his throat, as if to say "Get on with it." Eliza ignored him but felt slightly embarrassed.

"I have no reason to lie to the constable or judges. I'm a businessman, not a politician."

How many times had Eliza listened to similar statements? "And?"

"When a man approached me, suggesting I might say that your son continued the fight until the man's death, it raised my hackles. I may not be a godly man, but I have principles." His eyes darted back and forth again as McNally grunted. Jinkins's eyebrows lifted as he glanced at McNally. "Principles that have served me well in business and life."

"Who was he?" Eliza's patience was wearing thin. She didn't care about his principles or godliness. She was trying to be polite, but it was getting difficult.

He shrugged. "I don't know. I've never seen him before, and I've not seen him since. But then again, I've since moved to this side of town to conduct my business."

McNally crossed his beefy arms.

"What can you tell us about him?" Eliza persisted.

"Not much more than a boy, really. More a messenger, not the man pulling the strings. He was well dressed, wore some interesting jewelry—"

"Jewelry?" McNally interrupted and rolled his eyes.

Eliza shot him a glare of reproach. The man in front of them wore a pinky ring on one hand and a wedding ring on the other.

"I notice such things because one of the products I trade in is gemstones."

"Fascinating," Eliza said. She was not one to wear a lot of jewelry, but she did admire it on others. "So he was young and wore jewelry. Anything distinctive about the jewelry? What else can you tell us?"

He squinted his eyes. "He was tall, carried himself well, had dark curly hair and dark eyes, I believe. He wore a gold ring with some sort of insignia on it. I'm sorry I didn't get a closer look. But he wore it on his right hand. It was not a marriage ring."

"Will you talk with the constable? Tell him about this man who tried to sway your testimony?" Eliza's heart soared. Here was the man who was going to clear her son's name, who could prove there was intrigue afoot, that someone was trying to blame Alexander for murder. Of course, that left the question as to why. But she'd figure that out as well. Oh yes, she would.

"Indeed, I will."

After accompanying Jinkins to the constable's station, where he gave a statement, Eliza almost flew back to Harlem. Even though Alexander was not completely cleared, because it was only one man's word, it appeared better for him, and her spirits soared so much that she didn't pay attention to her usual landmarks. She didn't know if the river ran high or low or if the blackberries along the road had ripened.

Though her spirits were high that Alexander would be cleared of any wrongdoing, doubt began to creep in as she considered that someone was trying to blame a murder on him. And someone had indeed killed poor Van Der Gloss, and perhaps Peabody as well. All of this trauma on the heels of the loss of her husband.

She tugged at her collar, a blasted wooly thing that scratched her the more she sweated. She hoped there were no connections here. She hoped she was creating trouble where there was none. Maybe all she needed to do was focus on the good news, sleep on the rest of it, and tomorrow would be a brand-new day.

CHAPTER 14

Mrs. Cole helped Eliza peel off her heavy mourning wear, which needed a good washing after a day in the city. Eliza slipped on a more comfortable lounging dress while Mrs. Cole coughed and glanced at her.

"I'm not going anywhere but the garden. The children have been fed and are in bed. I've no appetite for an evening meal. Let me take in the garden air unfettered," Eliza reassured her.

What she needed right now was fresh air and to sit in the gardens. It was a good place to think.

Mrs. Cole nodded briskly. "Of course."

Dusk fell across the Grange as Eliza stepped outside into the cooler evening air, and a breeze rolled in from the river. Earlier this year, tulips, hyacinths, and lilies dotted the landscape. Now the roses and lilies bloomed, planted near the thirteen sweet gum trees, one for each state. Thirty-two acres of her husband's dreams made into reality. Not only did he have a hand in the design of their home, but also in the details of the gardens. Hamilton had considered each detail of their home thoughtfully, even naming the place after his grandfather's estate in Scotland. An emptiness sank into her chest.

Eliza's home brimmed with children and family, yet with him gone she felt so achingly alone. A memory washed over her of playing barefoot in the garden with her parents and sisters back in The Pastures, her girlhood home. The recollection sprang so vividly she could practically smell the rich earth of home. If only she could travel back to that more innocent time. She slipped off her house slippers and strolled to the wild rose bed. The scent soothed her. The earth cooled her feet as she curled her toes and watched as the dirt slipped through them, then turned her face to the heavens. *This too shall pass.*

"Mrs. General Hamilton," a male voice said.

She gasped and almost tumbled over. She turned toward the voice.

Mrs. Cole trailed the man. "I'm sorry, madam. I told him not to disturb you." Her jaw was firm. "He was supposed to wait in the parlor."

"I observed you through the window. I'm sorry to disturb you, but the matter is most urgent," he said, tipping his hat. It was Mr. Jeremiah Renquist, the solicitor. Hamilton had been dead just over two weeks. What news could he bring her now?

Eliza met his gaze. She had rejected his cards for a reason—her mind was not as sharp as it needed to be to speak with this peevish, impertinent man. "What can be so important?" she asked.

His face softened and his eyes darted from side to side as if he didn't know where to gaze. "I'd hoped to bring this up over a cup of tea, in a more genteel manner, but you've refused my cards."

He used words like "genteel," and yet here he was unannounced, sneaking into her garden.

Eliza lifted her chin. "Sir, I am in mourning. I don't wish to speak of wills and money."

He cast his eyes down at his clasped hands. "I'm sorry, Mrs. General Hamilton. But you need to stop spending money. You cannot pay for the apple trees you ordered."

Her heart plummeted to her feet.

There must be a mistake.

"No mistake," he said, as if he read her mind. "I've gone over the accounts several times. You will have to stop spending unnecessarily."

But the trees *were* necessary. She and Hamilton planned to grow apples, for pies, cakes, and for the children to pluck and eat. The trees were the next step to their dream garden. The very one where she stood. "Be forthright with me, sir." Eliza had assumed her finances were tied up because of Alexander's death, that soon they'd work themselves out, but she needed to be certain. She knew they had many debts but was uncertain of the money coming into the household.

He stepped forward. "Your husband's executors are meeting to discuss details. I don't have them yet. All I know is there's very little cash for you to live on. You must be cautious."

Eliza was aware of insufficient monies, as she maintained the household budget. But for special purchases, like the apple trees, she relied on different accounts. Her own accounts were set up by her family and they were dwindling, as she and Hamilton had been forced to avail themselves over the years. Could it be that Hamilton had not considered money when he dueled Burr? Knowing he might die? Hard to believe. Her stomach turned.

Oh, Alexander, what have you done?

"Fine, Mr. Renquist, I'm certain this is a mistake. I'll wait to purchase anything large, even my apple trees."

He cleared his throat. "One more thing."

She lifted her face.

"Are you quite well?"

Of course, he'd been hearing the stories about her visiting—unusual for a grieving widow. But as his eyes swept to her feet, Eliza gathered she'd been standing barefoot in the dirt for the duration of the conversation. Her face heated. Hamilton had been the only man to ever glimpse her feet. And this man had the audacity to not only observe them, but to remark on it.

"Mrs. Cole? Please show Mr. Renquist out." She turned her face to the setting sun, as she didn't want him to see how flustered she was.

She gazed at the bright pink and orange colors spreading across the sky. She listened to the sound of footsteps fade away. Thank God he was gone. Now, what to do?

The evidence could not be plainer. It wasn't that their accounts were poorly managed. It was that they lived from month to month. They no longer would have Hamilton's income from his law practice. Her husband hadn't planned to die, even as he marched off to fight. They were in serious debt. She'd go to her father, eventually. But in the meantime, she needed to find a way to bring money into the household.

From her years helping with the Widow Society, she had witnessed how creditors would come into homes and take the family furniture, jewelry, and housewares. As with the other families, hers had worked so hard for what it had. They'd only been in this house for two years. She could go through the place and identify where each item had come from and could remember how they'd saved until they could purchase everything. What did it matter now that he was gone? Something caught in her throat and it escaped as a scream. She dropped to her knees and sobbed.

CHAPTER 15

As morning broke, Eliza awakened with a start. She'd been dreaming. Images, movement, smells dipped into her memory but left her afraid. Her heart raced. There was someone who'd tried to blame Alexander for the murder of one of his father's friends. Another one of his father's friends had died mysteriously. There was a killer afoot.

And what's more, Eliza had no idea how she'd provide for her children. Which of those things were tormenting her mind so that she had bad dreams?

She untangled herself from the bed covers and placed her feet on the floor. Mrs. Cole had washed her second mourning dress and had it draped over the dresser. Next to it was the black lace collar she'd worn the day Alice had visited. The collar her grandmother had made. Soon the staff would need to be paid. Not to mention the university. And the mortgage. Had Alice been correct when she said the lace collar would fetch a pretty price?

Eliza's stomach tightened. Women had sold their precious items for generations to feed their families. She was luckier than most. But now, she was on the cusp of desperation. And she was too humiliated to tell her family. That Hamilton had not prepared for this day stabbed at her already broken heart.

She ran her fingers over the fine lace. Her grandmother would forgive her. She was now in heaven and had no such worldly concerns. It was just material. Eliza needed to sell it. In fact, she'd sell several pieces.

Wasn't there an old story about a woman making and selling lace to feed her family? It rolled around in Eliza's memories. She couldn't quite remember the details, but it rang true. As valuable as lace was now, it was much more valuable a hundred years ago. And even though Eliza hadn't made this lace, it was the same principle. She'd give up anything to help her family.

She remembered her grandmother's words: "There is something sacred about lace. It's present at all of life's important events—baptism, First Communion, the marriage veil, and funerals and mourning. It's fitting that most lacemakers are women, for we are the keepers of all of it."

Eliza's heart warmed as she remembered. No, she couldn't work like Alice, as it would be frowned upon. But who was to say she couldn't earn money her own way? Earning for her family in their time of need? She had to think the woman who crafted her lace would understand and even be proud that she was selling the beautiful things she'd made by hand to provide for her family.

But where was Alice? She hadn't come when asked yesterday. Eliza hoped she was well. She'd send another note today and hope for the best.

★　★　★

"I don't understand, Betsey." Angelica's eyes were on her embroidery. She didn't look directly at Eliza. When she called her "Betsey," Eliza discerned she was feeling extra protective. "Why are you still concerned about this matter if your son is nearly free and clear of all accusations?"

"He's not quite free. There is only the testimony of Mr. Jinkins. They may need more, like the actual man who approached him. But in any case, someone accused my son of murder. It's not over until I find out who and why." Eliza tried to focus on her own needlepoint, but her rage made it hard to concentrate.

Angelica dropped her embroidery onto her lap. "I fear your grief has blinded you."

"If it's done anything, other than break my heart, it's sharpened me. I knew something was wrong when he left me that morning, and what did I do? I ignored it. I quarreled with him. But ultimately I ignored it." Angelica's eyes widened as she listened to Eliza's loud voice. "I won't ignore my feelings any longer. What is the point? I can't bear any more losses!"

Angelica engulfed her sister in her arms as she sobbed. Anger plucked furiously at Eliza's chest and throat and escaped via hot tears. If only she'd listened to herself! If only! Maybe her Hamilton would be next to her right now!

She pulled back from Angelica. "Someone tried to say my son murdered one of his father's good friends. And then alluded he had something to do with Peabody's death. Don't you see? Not only is there someone trying to harm Alexander, but perhaps there is another person who will be harmed in the meantime."

"You mean—"

"I mean I'm afraid that two deaths within two weeks of our Hamilton's death, both friends of his . . . and someone trying to frame his son . . . something is going on here. If I don't figure this out, maybe someone else will be killed. Don't you see?" Eliza herself had just now verbalized what she'd been feeling. Her intuition was on high alert.

Angelica and Hamilton both often disregarded her intuition. But it was always spot-on. Many times she'd just kept it to herself and watched it unfold. Her Iroquois friends had respected intuition when she was a girl playing with them. But as she grew up and became a woman there were too many other concerns rather than listen to that voice in her head, that sinking feeling in her stomach. Or prickling at the back of her neck. She appreciated now how important it was to listen to her intuition.

Angelica's face turned from an expression of concern to something else. "Eliza, you are scaring me. I fear for your health."

Eliza swallowed. Angelica lacked imagination, much to her detriment. Eliza found herself wanting to shake her. Why couldn't she see what was so plain to Eliza?

"I'm going to find Mrs. Cole. You need some refreshment." She was gone before Eliza could tell her that was not what she needed. As for what she needed . . . she remained unsure, but she would determine it in time.

It never did her any good to argue with strong-willed Angelica. She'd let her primp and care for her, as she was wont to do. But Angelica could not control her thoughts, and that's what Eliza needed—space to think. What should her next move be?

She listed things to do in her mind: visit with Mrs. Van Der Gloss, write to Mrs. Peabody again, talk with the constable again about finding the young man who'd approached Mr. Jinkins, and, not for the first time, she wished she could go into taverns and establishment that she was not allowed to by virtue of her gender and status. But there was nothing to do about that.

Mrs. Cole entered the room. "Alice Rhodes here to see you. Shall I bring tea?"

Eliza's heart lightened and she nearly stood and jumped. "Yes, please. Show her in."

Alice walked in with a slight limp and sat down on the nearest chair. "I must apologize, Mrs. General Hamilton. I'd hoped to bring you news of Mr. Jinkins much sooner."

"I found him yesterday." Eliza watched as Mrs. Cole brought in the tea service, with Angelica trailing her. "It's quite alright."

"Are you well, Alice?" Angelica poured the black tea. She handed Alice a cup and saucer.

Alice took the fine cup in her wrinkled, red hands, one with only half a pinky finger. "I'm fine. I twisted my old ankle the other day on the cobblestones. But I've done that before and know I'll be better soon." She sipped the tea and turned her attention back to Eliza. "So you found our man? Did he get you the information you wanted?"

Eliza nodded. "Yes, but I fear I've only uncovered the tip of the matter." She had no intention of telling Alice her family business. No, indeed. But she wondered if there was a way to allude to it without revealing Alexander's alleged involvement. "I'm very concerned that the recent deaths link back to my husband."

Alice smacked her lips. "That's good tea, mum. Tell me more."

Eliza struggled to find the right words. So she poured herself tea. Angelica eyed her in warning. "It just seems odd that there've been two deaths—a murder and a suicide within a week of one another and two weeks after Hamilton's death. And all of them knew each other."

Alice's bushy eyebrows hitched, but she didn't say a word.

"I fear the grief has muddled my dear sister's thinking." Angelica set her cup down.

"Perhaps," Eliza said, wishing Angelica would leave the room. She wanted to speak with Alice about the lace, but Angelica would only offer her money if she understood her circumstances. Eliza didn't wish to take money from her sister's family. She'd made up her mind to sell the lace.

Alice drank her tea. "Grief can take your mind. But I've no doubt Mrs. General Hamilton will be fine."

Eliza nodded. "Thank you." She turned to her sister. "Angelica, can you please get the headache powder from my bedroom? I fear I feel a headache coming on."

Angelica stood. "Certainly."

"I should be going," Alice said.

"No," Eliza said. "Please stay. Once I take the medicine, I'll be fine."

Angelica left the room with a swish of her skirts.

"You look well," Alice said as she sat her tea down.

She was canny. Eliza thanked God for her. She kept her voice low. "I have my lace. I want you to sell it for me."

Confusion played over Alice's face.

"I'm sure it will be fine." Eliza didn't want to embarrass Alice by revealing too much of her family's dire circumstances. "I just need some cash until things settle with the estate." She reached into her bodice and drew out the lace. "Please take it and sell it for me."

"Mrs. General Hamilton." Alice studied the lace with reverence. "Are you certain?"

She held her gaze. "I trust you."

Alice batted her eyes. Eliza was unsure if she were blinking away tears. She was most assuredly moved.

"I'll do my best and will bring you the money." She slipped the lace into her bag.

"I know you will." She sensed Angelica coming down the stairs. "Let's keep this between us. Shall we?"

"Understood."

Eliza was not one to take medicine when she didn't need it, but she downed the headache powder when her sister handed it to her. The bitter taste lingered. She reached for her tea. The flavor helped to wash away the bitterness, but not completely. She eyed the biscuits. Eliza had no appetite, but she feared she needed to eat. She held the plate up to Alice, who gratefully took one, as did Angelica. Eliza took a bite, then another. The bad taste was almost gone.

"I do despise the taste of headache powder," Eliza said and took another bite.

"Drink more tea," Angelica said. "I'm just flabbergasted by the dreadful news."

"There have been rumors, mind you," Alice said after swallowing a bit of her biscuit. "The rumors suggest that Peabody did not take his own life."

"We've heard those rumors," Angelica responded flatly. "Rumors."

"There were fresh footprints in the mud outside the barn. Not his prints," Alice continued.

"Where did you hear that?" Angelica said.

"I know the man who cares for the horses—or used to. They let him go along with most of the staff before they left town."

Eliza's heart sank. So it was true that they had left town. Was it due to humiliation? Fear? "I've been trying to write to Mrs. Peabody. Do you know where they went?"

Alice smacked her lips together. "I can't say for sure. But her family lives in New Jersey. If I were a betting woman . . ."

"But of course, you're not," Angelica nipped, which prompted Alice to cackle.

"Only if the odds are certainly in my favor." She beamed.

After they quieted down, Eliza spoke. "The post office can be so slow. Do you know how I might get a note to her?"

Alice cocked her head. "I believe I do."

Eliza and Angelica exchanged triumphant glances. Alice was well connected in ways they could never have imagined.

Eliza penned her note to Mrs. Peabody while Alice and Angelica chatted. When Alice left, she had two items from Eliza—only one of which Angelica knew about. Eliza sent Alice off with a silent prayer that the lace would sell and help her get her family through this rough patch—and that Victoria Peabody would see her.

CHAPTER 16

Alice was limping along down the hill, the Grange at her back, when a carriage pulled alongside her.

"Good Day, mum."

She turned to face Davey McNally. "Hello."

"I notice yer limping a bit. Can I give you a lift?"

Alice didn't like hopping into a carriage with a man she barely knew holding the reins. But she was in pain. The more she walked, the worse it hurt. She'd overdone it this time. "Does the missus know?"

"No," McNally said. "I'm on an errand from her, figured she wouldna mind."

She nodded and hefted herself into the carriage. "Thank you."

Alice sat on the leather seat and tried not to cry from the relief. *Silly old fool.* She turned her head and watched the Grange fade away, high on its hill, facing out over Harlem and Manhattan.

She sighed and turned to face front. Eliza Hamilton was not a fool. Of course, Alice had always known that—but she was still surprised by her cunning. Everybody in Alice's circle figured Peabody had been killed. But then again, servants and shopkeepers saw people and circumstances in a different light. People often spilled their worst business around servants and tradespeople, as if they were not people with their own minds and could hear every word concerning marital affairs, wife beatings, and lost money. But they did.

How did the great Alexander Hamilton leave his wife and children with next to nothing? So destitute that Eliza had to sell a piece of valuable lace? Images of Hamilton's bloody, battered body taunted Alice. She guessed he didn't think he'd die so soon. He had more living to do. You just never knew where life would take you. Alice twisted at her dress as her ankle throbbed.

"Where do you live, mum?" Davey yelled from the front of the carriage.

"You can leave me at the cabby stand."

"Are ye sure? I'm heading to the Fly to pick up some flour and sugar. Surely I can take you closer to your home."

"Aye, yes. The Fly is close by. I live on Pearl Street." She'd quite forgotten it was market day at the Fly, the biggest market in the city. She wondered if there might be a buyer for Eliza's lace there. Her ankle pulsed in pain. She grunted. Maybe she'd ask one of her friends to look into it.

The carriage swayed back and forth, its rhythm reminding Alice of early days in her life. If only things had turned out differently, she might have a carriage of her own. She cackled at herself. But why worry about these things now? She'd done well enough that it would send some people from her past into a shock to know it. She cracked a grin. That some woman could survive well without a man was beyond some folks' understanding.

Some women. Alice considered Victoria Peabody and what she'd learned from a maid who worked in the house. She didn't know if the woman would survive the death of her husband. Oh, she'd be provided for, but she was not sound. Adding to her troubles was the humiliation of a possible suicide. Victoria Peabody's life would surely be a shadow of what it was.

Eliza's concern spoke of her knowledge of the nuances of this matter. Eliza and Victoria had both lost their husbands in horrible ways. But Eliza's mind remained sharp and astute.

The country scenery gave way to buildings and crowds of people the closer they got to the market. Alice found herself laughing, imagining the faces of her housemates when she exited from a carriage.

CHAPTER 17

The Van Der Gloss family home was not in lower Manhattan—which Eliza was grateful for. It wasn't in Harlem, either, which would have been more convenient for her, but the world didn't exist to serve her. That she knew.

But the distance still required a carriage ride with McNally as the driver. He was just back with her flour and sugar. She'd rather walk anywhere than bear another ride with him. She couldn't understand why he'd failed at finding Jinkins when it only took her a day.

King's College loomed ahead. When she spotted it, Eliza knew the Van Der Gloss family home was close. As they drove by, memories of the college pulled at her heart. Hamilton went to school here, as did Phil, and now Alexander. She took in a breath and held it, as if by holding it the pain would subside. It did not. She turned her head away from the window.

Soon enough, the carriage was pulling up to the Van Der Gloss home, where Rose Van Der Gloss expected her. As McNally opened the door, Eliza tried to calm her mind. She was here to offer comfort first, and then to find out anything she could about the days leading up to John's death. But she didn't wish to be insensitive, even though her business was urgent. Two men had died. Two men who were friends of her husband, and who had probably witnessed the duel. Were there others in danger?

She walked toward the door and it opened, as they were expecting her. The housemaid nodded at Eliza. "Follow me, mum," she said. She led her through white marbled halls into the sitting room, where Rose Van Der Gloss stood. She walked unsteadily over to Eliza, looking as if she were going to fall over. Eliza opened her arms and the young woman fell into them, sobbing. Eliza held her there, rubbing her back until the sobbing stopped. She ran her hands up and down her shoulders as Rose pulled her head up and eyed her. The fear and pain in her blue eyes was almost too much for Eliza to bear. "There, there, my dear. Let's have a seat."

The women wore the same black dress but made with different fabrics. Rose's was silky and soft, whereas Eliza's was wool and cotton. Sometimes she wore black lace, but not today. Their white caps were almost exactly the same.

Rose and Eliza sat on the sofa together. The tea service sat in place already. Eliza was beginning to hate tea, but she must be polite. She poured tea for the young widow from a mourning teapot much like her own. They both sipped their tea. Rose sniffed. "I don't know what I'm going to do."

Eliza set her tea down on the table in front of them. "What exactly do you mean?"

"What will I do without him?" Rose's voice squeaked.

"You will take it one day at a time. Like the rest of us." Eliza lifted her tea. "I'm truly sorry for your loss."

"And I for yours." Her voice was lower and more controlled now.

Rose looked as if she was nothing but bones. She was as white as the clouds in the sky, even though she wore rouge and powder. "Have you been eating, my dear?" Eliza queried.

"Have you?" Rose's eyebrow lifted.

For the first time, Eliza wondered what image *she* must be presenting to the world. Certainly she'd lost weight, and she was suspicious of her own pallor. She didn't quite know what to say. Honesty was best. "I have no appetite. I have only eaten because Angelica insists."

Rose harrumphed. "You can't say no to Angelica."

Eliza smiled. "No, indeed."

"My own sister will arrive from Boston tomorrow." She sipped her tea. "Sisters are a blessing. For the most part."

Once again, Eliza smiled. "Aye. I know what you mean. What can I do for you? Do you need anything?"

"No. I think I'm well cared for. Except for the loneliness . . . and I don't mind saying this to you . . . but the sense of confusion. I've mentioned it to several visitors. I know people die, of course, and some die tragically, like our husbands." Her eyes met with Eliza's. "But I struggle to make sense of it."

Eliza perceived an opening to the subject. But it called for caution. "I completely understand."

"Of course you do!" She said it almost too quickly.

The room stilled, as if waiting for Eliza to say something else. The yellow curtain. The blue settees and chairs. The flowered carpet. All seemed to wait. "I keep thinking about the day before the duel." Eliza balled her fists in her lap. "The clues were before me. I begged him to open up. He would not." She watched for Rose's reaction. She gave a slight nod. "And thinking back, he wasn't himself for days, maybe weeks before. When I first learned he'd been shot, I blamed myself for not stopping him somehow . . ." Eliza faded off. She had nothing more to say.

Rose took her hand. "I felt the same. My husband had not been himself at all, especially right after Hamilton's death. But the week leading up to it as well. I can't quite put my finger on it. But I fear there was something I could have done to stop his death. Murdered in cold blood!" She squeezed Eliza's hand almost too tightly.

Eliza's suspicions were confirmed. Van Der Gloss had been involved with something. "Do you know I found a note from your husband to mine?"

Rose brightened and let go of Eliza's hand. "Do tell!"

"It mentioned that he'd found evidence that someone was setting Hamilton up about the Treasury theft years ago."

Rose gasped and her hands covered her mouth.

"What is it?"

"Victoria Peabody mentioned the same thing to me. A note about a conspiracy involving our husbands. She mentioned a list of some kind."

Sweat pricked at Eliza's forehead. She patted her face with her hand. Her theory was correct, yet queasiness churned in her stomach. "What note? What list?"

"I've not seen it. Victoria mentioned it to me. That's all I could get from her, as she was very distraught, as you can imagine. Trina!" Rose called and the girl who opened the door came into the room. "Please bring us some of that lemonade your mother just made. It's quite warm for hot tea."

"Yes, ma'am."

The idea of lemonade cheered Eliza.

"Is lemonade all right with you?"

"It sounds wonderful," Eliza said in a low voice. Until this moment, this conspiracy had only been an inkling. But now it was real. Her intuition had led her down the right path. But she didn't know quite what to do about it. She needed to ask about that list. To find that list.

Trina brought the lemonade into the room and the glass was cold in Eliza's hand. "Rose, I wonder if you might remember anything of the day you said your husband acted strangely." She sipped the cool drink. Its sweet tartness was a welcome—the inside of her mouth sparked with flavor.

Rose drank deeply from her own glass and then set it down. "He fretted about his will, for one thing. I've lost count of how many times he changed it in the month before his death."

Eliza's skin prickled. It was the same with Hamilton. She hadn't considered it strange, but now that she contemplated it, it was. There had been no circumstances she discerned that would have led to a change in Hamilton's will.

"Who is his solicitor?"

"Jonathan Drake. In fact, he switched solicitors two months ago. I don't know why he changed from dear old Mr. Barnes, but there you have it." Rose twisted at her collar. "Drake is a bit of a cad. Unmarried and appears to enjoy it. He's also quite a card player."

Jonathan Drake. Eliza recognized that name. Directly out of school, he worked briefly for Hamilton. But now he was an associate of Aaron Burr's. Of course. All roads led back to Burr. Was he at the bottom of this? Was he killing off witnesses to the duel? Killing off those who witnessed his most hideous crime? That made sense to her.

She shivered, considering that other men might be in jeopardy. But why? What was the web that linked them? Was it simply the duel? If she could figure it out, she might help to save a life. As she considered the Peabodys, she remembered Hamilton's statement once more, that if anything happened to him, she should take the children and go to her father's home. She herself would not go until this matter was settled. But she would send the children. Tomorrow. And if she could manage it, she'd send Angelica with them.

CHAPTER 18

"How did your visit go?" Angelica asked Eliza as she slid a disc across the backgammon board.

They sat in the parlor, attempting to amuse themselves with something other than talk of death and murder.

"Rose is doing as well as can be expected." Eliza mulled over the discs on the board, which was aging and cracking, as she'd owned the game since she was a child. It had been a gift from Benjamin Franklin, who had taught her how to play. She made her move. "She misses her husband terribly but is well cared for. She's lost weight and is quite pale."

Angelica studied the board. "You've left me very few options."

"I wonder if you might accompany the children to Papa's. I do hate to send them alone with Angel. Alexander is back at his studies, with the constable's permission. Angel is responsible, but at times, she's off with the fairies."

Angelica lifted her eyes and met her sister's. "When?"

"Tomorrow."

"Why aren't you coming?"

"There are things I need to attend to here and then I will be there in a few more days."

Angelica straightened. "That's why I'm here. To help you with everything. What is it you need to do?"

"Are you going to move your disc or not?"

She moved and Eliza snatched her disc from the board. "Ah-ha!"

"Honestly! Who can beat you at this game?"

"I learned from a master." Eliza grinned as she began to clean up the game. "What I need you to do is to take the children to Father's home, where they will be well cared for." And safer, which she did not say aloud.

Angelica stood. "Very well." She twisted around, her black skirts swishing as she did so. "With the quicker trip by ferry to Albany now it won't be a bad journey." She pointed her finger at Eliza. "But I'm giving you two days. If you are not home with us by then, I'll be back here to get you. Do you understand?"

Eliza's heart thudded in anticipation. Two whole days of freedom to research without question. To find more lace to sell, also without question. To hopefully figure out who was killing witnesses to the duel and stop any further harm. It wasn't a long time. It wasn't enough time. But it was a good start.

"Do you want to play again?" Eliza asked.

"No. I'm tired of never winning and I need to stretch my legs. I'm going for a walk. Care to join me?"

Eliza would normally say yes, as she loved to walk and had made it her daily practice until Hamilton's death. But she wanted to inspect Hamilton's office without questions from her sister. "Not today. I'm a bit weary from my visit."

Angelica slanted her eyes, as if in scrutiny. "Fine." She exited the room, leaving Eliza to finish packing up the board game and stash it on a shelf.

She waited until the she heard the front door of the Grange open and close. Eliza slipped downstairs into Hamilton's office, with the stacks of paper and books everywhere. She glanced out the window and spotted Angelica walking along the row of gum trees just outside the house.

Eliza's husband had been an astute record keeper. She'd assumed something in his desk drawers or the stacks of paper would shed some light on what linked all of the murdered men. But as she regarded the chaos, her mind was plunged into a swamp of memories of nights spent writing while her husband dictated, walking into this room and finding Hamilton slumped over, asleep on his desk after a night of writing, and the morning the desk was first brought to this room. How he was so thrilled with this small office, surmising that working from home would be better for his burgeoning family.

Eliza swallowed. Once again, she swore to herself to keep his legacy alive, and once again she was afraid of what she might find. She opened a drawer that she had yet to open during her other visits to her husband's inner sanctorum. This drawer was full of Hamilton's diaries. Her heart fluttered as she lifted out the first one. She set it on the desk, and as she opened it the spine made a cracking noise. The pages smelled of ink, as these entries were made only a day or so before his death.

There were the words penned by her love. The familiar loops, waves, and lines of her husband's writing. His pen and inkwell sat in wait on the table. She opened the ink. She inhaled the scent. It would always remind her of her Hamilton, as he often smelled of ink, his fingers stained with it, as sometimes hers were as well. She closed the inkwell and turned her attention to the diary.

She skimmed the pages for anything that seemed unusual. There!

My men inform me that there is now enough evidence. They know who stole the money for which I was unjustly accused.

Eliza's heartbeat raced. About the time Hamilton was blamed for stealing money from the Treasury, and whispers took root, Maria Reynolds's name was brought forward. Being accused of stealing money was more dishonorable to Hamilton than his hidden affair with Maria. So he had manipulated public attention away from the possibility of his thievery, and into the muck of his affair, making his accounting of it very public.

Many people imagined that the Reynolds affair was pure fiction, invented just to sway the attention of the public. Parts of it were, Eliza mused. But not everything, unfortunately. Of course she knew Hamilton was innocent of the theft. But it had never been proven as to who actually did steal the money. In many circles, Hamilton was still considered guilty.

The pain of that time had been put behind Eliza, but it was always just beneath her skin and could be called upon at any moment. But she was never one to lick her wounds for long. Her Hamilton had loved her. He loved their children. Maria Reynolds was in the past, where she belonged.

Eliza read on, but there was no more mention of the discovery.

She threw the diary down on the desk. He'd finally gained evidence proving that he did not steal the money, and then he was killed. Her throat ached from stopping herself from screaming. Did this evidence point to Burr—or one of his men? Is that what the duel had been over? Nobody seemed to know. Or they simply wouldn't talk about it to his grieving widow.

Where was this evidence? Who did it point to?

Hamilton! He'd lived his life for his country, and being accused in such a manner tore him to pieces. It would have meant much to him to finally be found innocent in the public eye.

She stood and faced the tiny room, filled with books and paper. She needed to organize the papers and find someone to write his life story. But first, she needed the identity of the man who killed Van Der Gloss and perhaps Peabody, so there would be no more killing connected to her dear husband's good name. Or her son's.

She'd bet good money that the man in question was Aaron Burr.

CHAPTER 19

With the children and Angelica off on their journey to Albany, and Mrs. Cole instructed to turn away visitors, Eliza had two days to roam about her home and her city unfettered.

First, she needed to find Alice to see if she'd been able to sell her lace so that she could pay off some of what she and Hamilton owed. And while she was in lower Manhattan, she'd query her solicitor about Aaron Burr's whereabouts. Where was the justice? If a man killed another man, should he not be imprisoned? At the very least, she'd hoped he would leave the city and never come back, but now she almost hoped he was still here, for it would make sense that his hand was at play. Of course, that may not matter if Jonathan Drake was doing his dirty work.

The day was steamy, and as Eliza sat in the carriage, she yearned for a breeze. But even when she poked her head out the small window there was no breeze.

She slumped back into her seat and sweated.

When they pulled up to the Widow Society, Eliza's mind jumped back to the years she'd volunteered there. She'd met so many wonderful women who'd fallen on hard times by virtue of their husband's death. McNally opened the door and helped her out of the vehicle. He gave her a quick nod and smile.

She slipped her finger between her collar and her skin, straightened her widow's cap, and drew in air. Where was the air? Sweat trickled down her back as she shuffled into the old building. Things were much the same as she remembered them. It smelled of the morning's breakfast and not quite clean linens. The front room was decorated with a hodgepodge of castaway furnishings. Announcements were hung on the back wall, along with the rules of the establishment. No imbibing, no bringing men into the establishment, and church attendance was mandatory.

Mrs. Schumacher, the matron of the establishment, walked out of the back hallway and spotted Eliza. A grin cracked her otherwise dour face. "Mrs. General Hamilton! I'm so glad to see you." She hugged Eliza. "I'm so sorry to learn of your dear Hamilton's death." She'd had a thick Prussian accent years ago and Eliza noted it was now almost gone.

"Thank you, Mrs. Schumacher."

"Whatever are you doing here? Can I offer you tea?" She pushed her spectacles up her nose.

"No, thank you, but can I trouble you for some water?"

"I'll see to it. Please have a seat and I'll be back with some cool water." She scurried off. Mrs. Schumacher was a large but quick woman, very light on her feet.

Eliza sat on the tattered settee. Mrs. Schumacher soon entered the room with a cool glass of water. Eliza wanted to scream with pleasure. She concentrated on not gulping it down.

A woman gripping her daughter's hand entered the room.

"Where are we going?" the child asked in a whiny voice.

The mother shushed her and pulled her along outside.

Eliza's attention turned back to Mrs. Schumacher. She couldn't get distracted. There were many women here, and some had children. Her mind could slip into helping them—as it would any other time. But now she focused on finding Alice. Once her situation was clear, she'd help them.

"I'm looking for Alice Rhodes. Do you remember her?"

Mrs. Schumacher shrugged. "Aye. She checks in occasionally to see if we need anything. She donates and helps clean sometimes."

Eliza sat forward. "I know this is an unusual request. But do you know where she lives?"

Mrs. Schumacher's eyebrows gathered. "Why yes. She lives in a group house with a few other women on Pearl Street. I believe it's 22 Pearl Street."

"Group house? I thought she was doing well," Eliza said before finishing her water.

"She is. But she is clever and a frugal woman. There's a group of these women. From what I understand they manage to pay rent together. Would you like more water?" She readied to stand.

"No, thank you." *Women renting a house? How interesting.*

"All of the women who live there are widows, and their children are grown. So they've no need to maintain their own homes. It's an interesting concept and it seems to work well for them, ya?" Mrs. Schumacher pushed her glasses back up on her nose again.

Eliza had never considered such a thing. But she supposed it was better than living at the Widow Society. It seemed like an in-between step, between the Society and a good marriage. "Very clever."

"Indeed. They make their own money, don't answer to anybody, and seem to come and go as they please." She waved her hands back and forth. "When you go to their home, you'll need to walk behind the main house. They live in a house behind it."

Eliza was familiar with such houses, sometimes built for in-laws or for servants. "How are things here?" Eliza asked.

Mrs. Schumacher sighed. "Better than they were. But we have women knocking at our doors frequently. I hate turning anyone away, especially those with children. But sometimes we are so full . . . it's heartbreaking." She appeared to gather her thoughts. "The child you just observed was leaving with her aunt for the day. She wants to adopt her. But there are complications. Her mother died a few weeks back."

Eliza's heart sank. "Does the church step in often?"

"Ach, yes. They do, sometimes. Thank goodness for their help." Her voice was hushed, prayerful.

Wishing she could help, Eliza bit her lip. She was impatient to find Alice, but found herself planted, mulling over the twist in life circumstances that anybody could find themselves in. "I need to find Alice." She stood. "Thank you for the water. I'll stay in contact." She wished she could tell Mrs. Schumacher of her own circumstances. But she could not. She was Eliza Schuyler Hamilton. She raised her chin.

"Thank you for stopping by." Mrs. Schumacher rose and walked to the door with her. "The heat is terrible today."

"Agreed." Eliza quickly hugged her. "I'll return soon. I promise. Perhaps when it's a bit cooler."

Mrs. Schumacher merely nodded.

McNally stood waiting at the carriage. He glanced at Mrs. Schumacher, who gave him the shuddering glare of a woman who'd seen too many women destitute, beaten, and neglected by men—widows or not. He turned his attention to Eliza and offered her his arm.

The carriage loomed in front of Eliza. What was worse? A cramped carriage or the harsh sun?

"I think I'll walk. It's only a few blocks away. I'll see you at 22 Pearl Street."

"Mrs. General Hamilton—"

She held up her hand. "I'm walking. You're driving. The question is which one of us will get there first."

McNally stiffened. "Yes, ma'am."

CHAPTER 20

The home that Alice shared with four other women sat behind a larger house situated in the middle of the crooked Pearl Street. Parts of the busy, mostly mercantile street dotted with houses belonging to merchants and shippers faced the harbor. As Eliza approached, she noted that McNally was sitting across the street. They made eye contact before she followed the dirt path that led her to the house where Alice lived.

A small, tidy vegetable and herb garden sat to the right of the modest house. A basket of fresh daisies sat on the stoop. The house was closed off from the city and bespoke of charm. What a perfect place for Alice and her friends. Just around the corner was New York's bustling harbors and markets, yet here in this space peace exuded. Something in Eliza uncoiled and relaxed.

She had not walked in the city for a long time. She felt eyes on her as she did so, as most women in widow's weeds stayed behind closed doors. But she focused on getting to where she needed to be. She used to delight in the many sights of the city— the women in their fashionable clothing, street vendors selling fruit and bread, and sometimes entertainers with animals, such as monkeys and dogs. But today, her mind was focused on finding Alice and getting her money, if there was any. Once that was settled, she'd focus on the other bit of urgent business: linking Aaron Burr to the murder of two men in addition to her dear Hamilton. Surely they'd lock him up then.

The house was a typical city townhome: red brick, three stories, and with stairs leading up to the door. Eliza knocked on the door. An unfamiliar woman opened it. "Can I help you?"

"Yes, Eliza Hamilton to see Alice Rhodes. Is she available?"

The woman brightened as she recognized the woman standing before her, "Yes, Mrs. General Hamilton. Please come in."

Eliza followed the woman into a room where Alice stood packing several cloth bags. She lurched when she noticed Eliza. "Mrs. General Hamilton! I'm quite surprised to see you!"

"I'm sorry I didn't send my card ahead. But I didn't know where you lived. I stopped by the Widow Society to get your address."

"No matter. 'Tis good to see you."

A woman who'd been sitting in the corner knitting came forward as they talked. "May I get you some tea?" She spoke with a heavy French accent.

"No, thank you." Eliza extended her hand. "I'm Eliza Hamilton."

"Lovely to meet you. I'm René."

"René is a gifted lacemaker, among other things," Alice said as she led them to a settee, where they all sat.

"I don't have much time, unfortunately. It's getting late and the drive is long." Eliza curled her hands on her skirt. "Were you able to sell my lace?"

"Ach, yes!" Alice cackled. "I shall go and fetch your money. Plenty more where that came from. The gentleman was pleased and asked for more."

Eliza's heart raced. "Good to know."

She and René were left alone when Alice departed to retrieve the money.

"You are a lacemaker? How long have you been doing that?" Eliza asked.

René nodded. "I've been making lace since I was a child. The women in my village were famous for lacemaking. Girls learned from their mothers, grandmothers, or from the local nuns."

"It's like the Dutch," Eliza said. "My grandmother told me about lace peddlers going from house to house."

"It was the same in our villages outside of Paris," René said and smiled. "The old women told of a miracle in our village. How one family was starving and destitute, but one daughter walked into the forest and spotted a delicate, glistening spider-web. Something about that web reminded her of lace. She went home and ripped apart some of her clothing and wove the most delicate lace, which she sold and saved her family."

"The tale is told across many cultures," Alice said as she strolled into the room.

"It does sound like a story my own grandmother told me," Eliza said.

"Some of the tales are much taller," Alice said. "They speak of miracles, angels' thread, mermaid webs, and so on. I love the stories."

Alice handed Eliza the money.

"Were you also able to get the note to Victoria Peabody?" Eliza asked.

"René?" Alice said to the woman who'd gone back to her lacemaking pillow. "You were able to get the note to Mrs. Peabody?"

Her face grew pale. "I was."

"Is there something wrong?" Eliza asked.

"My daughter Paulette was in service with them but was let go. She now needs to find work." René continued to move the lace bobbins. "It is a sad business. Suicide!"

"Very sad." Eliza wondered what René's daughter might know that could be useful. "Did you hear the rumor that it was not a suicide?"

She and Alice exchanged glances. René nodded. "I've heard that as well. But nobody knows."

Eliza didn't like to gossip, but this was important. "I spoke with Mrs. Van Der Gloss and she believes it was not suicide. We think both her husband and Mr. Peabody may have been killed by the same person."

Voices and some sort of activity erupted from another part of the house.

"Sorry—the women in the next room are weaving," Alice said. "We've got several widowed craftswomen who live here." She motioned for Eliza to continue. "But back to what you were saying. This is all so extraordinary."

René's hands continued with a rhythm all their own, causing clacking noises when the bobbins hit one another. "If I hear any more rumors . . . I'll surely let you know," René promised.

Eliza hoped she didn't seem too forward, but maybe Paulette knew more. "Perhaps I could speak with Paulette sometime?"

"I will see to it, madame," René said.

"Good." Eliza stood. "Now I must be getting back to the Grange."

★ ★ ★

As Eliza exited the house, she fingered the money in her bag. She'd never earned money. Is that what she had done by selling her lace? As she walked forward to the carriage, dodging traffic and other pedestrians, her heart lightened. Perhaps she would be able to support her family, at least until things were sorted out.

★　★　★

The solicitor's office was much as Eliza had imagined it. She was the only woman there, and as she walked in, several men stood and welcomed her. It reeked of pipe and cigar smoke, with a hint of soap. She coughed.

It was an office rented by several men. Desks were lined along the wall of a large room. Thick books in cases were lined up against the opposite wall. One enclosed office sat off to the right. Someone had tried to make it appear welcoming with a potted plant in the corner, but the wilted, dry plant needed a good watering. Eliza glanced around and glimpsed familiar faces, though she couldn't quite match faces to names.

Mr. Renquist, Hamilton's solicitor, stepped forward. "Mrs. General Hamilton. How can I serve you? Would you like to sit down?"

"No. I've come on business and don't have much time."

"Of course. I see."

"I've come into some money and wish to give it to you." Eliza handed it to him. "I'd like you to pay for my son Alexander's tuition at King's College and order my apple trees. Then you may take your payment from the rest. Is that clear?"

"Yes, of course."

Surrounded by so many lawyers, it occurred to Eliza that someone had to know something about the Van Der Gloss murder. "Have they found Mr. Van Der Gloss's killer yet?" She meant to say it too loud for comfort, and it worked. Several men sat up or stood and took notice of her.

Renquist placed his hand behind his back, fastening his hands tighter. "Mrs. General Hamilton, that matter is still under investigation with the authorities. We don't deal with such cases here."

"Oh, I see." But Eliza wanted to see more. "I'm sorry to hear that. I guess you know nothing about the other murder, either." She turned to go.

"What other murder are you talking about?"

"Mr. Peabody, of course. Anybody who knew him also knows he'd never kill himself."

The room hushed. A hush that allowed Eliza a glimmer of satisfaction. This would be enough for the law to maybe take Peabody's murder more seriously.

"How particularly devious for someone to kill a man and make it look like suicide," she said. "Good day, Mr. Renquist."

Mr. Jeremiah Renquist was not the only man Eliza left in that office with his mouth hanging open in shock.

When Eliza stepped out of the office, a breeze blew across her skin and the clouds in the sky had darkened. A storm was approaching. She hurried for the carriage. Davey McNally raced them against the storm as Eliza bobbed around inside the carriage, hanging on for dear life. The sky opened just as the Grange came into view, high on the hill, pale yellow and white against the dark, stormy sky.

CHAPTER 21

Why was Eliza Hamilton so interested in the Peabody suicide? Was it just concern for his widow? Perhaps. But Alice had an inkling there was more to it. There was a nervousness about Eliza, which was unusual. She was a steady sort. Alice shrugged. It would all come out eventually, if it was meant to.

She listened to the crackling thunder, hoping Eliza and her driver got going before the skies opened on them. She stretched out her ankle—better since René had been making her deliveries for her. Alice been using her lacemaking crochet hooks to fashion a stack of lace handkerchiefs and collars. They were fast to render and quick to sell, but not huge moneymakers.

Rain pelted the windows. Alice loved the sound of it. Always had. Even back in the old country. As a child, she had splashed through mud puddles and danced in the rain—much to her mother's dismay.

René entered the room. "Jo has finished weaving the blanket. It just needs finishing."

Alice grunted.

René peered out the tiny window. "It's pouring, isn't it?"

Alice nodded, trying to concentrate on her stitching.

"I'm so glad you sold Eliza's lace. I have a strange feeling about her."

Alice stopped crocheting and placed her hands in her lap. "Her husband didn't plan on dying and she's in debt. That is all."

But was it? Alice wondered. She was not one to gossip, especially about the likes of Eliza Hamilton.

"They say they have a suspect in the killing of Van Der Gloss." René sat down. "But that he's so well connected that they are keepin' his name away from the public."

Alice smacked her lips. "What is the point to this story, René?"

"What if it's someone she knows?"

"Who? Eliza?"

René nodded, her silver-blonde curls bobbing and brown eyes dancing. "Yes, and that's why she's so interested in all of this. She's trying to help and—"

"Stop right there." Alice held up her hand. "Mrs. General Hamilton does not keep company with murderers."

"That's not what I—"

"Hush, girl. You don't know what you're talking about. She's just lost her husband. She's a kindhearted woman concerned for other widows. She always has been. That's all there is to it. Do you understand?"

Alice would not have rumors flying about in her home. If Eliza knew anything about the suspect, it was her business. Plain and simple. René, one of the younger widows in the house, had a loose tongue and an overactive imagination.

René frowned. "Yes. I do."

Josephine entered the room with a blanket in hand. "What's going on in here?"

"Nothing," René said. "Do you need help making the delivery?"

"I don't think so. But thank you."

Alice stood and made her way over to Josephine. She ran her hands over the wool blanket. "That is fine work, love. Fine work indeed." She often mused about the differences in Josephine and René. Both in their work and their natures. The black-haired, dark-eyed "Jo" was tiny, wiry, and the youngest in the house, not a widow, but an orphan. She kept to herself, as most weaving women did. René, an exquisite lacemaker and embroiderer, was vivacious and talkative.

Josephine beamed at Alice's compliment. "Thanks. Well, I'll be off then, as the rain has slowed down." She left the room and René took her leave as well, leaving Alice alone with her needles and reflections.

What if René was right? What if Eliza Hamilton was trying to help the suspect in a murder? It was hard to believe. Very hard.

CHAPTER 22

Eliza fell into bed, exhausted but feeling as if she'd accomplished something. She'd actually earned money for her family. It wasn't enough, but it would help. Also, Rose Van Der Gloss had confirmed her own suspicions, which was deeply satisfying. But now she needed to find a way to connect Burr to the other two murders, as well as prevent him from killing someone else. Time was of the essence.

The next morning, Eliza ate quickly, then she and Davey drove to the empty Peabody farm. It was only thirty minutes away in upper Manhattan, for which she was grateful. But she needed to see the barn with her own eyes, even though she was almost certain the rumors were not rumors.

McNally shook his head as she stepped out onto the ground. "I don't know what you're lookin' for in here."

"Me neither," Eliza admitted. She stepped forward and took in the barn. A typical wood barn. There was nothing unusual about it. She walked toward it and noted the barn door was unlocked. "Perfect," she muttered and opened the door.

McNally muttered, but Eliza paid no heed. "I don't think you should go in there. It's private property." She also ignored that and stepped into the barn. Why was the man always trying to thwart her?

The barn smelled of animals, manure, and hay. She fluttered her eyes to help adjust them to the dimmer light. A chair stood almost in the center of the room. She assumed that was the chair Peabody had supposedly used. But as her eyes looked upward to the rafters, something didn't line up in her mind. Peabody was of short stature. Unless the rope had been quite long, she didn't see how he could hang himself. Not from that chair. It would have had to be higher.

Though Eliza didn't know all of the ways a person could hang themselves, she couldn't make sense of the scenario. Of course, this might not be the chair he had used at all. Maybe there was a ladder? She examined the barn, which had been packed up as if the family was not coming back. She saw no ladder.

"What are you looking for?" McNally asked.

"A ladder. Or something higher than that chair."

"Perhaps they took it with them."

"I don't think so. They left very quickly."

"Us being here is not sitting right with me, if you don't mind my saying. A man took his life in this barn," McNally said.

"Did he?" Eliza turned to face him. "I think he needed a very long rope or a ladder. He was a short man." It wasn't as if she didn't respect the dead. Perhaps she respected them too much. Peabody's story was connected to her dear Hamilton's story somehow.

He peered down at her, frowning. "Long rope is easy enough to come by."

"But it's not easy to place it so high and make a noose if you're a short man, I should think."

McNally stood and Eliza watched as his eye traveled to the rafters, to the chair, and back to her. "You're right, but who knows if that's the chair he used. Maybe a ladder or a higher chair was used and now is gone."

"That's a possibility." The air was cooler in the barn and Eliza hated to leave the space. But she worried they'd be caught here, and how would they explain their presence? "Let us go home."

He nodded. They closed the barn door and began to walk away from the barn. As they did, a man on horseback passed them, giving Eliza a start. Had he seen them? Who was he?

McNally offered a "Good day" to the man—as if it were a good day. The man tilted his hat at him. Eliza tried as hard as she could, but she could not get a good enough look at him.

After they had arrived back at the Grange and Eliza dismounted from the carriage, she asked McNally if he'd recognized the man.

"No, I've never seen him before. But I could pick him out from any crowd. He had a patch over his right eye."

Eliza's breath nearly left her body. Could it be one of Burr's men? She knew that one of his closest friends wore an eye patch.

"Can you get a message to the constable? I need to speak with him at once."

McNally nodded. "Yes, ma'am."

With this added bit of information, Eliza was certain Aaron Burr was behind the recent killings. Between seeing the man with the eye patch, and inspecting the barn where Peabody supposedly hung himself, she surmised that all was not well. Now her question became who else had witnessed the duel and would therefore be next? She shivered. It was time to get help.

★　★　★

Constable Karl Schultz sat down on the settee in the parlor. His rumpled dark uniform stood out against the silky green brocade.

Eliza seated herself in a chair adjacent to the settee. If she wanted, she could reach out and play the pianoforte Hamilton and Angel loved to play together. But she needed to focus.

"How can I help you, Mrs. General Hamilton?" Constable Schultz appeared as if he'd recently lost weight, as his uniform did not fit him well and his cheeks were sunken. His blue eyes, however, were alert and full of questions.

"Thank you for coming," Eliza said. "I fear you will think what I have to say is the words of a woman mad with grief for her husband."

"I'm so sorry again about your beloved husband."

She nodded in thanks. "But I want to assure you that even though I miss my dear Hamilton and am quite bereft, I'm still of sound mind. I've been thinking about the two murders since my husband's death."

"I'm sorry?" He tugged his ear, as if he thought he heard her wrong.

"Mr. Van Der Gloss and Mr. Peabody."

His eyebrows lifted. He opened his mouth as if to speak. Then closed it.

Eliza frowned. "I'm told both men were at the duel."

His mouth dropped, then he gathered himself. "Madam, I have no knowledge of that. It was an illegal act. I was not there and know nobody who was there."

"As you say, it was quite illegal, as is killing off the witnesses, I assume."

His thick dark eyebrows gathered. "I suppose it would be . . ."

"That is the thing the two victims have in common. I'm told they were both witnesses to Burr shooting my husband."

"Madam," he said in a softer tone, "I warrant you should not tax yourself with these matters."

"Tax myself? Why, I can hardly think of anything else." She gulped air. Her sweaty hands would betray her nerves, so she placed them on her lap. "I believe Burr is killing off witnesses to the duel and will continue to do so unless he's stopped."

"What?" The constable shook his head. "Madam, Burr is long gone."

Her heart sank. "What?"

He nodded. "Vice President Burr left the city shortly after . . ." He trailed off as he shifted his weight on the settee.

Nobody had mentioned this to Eliza as she was going from house to house campaigning against Burr. Campaigning to get him out of town, for New York's families to shun him. Had she done that for nothing?

"The last I heard he's taken refuge somewhere down south." He said it with as much gentleness as a large, tough Prussian man could muster.

Eliza worked to steady herself. Burr had escaped and would not see justice. Her hand went to her chest and she stood. She would not fall apart in front of this man. "Please excuse me."

She had managed to avoid running out of the room and flinging herself on the floor or pounding her fist into the wall.

Burr was gone.

Eliza stood in the hallway and focused on her breath, trying to compose herself. How could a man kill someone and just leave the city with no ramifications for him at all?

Alice's words came back to her: "Burr's money is what's keeping him from hanging."

Mrs. Cole entered the hallway. "Are you quite well?"

Eliza opened her mouth but could not speak. If Burr wasn't killing witnesses to the duel, then who was? And why?

"Mrs. General Hamilton? May I get you some water?" Mrs. Cole queried.

Eliza nodded. "I'll be in the parlor. Please bring two glasses and a pitcher." She withdrew her handkerchief from her bodice and patted her forehead.

It made a twisted sense that Burr would not want anyone who witnessed him take a life to live and spread the news of how he killed a man, but now . . . maybe one of his men was carrying out the killings? In any case, Eliza needed to find out who the other witnesses were.

Eliza reentered the sitting room. "I'm sorry, Constable Schultz. I asked for Mrs. Cole to bring us some water. It's been so warm this summer."

He smiled and nodded.

After Eliza sat back down, Mrs. Cole brought in the water and filled up their glasses. Eliza drank the cool water, feeling grateful for it.

The constable seemed to enjoy his drink.

"Back to our discussion . . . ," Eliza began.

"Madam, I—"

"Is there a way I can get a list of the men who were at the duel that day?"

"Madam, if there were such a list, I have no knowledge of where to find it. I am a constable. People would surely hide such a list from me, as anybody who was there could be arrested."

Eliza's thoughts tumbled around in her mind and she tried to calm them. There must be a list. But who knew what names were on it? Only Victoria Peabody. "If there were such a list and we did find it, and you were the one to deliver justice, how would that look to your superiors?"

Constable Schultz couldn't hide his shock at such a thing coming out of Eliza Hamilton's mouth. Nevertheless, he said, "I'm listening."

CHAPTER 23

Burr was no longer in town, a point that Eliza had mixed feelings about. Before she was aware of the two murders, she had campaigned to get him out of the city. It was all she had wanted, for her own and her children's safety. She'd yearned to see him in prison but suspected his station as Vice President of the United States would keep him from seeing true justice. But he was the person mostly likely to have killed both Van Der Gloss and Peabody. She was certain that he'd wanted to kill them off because he'd done something even more illegal than participating in a duel with her Hamilton. Maybe he fired before he was told? Maybe his men held her Hamilton down? She cringed.

It wasn't too much of a leap in logic to then assume that if the killer wasn't Burr, it may be his closest allies that were killing witnesses off. Jonathan Drake was Burr's solicitor's name; she remembered that name being uttered by Hamilton. But she could not remember exactly what he had said about the man.

Eliza slipped into bed wishing Hamilton was next to her. He was exactly what she needed. The person she could speak with about anything. His mind was so sharp and analytical, he'd have had all of this figured out already. Instead, she found herself resorting to seeking satisfaction in other ways. Like she had today, hoping someone would come to her with more information if only they knew she was seeking it.

"Sometimes the only way to get action is to stir the pot," Eliza's father, Philip Schuyler, used to say.

She hoped that she'd done just that during her travels earlier that day. Before she fell asleep, she said a prayer of gratitude. Her children and sister were safe with her father. She now had the help of both a constable and Alice's group, and she'd managed to leave the solicitor's office with tongues wagging.

Eliza had also paid some of her debts, which gave her deep satisfaction. She had always managed the finances of the house, but the solicitor and Hamilton had always dealt with the larger sums of money. Much of their money came from Hamilton's law practice. She had a few smaller accounts of her own, which paid for a new dress every season, as well as clothing for the children.

As she dozed off that night, Eliza contemplated the women she'd met at Alice's home. There they were, most of them women her age or older, all widowed, pulling together to share expenses and work. It was a curious and wonderful thing to behold. It spoke of the kind of freedom she'd never allowed herself to think about.

When Eliza awakened the next day, she arose with energy and enthusiasm. She now knew how to earn money for her family. It wouldn't be enough to pay for the mortgage or the servants, but it would be enough for other items, like tuition and household and medical expenses. She also had the new goal of finding the list of witnesses to the duel.

She opened her armoire, which was not just full of dresses and hats but also a few boxes of cherished items she didn't wish to keep in the attic. She was searching for a chest full of lace that her family had made generations back. Some tatted, some bobbin lace, and some finely woven crocheted lace, which was the kind she'd learned to make.

Her mother had made bobbin lace, and Eliza could still remember the delicate blue floral pattern on her mother's lap pillow intertwined with the needles and the sound of the clacking bobbins as her mother worked. Eliza's grandmother taught her to make crochet lace and also taught her tatting, but Eliza didn't care for the looping and shuttling movement, nor did she like the end product, which was bulkier than the fine lace she preferred.

She shoved aside several of her dresses and found the box she wanted. She sat on the floor and opened it, feasting her eyes on the lace. She'd forgotten how much of it there was. She had never before seriously considered parting with it until her recent conversation with Alice. She would have expected it to hurt a bit to sell that black lace, but it had not. After all, it was just an object. The only attachment she had to it was that it had been fashioned by her grandmother's hands. Eliza's grandmother had been a very rich woman who had never sat idle. She could've purchased all her lace, but instead she had made it. Eliza only wore pieces of it every so often. Tucked in a bow on a hat. Positioned on a dress as a collar or cuffs.

She liked to think her grandmother would be very proud to know these items would be used to help Eliza make ends meet.

As she held up each piece of the fragile lace, she marveled at the artisanship. Yes, it was very fine lace, indeed.

"Thank you, Grandmother," Eliza said as she tucked the lace back into the small trunk.

"Mrs. General Hamilton?" Mrs. Cole's voice rang in Eliza's room. She called her name again.

"I'm on the other side of the armoire, Mrs. Cole." She stood and wiped dust off her nightdress.

Mrs. Cole peeked around the corner. "Breakfast is ready."

"Be right there."

As she stood, Eliza glimpsed her favorite blue dress. She reached out and fondled it. Was it just three weeks ago she wore this dress as the wife of Alexander Hamilton, when she had hosted an elegant party with important, lovely people? They had dined and danced as if none of them had a care in the world. And they did not. But a week later, the world came crashing down.

One day at a time. One step at a time. Eliza walked forward.

★   ★   ★

Mrs. Cole handed Eliza the mail just as she finished eating breakfast. There were several sympathy notes and letters of condolence.

The last piece of mail she opened was plainer than the rest. Her name and address were written in what resembled a child's handwriting. Strange. She opened it and slid out the letter. She unfolded the paper and read: *Mind your own affairs—or else!* A poorly drawn pistol was next to the words. Eliza blinked. Was she dreaming? Was this real?

She dropped the letter. Oh, this was real. A gun. A warning. To her. Her stomach soured. She grabbed the letter, not wanting anybody to see it, and shoved it into her pocket. She then hurried to her room. She needed time and space to think this through. Who could've sent this to her?

"Mrs. General Hamilton, are you well?" Mrs. Cole said, having followed her.

Eliza drew in some air. "Of course." She tried to smile, not wanting to alarm Mrs. Cole.

"Madam." Mrs. Cole approached Eliza. "You've gone green."

Eliza rushed for the basin and threw up her breakfast. She wiped off her mouth when she was done. "I'm just queasy."

Mrs. Cole rolled her eyes. "Just queasy . . ."

Before Eliza grasped what was happening, Mrs. Cole had a cold cloth on her head, and she was lying in bed. "I've sent for the doctor."

Eliza wanted to say she was quite alright, but she didn't have the energy. Someone had threatened her life. That's what she got for stirring the pot yesterday. It didn't seem like such a good idea now. She had children to raise. With their father gone, it was imperative that she remain safe and healthy.

"I don't need the doctor," Eliza managed to say before closing her eyes and slipping into something like sleep.

★   ★   ★

"It's exhaustion, pure and simple. I want you to stay in bed for a few days." Dr. Jaquith clipped his case shut. "These pills will help you to sleep." He set them on her bedside table.

"I'm not exhausted. I just had a fright," Eliza said.

"About what?"

Her jaw tightened. "I'm sure it's nothing. I'll be fine."

"Let me be the judge of that." He stood. "Eliza, you've been through a traumatic experience. The loss of your husband was brutal for us all, but most especially you. You've been trying to put up a strong face for the children. I know they are off now with your father, so please take this time to rest."

But she had to find a killer and save the rest of the witnesses! He'd never understand. So she remained quiet.

"Sometimes our psyche protects us by inventing distractions to keep our mind occupied on something other than our great loss."

Was that what she was doing? Her mind fogged.

"The medicine I've given you will make you sleep."

Eliza didn't even remember taking the medicine. She laughed. Maybe her mind was slipping. Maybe the loss of her dear Hamilton had been too much for her.

The doctor smiled down at her. "I'm so happy to hear you laugh. I've given Mrs. Cole instructions for your care. I'll check in on you tomorrow."

"Thank you." She bit her lip and was surprised by the numbness. She laughed again before drifting off to images of flowers, beautiful dresses, and stacks of lace in old trunks.

CHAPTER 24

The next morning Mrs. Cole knocked on the bedroom door and opened it, awakening Eliza. "Good morning, Mrs. General Hamilton. I've brought you something to eat."

Eliza swallowed hard, trying not to retch from the scent of the food. "Take it away." She buried her head in the pillow.

"Are you certain?"

"Yes! I can't stand the smell of it!"

"Very well." Mrs. Cole left the room and Eliza gradually made her way to the wash basin.

She was dizzy and felt as if she'd been dragged by a horse. She was certain it was the medicine the doctor gave her. She wasn't sick. She'd had a scare. That was all. Anybody would have been startled if their life had been threatened.

And her life had been threatened. A sharp wave of fear and anger pounded in her chest.

She stood and walked to the stand where a jug of water sat and poured herself a glass while surveying the foggy morning outside. Green hillsides poked up through white patches. Beyond, patches of the ghostlike river snaked through the mist. She drank the water, trying to clear away the fog in her own mind. She considered the note she still had buried in her dress, now flung across a bedroom chair. She'd most definitely stirred the pot. Word of her visits yesterday must have gotten around very quickly. She had to admit that, in some queer way, a sense of satisfaction grew within her.

Now to untangle the web she'd created.

But how? Where to start?

She wished she could strategize with Hamilton, but the next best person was her father, who she didn't wish to alarm. And she wanted his attention and energy focused on the children. Angelica would be back tomorrow. She was as intelligent as she could be, but she lacked the thread of desire for anything like strategy. Eliza supposed she'd have to rely on herself to figure this out.

She didn't want another man to die.

Hamilton.

Van Der Gloss.

Peabody.

What did they have in common, besides the duel and being friends?

It was so hard to get any information from anybody concerning Hamilton's duel, as if they were all sworn to a deadly secrecy. Or maybe they didn't wish to upset her further with details. But for some strange reason, she craved details. Hamilton himself could not tell her more than what was in his letter to her. He had written her a note before he went to the duel, to be delivered to her if the worst were to happen. And it had. Men believed women could not handle such matters, which Eliza had always considered ridiculous. Women were not children. Though she realized that some women did not have the experiences and opportunities she'd had. They had not spent weeks in the forest with the Iroquois or eavesdropped on her father as he discussed strategy with other men involved in the French and Indian War. Nor had some women had her education, which her own mother and father saw to. She and her sisters were unique—but not so much so that they were vastly different from other women. Men seemed to assume all women were childlike.

Some women, she realized, used that to their advantage. More power to them.

With each sip of water, Eliza felt more herself. She did not like that medicine the doctor had given her.

Mrs. Cole knocked on the door again then opened it. "Breakfast, Mrs. General Hamilton?"

Eliza was still a bit queasy, but she knew if she refused, the doctor would be along sooner than she could stomach. "Please leave the tray and I'll try to eat."

Mrs. Cole nodded. "The peppermint tea there will help with the upset."

"Of course. Thank you."

"Will you be seeing any visitors today?"

Eliza didn't answer right away. Would she? Did she want to see anybody? Who could she trust? She had already visited with Rose Van Der Gloss, Alice, and the solicitors. Had any of them sent the threatening letter? Or had one of them told someone about her visit and that person had threatened her? Her idea about drawing attention had worked, but it was the wrong kind of attention.

She didn't think any of the others who knew of her suspicions were quite trustworthy, and Rose Van Der Gloss was a gossip. Eliza did think Alice was trustworthy, to a point. She could trust Alice with a secret. After all, word had not gotten round about her dire circumstances and Alice had helped without spreading gossip about it. Maybe she could trust Alice more than she'd believed.

"I will see Alice if she stops in."

Mrs. Cole eyebrows lifted. Then she nodded. "Very well."

"But please let me know if someone else stops by. I want to keep track." She added, "I do not want to see Dr. Jaquith."

"But—"

Eliza held up her hand. "I'm feeling much better, I assure you."

"Very well," Mrs. Cole said again, then exited the room, shutting the door quietly behind her.

Eliza poured herself some tea and drew in the scent of fresh peppermint, harvested from their own garden. It comforted her, and as she sipped it her stomach settled.

She'd told Mrs. Cole she'd have no visitors other than Alice today, but the more she drank the tea the better she felt, and she couldn't quash the feeling that she needed more information about Jonathan Drake, the young solicitor. And there was only one way to do that: go into the city and visit with Hattie McClure. She was the biggest gossip in town.

Of course, Eliza could also go to the courthouse on the pretense of seeing the newly constructed building. That way she might see the man himself or catch a glimpse of his group of friends. Any one of them might be the man who was killing off witnesses to the event that had stolen her husband's life.

CHAPTER 25

Before leaving the house, Eliza spotted a stack of mail on the table in the sitting room. She rushed to it, hoping for more than just letters of condolence and payments needed. She also hoped there'd be no more threatening notes.

She sorted through the stack. In an off-white envelope was a note from Victoria Peabody. Eliza wanted to rip it open. Instead, she slid a letter opener in between the sealed papers and read:

My Dearest Eliza,

Thank you so much for your warm and thoughtful letter. We are living with my parents in Long Island. They have kindly taken us in.

I beg of you not to trouble yourself and to let sleeping dogs lie, my friend. Please do not inquire anymore about the situation. I don't wish to see anything happen to you. Your children need their mother.

Eliza's heart raced. It was as clear as day. She was warning her. She read on:

Know this, my friend—I wish I could turn back time and pay more attention to my dear husband and his business. He was not

*himself and I tried to speak with him about it but was put off too
easily. Something was amiss. But for him to commit the unspeak-
able? I'll never believe it.*

Eliza's heart nearly stopped. It was the same story with Rose
and herself. What had their husbands gotten involved in?

She read Victoria's sign-off and then mulled over the entire
letter. Obviously, Victoria knew that Eliza had been asking questions. Word got around very quickly. Maybe she should heed Victoria's warning. She swallowed. Could she do that? She certainly
wanted to be there to care for her children. But at the same time,
other lives might be at risk.

To help others any time you could—it was the Christian
thing to do. Would she turn her back on her fellow human beings
to protect herself?

Her children were well cared for and protected at the present
time. Except for Alexander, who was back in school taking his
final exams, even though he officially was still a suspect as the
police continued their investigation. Which was another reason
for Eliza to persist with her own inquiries.

The letter trembled in her hand. She needed to proceed carefully. It was unwise to go about town as she had been, trying to
stir the pot. She could see that now. There had to be another way.

She tucked the note into her bag with the earlier threatening note and made her way to the front door, outside of which
McNally awaited with the carriage. But when she opened the
door, she was surprised to find Alice and a young Black woman,
both of whom were hunched over examining their shoes, standing in their stocking feet. Eliza's mind took her to her youth and
her well-loved nanny, who was a Black woman who'd looked
similar to the young woman with Alice. Shame spread through
her as she considered how she and her family had prospered while

using the labor of others. It sickened her. And it sickened her that it was still legal to own another human being. Hamilton had been working with his friends in the Manumission Society to help ease their plight. As for Eliza, she did her best by helping where she could, for she believed with all her heart that all men—and women—were created equal.

"Alice?"

"Oh!" Alice turned to face Eliza. "I'm sorry, Mrs. General Hamilton." The young woman froze. "We ran into some mud and were scraping it off. Not wanting to bring dirt into your lovely home."

Eliza turned around and observed McNally standing at the carriage. Where was Alice's carriage? Realization moved through her and she cringed. Alice didn't have a carriage. She had probably hired one and the driver would not bring people past the forest between upper Manhattan and Harlem. These women must have walked for miles. Eliza felt ashamed of herself, as she grasped that she'd bidden Alice to her at least twice without considering her circumstances.

"'Tis no bother," Eliza finally said. "Leave your shoes here and come inside. I'll have Mrs. Cole find someone to clean them for you. And we must take refreshment."

"It looks as though you were leaving?" Alice asked.

"I was, but it can wait until after our visit. In fact, we shall give you a lift home." Eliza said it loud enough for McNally to hear. He nodded, at the ready. "Please come in."

The young Black woman hesitated. "You are most welcome here," Eliza said. "Come inside before you soil your stockings."

She smiled at Eliza and nodded. Eliza stood with the door open as the two women walked through.

"Mrs. Cole?" Eliza called.

The woman entered the hall immediately.

"A pitcher of water and some sandwiches in the parlor, please."

Confusion played over Mrs. Cole's face as she took in the two guests in their stocking feet. "I trust you have come a long way."

The young woman nodded. "Yes, ma'am."

"And can we please find someone to clean the ladies' shoes?" Eliza queried.

"Of course," said Mrs. Cole, and then she departed for the kitchen as the other women settled into the light-filled parlor.

"Mrs. General Hamilton, this is Paulette, René's daughter." Alice gestured toward the young woman.

"I'm pleased to make your acquaintance." Eliza reached out her hand and shook Paulette's hand gently.

"Likewise, I'm sure," Paulette said.

"Paulette's father was from the West Indies," Alice said. "When he died, she and her mother came to the Widow Society, where I met them. And now she is a grown woman with her own family." Alice beamed.

"So you have children?" Eliza asked her.

Paulette nodded. "I have two daughters. Mary and Rachel."

"Lovely names." Eliza loved the biblical names. Hamilton had not been a fan.

"Thank you."

Mrs. Cole carried in the water and plates of sandwiches.

As the women ate, they talked of the hot weather and the latest ship that had come in from China, carrying silks and teas that every person in the city was talking about.

"Paulette is a good seamstress, like her mother," Alice offered.

"Wonderful! We've been using my sister's seamstress, but we certainly need our own. Are your services available?" Eliza caught herself. Why was she offering Paulette employment when she was uncertain she'd have the money to pay the staff she already had? She swallowed. She'd find the money. With the way the children were growing, it would be worth the investment.

"Yes, I am."

"Fabulous. It is done, then. We can talk more specifically later. But in the meantime, Alice has brought you here for a reason?"

Alice smacked her lips. "Aye. I have. She worked for the Peabodys, as you know."

"I am in receipt of a letter from Mrs. Peabody." Eliza pulled it out of her bag and read it to them.

Paulette set her sandwich down on her plate. "I fear she is correct. I don't think Mr. Peabody harmed himself. As I told the constable, I heard men's voices in the barn that night."

"More than one?"

"I believe so."

Eliza's heart raced. *More than one.*

"Who did you tell that to?" She asked.

"Constable Andrews."

"The time line is an issue." Alice straightened her collar.

"What do you mean?" Eliza asked.

"They found Mr. Peabody at five in the morning. Nobody can say for sure what time he went into the barn, let alone if he was alive when he went in."

The women sat in silence for a few moments, letting those words sink into their minds.

"The bigger question, I suppose, is why they dismissed Paulette's testimony," Eliza said, breaking the silence. "Also, who were those other men?" Eliza's breath quickened. What was going on here?

Alice and Paulette exchanged looks.

"Burr and his man Drake, along with another gentleman whose name escapes me, had been visiting in previous weeks. But last week, Mrs. Peabody was quite frightened after the men left. And Mr. Peabody yelled at her," said Paulette.

Burr and Drake!

"What? That doesn't seem like him . . . to raise his voice to his wife . . ." Eliza set her glass down.

"I'd never heard it before, that is certain." Paulette's eyes widened. "It was shocking."

"Tell her what he said," Alice prodded.

"That she needed to mind her own business, take the children far from here, and the other thing was . . . something about signs. Symbols. A society? I couldn't quite catch it." Paulette lowered her eyes. "I fear you'll think me a gossip. But I think this is an extenuating circumstance." She met Eliza's eyes. "I don't know what's going on. Do you?"

Eliza sank back into her chair. "I can't be certain. But I think Peabody witnessed the duel between Hamilton and Burr. I think Van Der Gloss did as well. Besides that, all three were friends. But there must be other witnesses."

"Something must have happened at the duel that someone wants to keep quiet." Alice crimped her hands in her lap.

"He killed my Hamilton in an illegal duel. It's public knowledge. What could be worse? What else could they all have witnessed? Or done?" Eliza said.

She was educated in the rules of engagement. There were not supposed to be any witnesses to a duel. However, Eliza figured the nature of many men would preclude them from caring about those rules. There would have been others who knew about the duel, certainly. There were men who rowed the boat across the Hudson River to Weehawken, New Jersey, where the duel had taken place. A sea captain who lived nearby had been written up in the papers about it, as he'd ended many duels before. But Hamilton's duel had taken place too early in the day to stop it. The shots had awakened the sea captain shortly after seven.

The three women sat in silence.

Now that Paulette had told Eliza what she had witnessed, confirming the rumor and her own intuition, Eliza was certain other lives were at risk. But whose?

Her brain churned. The journal entry. The note. Obviously, someone had been trying to set up Hamilton in 1797 to make it look like he robbed the Treasury. But Van Der Gloss wrote that he had proof that wasn't the case. Proof that would vindicate her husband should anybody have believed that nonsense. Some people did. All of these men must've known who that person, or group of people, was. Someone wanted to keep them quiet. They must have all gathered to watch the duel between her husband and Burr. Was something said? Done? Something that led to further deaths?

"We need to find out who else was at the duel," Eliza said, not for the first time.

"I know of one other person," Paulette said. "I overheard him and Mr. Peabody speaking. It was Jonathan Drake. He was there."

"He's one of Burr's men," Alice said. "I reckon he must be behind all of it."

Eliza searched her memory. "I don't believe I know the Drake family."

"He's not a New Yorker, has no wife." Alice chimed in. "I think he's from Philadelphia."

Philadelphia? Eliza and Hamilton had lived there for years. She had fond memories of Martha and George Washington during that time. She'd make a few inquiries with some of the friends she still had there. It was one place to start.

CHAPTER 26

The conversation wasn't quite so dark as before as the group made their way into lower Manhattan. The women spoke of the heat, the flora and fauna, and the lovely views of the North River and surrounding landscape. Harlem was a beautiful respite from the ever-busy and crowded city. Respite is what Eliza, Hamilton, and their family had needed. But as Eliza listened to the women in the carriage with her, she concluded everybody could use that same respite.

The rolling hills and grassy knolls gave way to cobblestones, dusty streets, buildings, crowds in the streets, noises so loud that the women gave up trying to have a conversation. When they pulled up to Alice's house, the creaking carriage tilted off to one side.

McNally swiftly opened the door and helped the women out.

"What's happened?" Eliza asked.

"I fear a wheel has broken. I'm not sure I have what I need to repair it." McNally's voice was full of concern.

"You must come inside then," Alice said to Eliza. "And take rest before your long journey back."

"Thank you, but I need to walk after that long journey. And I'd like to find out more about Drake."

"I'll go with you," Alice said. She turned to Paulette. "I believe your mother is inside and waiting to see you."

"Yes, ma'am. You're right. She frets so! Honestly, I am a mother myself, but she frets more than any other I know. It was lovely to meet you, Mrs. General Hamilton. I eagerly await your instruction on when I will start my new situation with you." She beamed.

"Very nice to meet you as well." Eliza extended her hand and the two women shook.

Before departing, Eliza told McNally they were heading to her solicitor's office to find out where Drake's office was. Eliza and Alice walked along the path on the side of the cobblestone street. It felt good to walk after being curled up in the carriage for two hours, even with the pleasant company.

A drop of sweat trickled down Eliza's back. July in the city was a sweltering cesspool. She pulled out her lavender-scented handkerchief, as the smells of the city were too much for her at times. She whiffed in the lavender as Alice walked next to her.

A rush of something like disbelief swept through Eliza. Here she was: Hamilton was gone, and yet she walked along arm in arm with Alice, as if she had not a care in the world.

★ ★ ★

"Mrs. General Hamilton," Mr. Renquist stood up from behind his desk. The room was open, with several desks where men sat hunched over or talking in hushed tones.

"Good day, Mr. Renquist. This is my friend Alice Rhodes."

"Nice to make your acquaintance."

"Likewise."

"Now, how can I help you?" He leveled a look at Eliza. She was convinced he didn't actually want to help. What he wanted was to collect payment.

"I'd like to know where Jonathan Drake's office is."

Several heads turned in their direction.

"Surely you don't have business with him. I handle all your affairs," he replied.

Eliza smiled to alleviate his apparent insecurity about losing her business. "I'm sorry. I don't wish to speak to him about anything relating to business. It's a personal matter."

"Personal? My dear Mrs. General Hamilton, are you quite well? Shall I call for tea?" He spoke with obvious distaste. He was clearly not fond of Drake.

"No, thank you." Why was it that a man immediately thought a woman was unwell if he didn't understand what she was doing? "I'm quite well, I assure you."

"You do know that . . . Drake was no friend of your husband," Renquist said haltingly.

Eliza narrowed her eyes. "That's exactly why I'd like to see him." She lowered her voice. "He's Burr's man, correct?"

Renquist's face whitened. "Madam, you must not go to—"

"Mr. Renquist, I believe he knows something about the recent murders. I'd just like to speak with him."

"Madam, you mustn't accuse people of such things!"

"I'm not accusing anybody. I just have some questions."

He looked as if he was searching for the right words. "Madam, he is a nasty piece of work. I couldn't possibly allow you to visit him alone."

Eliza glanced at Alice. "I have my friend with me."

Renquist sighed. "Then please let me escort you to see him."

Eliza could see that was the only way she'd get her face-to-face with the man. "Fine."

Renquist led the way outside and down Wall Street, then around a corner. Eliza stopped momentarily to study the place where she and Hamilton had once lived. A tiny townhouse filled to the brim with small children. It was in the thick of the town. Bright blue curtains hung in the windows. There must be another family living there now. A wistful pang swept through her. She turned her face away and moved forward.

When Eliza had left behind the city life, she also left behind her Wednesday morning social calls, which she had dreaded. Chinese tea with the ladies of society bored her to tears, and she despised the gossip. She had been expected to be a part of the social circle when living in the heart of the city. Moving to Harlem didn't remove all of her social responsibilities, but it did take her out of the melee.

When they opened the door to Drake's office, Eliza was immediately struck by the differences between his office and Renquist's. Drake's was much more elegant.

"May I help you, sir?" The clerk completely ignored the two women, even the famous one.

"Is Jonathan Drake in?" Renquist asked.

"I'm afraid not. He's in court all day, sir. May one of our other solicitors help you?"

Renquist sneered. "No, thank you. We'll return another time."

After they left, Renquist turned to Eliza. "Maybe it's best if you go home to your lovely Grange."

"I will," she said. "Thank you." No need to tell him that her carriage was in disrepair.

"Mr. Renquist? You said that he's a nasty piece of work. Can you be more specific?" Alice asked.

He shrugged. "You know, the usual."

"I'd heard he's a bit of a cad," Eliza supplied.

He stuttered at first. "I—I—I know nothing about such matters. He's been known to . . . twist the truth in court." He gawked around and then leaned toward the two women. "He's a gambler and is in debt to several institutions." He held the guise of smoldering satisfaction, apparently hoping this would dissuade them from asking more questions.

Eliza recognized that money could make even good people do horrible things. "How much?"

"Hundreds of dollars, madam."

"I see." A man who owed gambling debts was a desperate one, for sure. Desperate enough to murder for money? To take hush money? "Thank you, Mr. Renquist."

He tipped his hat. "Good day to you both."

Eliza nodded, keeping Alice's arm through hers. After they were out of earshot, she pulled Alice to the side of the walkway. "Let's go to the courthouse. It's not far from here."

"Why? You can't barge into a courtroom. I've tried."

Eliza made a mental note to ask Alice more about that later. "I just want to set my eyes on him."

"It's getting late in the day. The courts will be closing soon and there will be a parade of people exiting to go home. There's a park across the street. We can sit there and watch the courthouse."

"Splendid."

As they walked, they passed a girl selling hot buttered corn on the cob. The smell of the butter and corn turned Eliza's stomach. The girl couldn't be more than nine years old. Eliza dipped her hand into her bag and gave the girl some coins.

The girl, dressed in a garment that was at least two sizes too big, handed her a cob.

"No, thank you," Eliza said.

"I don't understand, mum." The girl's big brown eyes held confusion.

"Just keep the money and sell your corn to others," Eliza said. She and Alice exchanged knowing glances. Just then a man came along and bought two cobs, and Eliza walked off, following Alice to the park.

Passersby were turning their heads. Some looked more familiar than others. As they walked toward the park to find a bench, Eliza searched for one in the shade and found it. She didn't want to be seen, especially by any of Hamilton's friends.

Eliza and Alice sat in companionable silence as they watched men scrambling into or out of the courthouse. Finally they were rewarded with the presence of Jonathan Drake. As he drew closer to them, Eliza noted his youth. He was boyish. Lanky. As if he'd just stepped out of school. She remembered what Paul Jinkins had told her about the man who approached him and the jewelry he was wearing. "Do you see a ring on his finger? On his right hand?"

"Aye, I do," Alice said.

Eliza's heart raced as she watched Drake walk off with two other men. She was certain he was the man who'd approached Jinkins. But why? And now that she knew it, what could she do about it? He was the key to proving Alexander's innocence.

She stood. "Alice, we must follow him."

"What? Oh. Fine." She accompanied Eliza as she crossed the street. Eliza spotted Drake from behind between the other two men on the path. If only they'd move, she'd have a better view. All three soon ducked inside a tavern.

Alice pointed to the tavern sign: *No women allowed.*

Eliza's heart felt like it would thunder right out of her chest. Once again, thwarted by her gender and her status. Eliza Hamilton could never step into a tavern, and now neither could Alice.

"We could wait for him to emerge." Eliza yanked at her collar. The sun beat on her and sweat trickled down her back.

"I'm happy to do so, but it could be a long time, maybe even into nightfall," Alice said.

But just as she said that, Drake exited the tavern and he glanced straight at Eliza. He nodded his head. "Mrs. General Hamilton."

She composed herself. "Mr. Drake."

He folded his arms behind his back. "Are you lost?"

"I am not lost, sir. My carriage is being repaired." She waited for a reaction, There was none. "Are you lost?"

He laughed. "You are quite charming."

"Alexander, my son, will be here momentarily." She thought quickly. "Do you know him?"

The smile dropped from his face. "No, madam." His eyes darted from side to side.

"Funny, I'm sure I saw you speaking to him the other day," Alice spoke up.

"And you are?"

"Alice Rhodes, she's a friend of mine," Eliza explained.

His nose went up. "I'm sorry, I've never spoken to him in my life. Now good day, ladies."

He left them standing on the street just as another gentleman came out of the establishment, calling his name. He ran to catch up with him.

Eliza and Alice exchanged glances.

"Did you really see him speaking with Alexander?" Eliza asked.

"No. But were you expecting to meet him here?" Alice cracked.

"It disturbs me how easy it is to lie. I'm not a liar, and I know you're not either."

"Aye. I'm as honest as they come. But when there's a reason to, our instinct kicks in, I'm sure."

"One thing for sure is that he does know Alexander and he fits the description Jinkins gave me. Maybe I should go to the constable with this information."

"Maybe. But have they been helpful so far?"

"Not really."

"Maybe we need more evidence before we go to them."

Eliza wasn't certain that she agreed with that logic. But she would think about it. In the meantime, she should get back to check on the carriage. It was getting late and the drive home was long.

CHAPTER 27

When Eliza and Alice arrived at Alice's house, the carriage was not in sight.

"Please come in and wait until your driver returns," Alice said.

"I don't wish to impose." Eliza grew increasingly agitated thinking about her carriage. What would she do if they couldn't fix it?

"'Tis no imposition at all and we've got plenty of room," Alice said, almost dragging Eliza into the house. Despite herself, Eliza felt a bit like a girl visiting a friend, long before she became a woman, a wife, and a mother. When she crossed the threshold in Alice's home, she felt something akin to freedom.

But when she entered the sitting room, there sat McNally with René and another resident, enjoying a glass of lemonade. He stood. "Mrs. General Hamilton."

"What's this?" She gestured toward the glasses and plates of half-eaten sweet cakes.

"I'm just back from the wheelwright. The wheel won't be finished until very late this evening or maybe tomorrow morning. I shall take the horse back to the Grange and return in the morning with a fresh one and hopefully a fixed wheel." McNally stood.

"Very well." Eliza's heart raced. Obviously, there was nothing to be done. "I must find a hotel immediately, McNally."

"Yes—"

"Hold on," Alice interrupted. "We insist you stay here. We've got plenty of room. No need for a hotel."

"I simply couldn't impose on you," Eliza said.

"It would be an honor for you to stay here," René said. "You are a kind Christian woman. Everyone knows that. And as such you will allow us to help you, as it is our duty, milady."

Eliza considered the hopeful faces around her. "Very well. But I must send word as to where I am."

It was as if the entire room sighed in relief. Eliza did not have the energy or fortitude to argue with this group of formidable women—or even McNally, for that matter. It had been a taxing day. Her carriage broken. Having to deal with Renquist, who, though she tried to like, she could not. And she'd stared into the eye of the man she was certain was trying to blame her son for murder and may even have killed two others. She needed some time to consider her next steps.

The women gave McNally a satchel of food for the long journey back to Harlem. Before he took his leave, he turned to Eliza. "I will see you early in the morning, Mrs. General Hamilton."

She nodded. "Safe journey to you, Mr. McNally."

After McNally departed, Alice led Eliza through the rowhouse, which was familiar to her in some ways, as she and Hamilton had lived in a similar one. Behind the front parlor was a back parlor, where families often gathered. But in this house the back room was set up with a loom and shelves of fabric and thread, along with baskets of wool to be spun.

The kitchen and dining area were on the very bottom floor. There was an entryway just outside the dining area, as in the older houses, for servants to enter.

The women of the house shared bedrooms, which were on the second and third floors. Eliza was given her own room, where, the moment she was alone, she fell into bed and napped, dreaming of nothing.

★ ★ ★

Later, after a simple, light dinner of oysters, salad, and brown bread shared with the other residents of the house, Eliza went to bed. The room that she had been given for the night was plain and small but likely was the best in the house. The bedclothes were a bright butter yellow shade and well used, as were the curtains hanging over the one window. A cream-colored wash basin filled with water sat in the corner. Eliza peeled off her clothes and splashed water over herself.

She was taken back momentarily to the homes she and Hamilton had shared before they built the Grange. They'd lived in a very similar place in Philadelphia for a brief time. During the War for Independence their accommodations bordered on rustic, often just a single room.

"I'm sorry I can't do better now, Betsey. I know you're used to more," Hamilton would say as she was lying in his arms.

She hadn't minded. Not one bit.

Much like today. Perhaps she should have considered herself put out, as her mother or sister might have. But she was pleased to have a bed and fresh water to clean herself with. As she mulled over what may lie ahead of her, she appreciated it even more.

Hamilton had loved her, that much was true. But he hadn't left her anything to live on. As much as she hated to feel so angry, she did. He'd gone off to a duel, leaving the family in debt. Leaving her to deal with this mess as best she could. The money, Alexander, and the pending murder charges.

She lay down on the bed, noting the lovely embroidery on the bed linens, which reminded her of her childhood home in Albany. She whispered a prayer of gratitude, knowing her children were safe there. She had no idea what treachery tomorrow would bring.

★ ★ ★

The scent of fresh biscuits baking woke Eliza the next morning. She rose from the bed and dressed, making her way to the dining room, where three women and a young man sat with tea, biscuits, and a dish of hard-boiled eggs.

"Good morning," Eliza said.

"Good morning, Mrs. General Hamilton," René said. "Alice sends her apologies. She had an early meeting this morning with a lace broker. She could not miss it."

Eliza felt the shame of imposition. Of course these women were quite busy. They were earning their way in the world, a foreign concept to her in many ways, but she respected and admired it. "Of course not." She sat down. "I hope to be on my way as soon as possible."

She glanced around the table. There were René, Mary, and Rosa. All of whom she'd met last night. But the young man? There was something familiar about him, but she couldn't quite place him. She examined him.

He smiled vaguely back at her. "Good morning," he said, not sounding at all like a young man.

Eliza must have seemed confused, as René placed her hand on the man's shoulder. "Meet Joseph. Better known as Josephine."

Eliza's mouth flew open. "What are you saying?"

"Sometimes I dress as a man," Josephine stood up to emphasize her garb and yanked on her trousers.

"Whatever for?" Eliza asked.

"Because often we women can't get into the places we need to go, madam. Some shops don't engage with women. Or if they do, they underpay us by virtue of our gender. So sometimes we play a little trick on the men."

Eliza's thoughts tumbled. It was preposterous. A young woman placing herself in such jeopardy. It was unheard of . . . but as her eyes darted from woman to woman to woman, she sensed confidence in them and even some kind of . . . joy.

"We've figured out more than one way to beat men at their games," Mary said and cackled.

"But what of her safety?" Eliza finally found the words to ask.

"We'd never place her in jeopardy," René said. "You must believe us. She's been quite successful at it for a while now."

Something flickered in Eliza's breast, and a giggle erupted. "I don't think I've ever considered it . . . but it is quite ingenious." She lifted her teacup in salute. "Here, here. To women and . . . boys!"

Laughter erupted across the table.

Chapter 28

By the time McNally arrived with the carriage, Eliza almost didn't want to leave. She felt lighter in this house, unburdened by her troubles.

"Come back any time," René said. "Our doors are always open to you."

Eliza beamed.

McNally's face was unfriendlier than usual.

"What is it, McNally?" Eliza asked.

"It's Mrs. Church. She's back and furious with me for allowing you to stay here last night."

"*Allowing* me?"

He nodded, stiff-jawed.

"We'll see about that."

The drive home was as pleasant as it could be and gave Eliza plenty of time to consider Jonathan Drake as the man behind all of the murders—and the blaming of Alexander for at least one of them.

When she recalled Drake, more memories came back to her. He was Burr's man, and she remembered Hamilton saying as much, calling him "Burr's pup." She also remembered him being at a ball, alone, and she understood he was still alone, unmarried, as she kept abreast of marriages as best she could. She also remembered a conversation she overheard between Hamilton and her father about Drake, Burr, and someone named Calvin Evans. Something about a ridiculous secret society. "Could they be serious?" Hamilton had said.

Eliza's notions flooded her mind. Her imagination had taken hold of her again. Secret societies? The city was full of them, and this had irritated Hamilton, who used to jest about them. How secret could these societies be if everybody knew about them? She vaguely remembered him talking about this particular group. As far as Eliza was concerned, just the fact that Drake worked with Burr made him highly suspicious.

As the Grange came into view, sitting like a dollhouse in the distance, placed among the gardens and rolling hills of Harlem, her stomach flip-flopped. *Home.* Would she be able to keep it?

As they drew closer to the house, Eliza could see through the large windows, where a woman in black paced back and forth. Angelica. She stopped and gazed in their direction. Eliza figured she'd meet them at the front door.

The carriage stopped. McNally opened the carriage door and helped Eliza out. Angelica stood before them with her hands on her hips.

"Angelica! You're back, dear sister!" Eliza embraced her somewhat stiff sister.

"We have much to talk about," Angelica whispered into her ear.

Eliza ignored her and walked toward the front door. "I'm so thirsty. I hope there is lemonade."

She walked into the foyer and was stopped in her tracks by the bust of her husband. She stood a moment and gazed at it. *Oh, Hamilton, how I miss you.*

"Eliza!" Angelica came up from behind her. "What were you thinking, staying in town last night with someone we barely know?"

She turned to face her. "Angelica, I know Alice very well. You know I met her during a rough period in her life. I can certainly trust her. Besides, the carriage was broken, and it was either that, stay at a hotel, or hop on the horse with McNally."

Angelica gasped.

"Precisely."

Mrs. Cole met them as they headed into the family room. "Can I get you anything, Mrs. General Hamilton?" she asked.

"Lemonade?"

Mrs. Cole nodded. "I'll bring the pitcher and two glasses."

"Good." Eliza turned to Angelica, who was fuming quietly. "Join me, sister."

"What were you doing in town anyway? We've discussed this. You're in mourning. You shouldn't be flitting about town."

Eliza opened the window and gazed out over the gardens. "I much prefer this view of the city, but I had business to tend to."

"Business?"

"With Mr. Renquist."

"The solicitor?"

"Indeed."

Mrs. Cole brought in the lemonade and set it up on the tea table, pouring them each a drink.

"I also wanted to get a peek at Jonathan Drake," Eliza added.

Angelica stopped her glass half-lifted to her lips. "Whatever for?"

"He fits the description of the man who paid off people to lie about Alexander."

"Eliza, a million men must fit that description!"

Eliza drank the cool, sweet elixir. *Heaven!* She hadn't fathomed the depth of her thirst. "Perhaps, but, curiously, he wears a ring on his pinky finger. I don't think many men do that."

"It's very European."

"We are not in Europe."

"So, did you talk with the constable?"

"Not yet."

"Why ever not?"

"I think Alice might be right. We need to be more certain before we go to the law. It will better help Alexander's case."

"I agree with her there."

"I also need to do more investigating to find out what exactly linked the two other murder victims with my Hamilton."

Angelica sat her glass down. "What? Are you well, Eliza?" She drew closer to her sister.

Eliza drew away from her. "I am very well."

"I think not. What have you concocted? You are sick with grief." She nearly swooned toward Eliza and wrapped her arms around her.

"My grief is a part of my breath, sister." Eliza pulled away. "But I'm not ill. I'm reporting to you things that are quite clear to see. Open your eyes."

Angelica's beautiful face twisted into fright. "I'm calling for the doctor."

"You'll do no such thing."

Angelica's jaw twitched before she said, "How can I help you if you won't let me?"

"Angelica, you've been a great help to me." Eliza drank the rest of her lemonade and set the glass down. "I don't know what I would've done without you. And yet . . . you are grieving too. I know you loved him." Eliza tried to soothe her sister. She needed to gently change the subject. Her sister's stance was getting more and more worrying. "How are the children?"

Angelica's face lit up. "They are quite happily ensconced with our father."

"It's the best place for them right now, though I do miss them." Once again, Eliza was glad about the new ferry to Albany. Even though her children were farther away than she wanted, it would take less time to finally get back to them.

"They will be much happier when you can join them," Angelica said flatly.

"As will I, dear sister. But first things first." Eliza ached for her children and tried not to think about them. She also longed to speak with her father about the things she'd learned and the theories she had, and longed for his opinion on the subject. He'd know the right move for her to make now. He'd also grasp the importance of it. She was on to something, which is why someone had sent her that threatening note. This was not a tale she'd woven to entertain herself during long nights, as when she was a child. If only it were.

CHAPTER 29

The pain in Alice's foot had subsided. As she moved along the street, she paid close attention to her steps, so as not to hurt herself again. With a basket full of handkerchiefs, she marched herself toward the Fly to sell them to vendors. She'd inquired about setting up shop there for linens, but rent and upkeep were expensive and it didn't make sense for the women in the house on Pearl Street, who managed very well to work and sell from home without a shop.

The heavy scent of baking bread filled the air. Alice never allowed herself to buy bread made by others when she could make it herself. But she had to admit that the temptation clung to her as she moved forward.

A spice vendor peered at her through his strung-up herbs. He nodded politely and she nodded back, inhaling the scent of the familiar rosemary, along with unfamiliar scents that made the back of her throat itch. She made her way beyond his barrels of powdered red and yellow spices.

The crowd thickened the closer into the market she moved. A dog sat in front of a hot pretzel vendor, looking very pleased with itself as some dogs do. Alice resisted the urge to reach down and pet it, or, God knows, it might follow her home—she'd learned that lesson the hard way.

There, between a fruit vendor and a hat seller, was the man she'd come to see. He didn't appear to notice her as she made her way to him. Very few people did notice her. It was one of her greatest assets.

"Monsieur DeSoirre?" Alice said loudly to be heard over the din of the crowd.

He turned to her and smiled. "Mrs. Rhodes, how lovely to see you." His eyes went immediately to her basket. "What have you brought for me today?"

She opened the lid of her basket and he peeked inside, pulling out the delicate handkerchiefs. "*Mon dieu*. You've been busy. I recognize your fine hand."

Alice beamed. Of course he did. "Thank you. Do you want to purchase them?"

He didn't hesitate. "Of course. I'll give you a fair price."

"I know you will." She lifted the handkerchiefs from her basket and handed them to him. The lace work seemed so delicate next to his ruddy, rough skin. A fiddle played in the distance as he took the cloths from her and handed back money.

"Good day and thank you for buying." Alice walked away toward a small tavern where she often treated herself to a cider.

She entered the dark space gingerly, stopping to allow her eyes to adjust to the dark. She spotted a chair near two other women, one of whom she recognized, so she made her way to them.

"Alice, how are you, love?" Brigid Monahan slurred.

"Busy. How are you?"

"Busy with my fourth here." She laughed. Too hard.

Her friend rolled her eyes. "I'm afraid she's had a bit of a scare."

"I was let go again. I don't have nothing. I don't know what I'm going to do," Brigid wailed.

"Well, drinking away what you do have ain't the way to go about it, love," Alice said in a gentle tone.

Brigid shrugged.

"Who were you working for, then?" Alice asked.

"The Peabodys."

Alice's brain kicked into gear. Another Peabody family connection. It had been quite a day. She'd sold all of her handkerchiefs at more than a fair price, her foot was in good shape, and now look what Lady Luck had delivered to her. Even a little drunk, Brigid's word was as good as gold. But sober would still be best.

"I loved him," Brigid slurred.

"Who?"

"The mister. He was a good man." She sobbed.

Brigid's friend rolled her eyes again. "I don't know about that . . ."

"He is kind . . . handsome . . ." Brigid moaned.

Alice's instincts kicked in. This drunken conversation needed to stop. The Peabodys had enough to worry about. They didn't need someone overhearing a drunk servant talking about how handsome Mr. Peabody was. They might get the wrong impression. And then Brigid would never find good work again.

Alice took her arm. "Why don't you come home with me, love, for a spot of tea?"

"That's a grand idea!" Brigid's friend said, helping Alice get Brigid to her feet.

Brigid didn't put up a fuss. She complied as Alice and her friend helped her out of the dark tavern and out into the bright day.

CHAPTER 30

Eliza was not thrilled to be in church the next day. But Angelica insisted. Eliza was a woman of faith, but she had no place in her heart for it at this moment. She found it difficult to follow the sermon. But she nodded politely and smiled, shaking the minister's hand on the way out of Trinity Church. She was not ready to visit her husband's grave in the churchyard. There was no comfort in knowing he lay in the ground there. She'd rather recall the many mornings here, next to her Hamilton, worshiping side by side, the warmth of their commitment to one another and to God. But she had not experienced that today sitting next to Angelica.

As the sisters made their way to the carriage, a voice stopped them. "Mrs. General Hamilton." Eliza turned to face Jonathan Drake. Her heart nearly tumbled out of her mouth.

"Mr. Drake, sir."

Angelica tightened her grip on Eliza's arm.

"I understand you've got a quarrel with me." His chin jutted out, as if he were considering a fight.

Eliza studied him. *Never let your enemy see emotion.* "Quarrel, sir?" She smiled sweetly at him. Eliza could not look at her sister, lest emotions bubble up.

The other exiting churchgoers did their best to ignore them. But Eliza could feel their attention, and her embarrassment was almost too much to bear.

Drake nodded. "Yes. I believe that's the word for it when one gads about town asking ridiculous questions that could ruin a man's reputation."

If only he'd lower his voice.

"Come along, Eliza." Angelica tugged on her arm.

McNally suddenly stood next to her. Drake, a smaller, thinner man, crumpled into himself.

"I don't understand, sir." Eliza pulled her arm away from her sister. "People who've done nothing wrong certainly don't care about others asking after them."

Drake lowered his voice. "Be careful, madam."

McNally cleared his throat and shifted his weight. "The carriage is ready, madam."

But Eliza's attention was focused on Drake. "Whose pocket are you in, sir? What do they have against my son?" She matched her tone with his.

His mouth dropped and eyes widened. "I, ah—"

"Good day, sir," Angelica said, as she and McNally each pulled Eliza away from the scene.

McNally nearly lifted Eliza into the carriage. Angelica threw herself down in the seat. "What was that about?"

Eliza shrugged. "I asked our solicitor about him. He must have told him." She neglected to mention she'd spoken with Renquist only yesterday. It had been a pleasant enough exchange.

"Renquist! John has never liked him. I don't know why Hamilton kept him on. We should find you a better solicitor. He should not be discussing your business all over town. Wait until John hears about this!"

It wasn't just the solicitor; there were also his colleagues in the office. It could've been any one of them. And the ladies in Alice's house all knew of her theory. She had effectively stirred things up all right.

Angelica continued. "Besides, who does he think he is to even speak to you, let alone speak in such a tone. You are the Widow Hamilton. Who is he? Some young upstart solicitor . . . Burr's dog. That's who he is."

Eliza watched out the small window of the carriage as buildings and people moved in and out of her view. She was getting close to something. Drake wasn't just warning her about himself. "Be careful, madam," he'd said. But it held a note of concern, not just malice. She had no proof of that, just her years of listening to generals and politicians . . . and their wives. Her instincts were usually spot-on.

"Drake is thoroughly unpleasant," Eliza said.

"That he is," Angelica agreed.

"But he's Burr's friend. What can you expect?"

Angelica grunted and gazed out the window with a faraway expression on her face.

As the carriage turned right onto Bloomingdale Road, the traffic thinned out and the sound of horses on the road, mixed with the jangling of horse harnesses, filled the air.

When they pulled up to the house, Eliza was surprised to see the doctor's carriage. She turned and looked at Angelica. "What is this?"

Angelica sighed. "It won't hurt to have him examine you. You are not quite yourself."

Eliza's ears throbbed with fury. "My husband was murdered in broad daylight. Two of the witnesses have been killed. Alexander is a suspect. And since he did not commit these murders, there is someone out there who's at large and may commit another one. Of course I'm not myself. But I'm not ill."

Angelica raised her eyebrows. But she said nothing.

Eliza neglected to mention her financial circumstances. She also neglected to mention that the very thing that had weighed on her Hamilton—the notion that people would suspect him of stealing money from the Treasury—would have come to a different conclusion had he lived. They'd found proof of the culprit, but Eliza still had no idea who that was. Telling the truth of Hamilton's story burned in her chest. She would not rest until it was set right.

McNally helped Angelica out of the carriage. Eliza gathered herself before receiving his hand to exit. There was no relief from the heat. It was warm in the carriage and warm outside. She entered the house and opened the windows in the foyer further to allow the crosswind from the Harlem River into the house. Angelica had gone into the parlor, where the doctor waited.

"I'm sorry to keep you waiting, Dr. Jaquith," Eliza said as she entered the room. "But I assure you that I am quite well."

He stood and took her hand, shaking it politely. "That is good to know, Mrs. General Hamilton."

They both sat down. Angelica remained seated.

"You certainly look better than the last time I saw you." He pushed his spectacles back up on his nose.

Eliza nodded. Angelica was unaware of that episode. She'd been frightened and Mrs. Cole had insisted on the doctor.

"My sister has been very busy," Angelica quipped. "She's trying to prove that her son Alexander is innocent in the suspicious deaths of two men."

Angelica! Great anger rushed through Eliza's body. She balled her fists onto her lap to prevent herself from combusting.

"We can count on your discretion, of course." Angelica smiled sweetly at the doctor. Eliza wanted to smack her.

The doctor closed his gaping mouth. "Ah." He cleared his throat. "Absolutely." He paused. "I know I've spoken about this before, Mrs. General Hamilton, but grief takes many forms. Sometimes people take to their bed . . . other times they become restless . . . it works differently on the mind." He was patronizing her.

Eliza stood. "I won't be spoken to about grief as if I'm a child."

"Eliza! Please sit down." Angelica tugged on Eliza's arm.

"My son is in trouble—is it not suitable to try and help him?" She stepped over to the window and tried to fix her gaze on the gardens. *Calm down*, she told herself.

"Yes, of course." The doctor stood and came over to her. "But you must take care, madam. You are not thinking clearly."

A wave of doubt struck her. Was he right? Was she not thinking clearly? It would be so much easier to believe that. But she had proof. Proof that she was not following fanciful ideas. She had stepped on someone's toes—she'd received a warning note. Which she had not shown to either of them. With the fuss they were making over all this, she determined it best to keep it to herself.

"I think sleep is the best thing to calm your mind, if you can do it," Dr. Jaquith went on. "I can give you something to help."

"No, thank you." Eliza well remembered the last pill he'd given her, which did the opposite of clearing her mind. But she longed to be alone in her room. Alone with her thoughts. "But I think I will take this opportunity to get some rest." She turned to Angelica. "I'll see you in the morning."

CHAPTER 31

During breakfast the next morning, John Church stormed into the dining room.

"John?" Angelica stood. He greeted her with a peck of a kiss.

"Angelica." He turned to Eliza. "Eliza."

"Please have a seat and help yourself to breakfast." Eliza gestured toward the long table with only two place settings, but enough food for an entire family or more.

"I've already had my breakfast, but thank you. I'm here because there's news." He sat next to his wife.

Angelica dropped her fork onto the plate. "Get on with it, man."

"The authorities have found the blade they believe was used to kill Van Der Gloss."

Eliza stopped chewing her biscuit.

"It's a blade with 'AH' carved into it."

Eliza's heart raced.

"Does Alexander own such a thing?" Angelica asked.

Eliza tried to remember if he did.

"I spoke with the boy today before he went to exams. He claims he does not, never did. Eliza?" John queried.

"I cannot recollect. I'm certain he's had a blade, carried one like most young men do. But one with his initials on it? I don't recall such a thing."

"I've got a man on this thread of inquiry," John said. "We need to know where the knife came from. It's unusual looking. It doesn't appear to have been forged in this city."

"Thanks, John." But Eliza did not feel any sense of relief. She would not rest until the real culprit was found and her son was no longer being investigated. Once again, to her it appeared as if someone were trying to set him up. What she didn't know was why. "Where did they find it? And who found it?"

"It washed up on the riverbank, near where Van Der Gloss was found, evidently with a lot of other little trinkets. A few buttons with the Bavarian Illuminati symbol on it, which I find intriguing. The police don't think one thing has to do with the other. They went on about tides and ebbs. They wouldn't tell me who found it."

"What on earth is the Bavarian Illuminati?" Angelica spread butter onto her biscuit.

"Just some silly secret society, nothing for you to worry about."

But Eliza's chest burned. She knew who they were. Hamilton had talked of them. They were anti-Christian. They talked of enlightenment and intellect, as if Christians were the opposite of those things. Hamilton had gone to a meeting or two, but he didn't care for it.

"Hamilton told me about them. I doubt there is nothing to worry about," Eliza volunteered.

John's face reddened.

"What would they have against Alexander?" Eliza asked.

"I don't follow," said John.

"Why would they want to make it look like he killed some-one, especially someone who witnessed the duel?"

"I fear your grief has taken a turn for the worst, my dear sister."

"John!" Angelica interrupted. "We are not children. Please don't patronize us. Something evil is afoot. You must surely see it."

He stood quickly, knocking over his chair in the process. "I have no time for this folly. I live in the real world. All matters you are discussing are purely circumstantial." He turned and picked up his chair. "The important matter is that Alexander may be in real trouble. We need to find out about the blade. As I said, I have someone investigating it."

"We don't know that it was his. And what if it wasn't, John? What if someone just wanted it to look like he killed a man?" Angelica persisted.

Eliza's thoughts exactly. But she could see John was in no mood for conjecture.

"Honestly!" He raised his voice.

"Please sit down, John, you are quite agitated. Please relax." Eliza gestured toward his chair. "We all need to remain calm if we're to figure this out."

He remained standing for a moment, his eyes darting from one woman to the other, then finally sat down. "I apologize. I admit I am on edge. Have you seen the papers?"

"Not yet." Angelica folded her arms. "It takes a while for them to get the paper here. We are in the country, husband."

He slumped into his chair. "Jonathan Drake was murdered last night."

Eliz stopped chewing and coughed her biscuit into her napkin. Her throat tightened. She tried to swallow.

"What?" Angelica said. "We just spoke with him yesterday."

Eliza's ears thrummed with the beat of her blood pulsing. She grew dizzy, placing her elbows on the table and her head into her hands. *Breathe, breathe, breathe,* she commanded herself.

"I heard." John's lips pursed. "The conversation spread through town, of course."

Heat crept up Eliza's neck and face. Was seeking out Drake a mistake? Had she made the wrong move?

"People have nothing better to talk about!" Angelica tried to sound flippant. "Eliza spoke to him very briefly. And as I've said before, he had no business speaking with her. A woman of her stature."

John sighed. "I love you, Angelica, and I adore you, Eliza, but women of your stature should not be gadding about town asking questions about . . . murder." He lowered his voice. "You are both ladies. Ladies in mourning. It's only because you are so beloved that people have turned a blind eye to your escapades."

A vibration moved through Eliza. Shame? Anger? Fear? Her skin tingled as the movement traveled up her spine. Thoughts tumbled in her mind and spun into a single word. "No." It came out solid, unshaking.

"Pardon?" John said as Angelica reached across the table for her sister's hand.

Eliza remained calm, even though she burned on the inside. "I have lived my whole life following the rules, John. Keeping my mouth shut when I wanted to ask questions. I appreciate you investigating the knife. That will help, I'm sure. But we need to dig deeper to find out why someone wants Alexander out of the way. I won't stop until I have answers and my son is completely free." She hesitated. The fact that Drake had been murdered only lent credence to her theory. He had been seen speaking with her. He'd warned her, hadn't he? "I fear I may have caused Drake's murder. I pushed him. He warned me." Her voice was only a whisper and John and Angelica bent forward, both blurs in Eliza's sight. She tried to focus her eyes on the lace tablecloth but the surface of the table rose to meet her. When it hit her, it thwacked her hard on her head.

CHAPTER 32

"Nothing more than a bruise on your head. With ice, it will subside in a few days," a male voice said. Eliza fluttered her eyes open to see Dr. Jaquith leaning over her. "There she is." He smiled a fatherly smile. If only it were her own father. "How does your head feel?"

"Hurts." Eliza ran her fingers along the painful bump on her forehead. "What happened?"

"You fainted." John's face came into view.

"Where is Angelica?"

"She is with a guest who wouldn't be deterred," John answered. "No worries, my dear. Everything will be alright. I should have been more patient with you in your state. I apologize."

"Indeed," Dr. Jaquith muttered.

John shot him a glare.

"She needs peace and quiet." Dr. Jaquith stood up from her bedside. "I've given you more medicine and it will force you to rest."

"What?" Eliza tried to sit up and the room spun. *No!* She could not lie on her back in a drug-induced state while her son was in trouble and perhaps another person's life was at stake!

John stared down at her and smiled. "Rest is the best thing for you now. Please take the doctor's advice."

"I have no choice . . . he drugged me. But John, listen . . . please . . ." But as hard as she tried to fight against sleep, she couldn't win, and she drifted in dreams of clouds.

Eliza made out the sound of voices. Women. *Angelica?* But she couldn't lift her eyelids.

"Alice! Are you quite sure?"

"I am. When René delivered the linens, she saw that very knife sitting on the table in the entryway. She deemed it odd, out of place, and examined it further. She said it looked as if the initials had just been carved into it."

Initials. Carved. Knife.

"How long ago was this?"

"A few days ago."

"Drake turned up dead last night, the same day the knife was found," Angelica said.

Eliza tried to open her eyes. But the more she tried, the more weariness swept through her.

"Can't be a coincidence, can it, mum?"

"I fear you're right."

Those were the last words Eliza heard before the glass shattered. The sound rang in her head as she tried to make sense of it. Was it a dream? But soon her door swung open and people were in her room.

"Get her out of here, McNally."

"Pardon me, Mrs. General Hamilton." He lifted her out of bed as if she were a child. She batted her eyelids furiously, trying to focus her eyes, but glassy stars shining on the carpet were all she glimpsed. She hadn't realized McNally was quite so strong, nor so warm.

He carried her down the hall, placed her gingerly into Angel's bed, and wrapped her in a quilt. Her shivering stopped.

She couldn't make out what the voices in her room were saying. Nothing made sense. It was a strain to try to figure it out, so she gave way to more sleep.

★ ★ ★

The next morning Eliza awoke with the sun streaming into Angel's room. Angelica was in a crumpled heap on the sleeping settee next to the window. Eliza untangled herself from the damp quilt. She'd sweated all night, evidently.

She held her hand across her forehead against the sunlight and quietly stood to close the curtains. The light met her eyes and sent a shard of pain through her head. Relief swept through her as the room darkened with the closing of the curtains.

"Eliza?" Angelica sat up.

"I didn't mean to disturb you, sister." She sat back down on the bed. "But it was too bright in here." Hamilton had designed the house to be as light-filled as possible. But today, that wasn't a good thing.

"How are you feeling?" Angelica continued her battle with the quilts cocooning her and finally sat up.

"My head hurts a bit. But I no longer feel so sleepy. I may be able to form a thought."

"Good." Angelica's expression reminded Eliza of her when her sister was sixteen years old and they'd stay up all night talking about the men they'd met through their father's work. "I've packed a bag for you."

"Why? I'm not ready to go to Father's."

"No. Listen. You are in danger. I see that now. You will not be going to Father's. That is the first place they will look for you." Angelica's eyes were sincere.

Why was Eliza in danger? What had changed her sister's mind? She gradually remembered the shattered glass. "What happened? Why am I here?"

"Someone threw a rock through your window. Alice witnessed it. She also thinks it was Drake who carried the knife now being used against Alexander."

Eliza's mind was still a little too foggy to catch what she said. She slowly remembered the words Drake had spoken to her. "Drake tried to warn me."

Angelica held up the rock. "This is what came crashing through your window."

Eliza squinted. "What's painted on it? Is that—"

"It's an owl." Angelica set it back down on the bedside table.

"An owl painted in red?"

"With an X over it. Or maybe those are swords?"

Eliza struggled to understand. "Does it mean something? Anything?"

Angelica nodded. "Probably. But who knows what. Today we will rise and eat as usual with our guest, Alice. Then you will accompany her to her home and stay there."

"I don't wish to burden her." The tranquil house on Pearl Street appeared in her mind's eye. It was small, yet the women who lived there had everything they needed.

"I will see that she is not burdened. We think it's the safest place for you. I will join you when it's safe for me to do so."

Eliza opened her mouth to argue with Angelica. This was her home. She didn't want to leave it. But then she judged the better of it.

"You've got it all planned out." Eliza stood. She was impressed. Now her sister was thinking like Eliza knew she could. Now she perceived the danger. What might happen next? Eliza would need to be more careful in her investigation. Her children needed her. But that also included Alexander. She needed to think quickly, gather her resources, and make a move. Being on Pearl Street would be very convenient, indeed.

CHAPTER 33

Before Eliza and Alice left, Eliza paid the staff with the money Alice had brought to her. A huge weight had been lifted from her shoulders. The staff had been loyal and good to her and the whole family. That they had been forced to wait for their wages weighed on her.

Also, the burden of keeping recent events a secret had now been lifted a bit. Alice, McNally, and Angelica all believed her. She found it meant more than she had realized, for she no longer questioned herself. Now she only questioned what was next.

And she also questioned her original theory that all of the men who had been killed since Hamilton's death had witnessed the duel. Perhaps they had. But it was hard to believe that Jonathan Drake would have been at the duel. Though odder things had happened, he seemed very straitlaced. And duels were illegal, even in New Jersey.

"Be careful, madam," he had whispered to her. She shivered, even in the stifling heat within the carriage. She patted the sweat off her face.

Poor man. Found dead in Trinity's graveyard, splayed over a tombstone. Someone wanted to make a point. But what was it?

Eliza shivered again. What was happening, and what did it have to do with Alexander?

When he was a small boy, she knew of all of his comings and goings, knew his friends, but now that he was at school, Eliza had no idea what her son was doing and who he was doing it with. She'd expressed her concern to Hamilton about sending Alexander off to live in rooms near King's College.

"Eliza, my love, we must trust that we've raised him well and that he will carry our love and our decency with him," Hamilton had said.

But Philip, their oldest son, had not. He had died in a duel. Just like his father. "Because of his father," a tiny voice whispered in her head.

Eliza had every cause for concern.

Philip, their oldest son, had been a beacon of hope, and he'd also had a great deal of pride in his father. When he overheard one of his schoolmates voicing a strongly negative opinion of Hamilton, he challenged the young man to a duel. Hamilton swore he knew nothing about it, but Eliza knew otherwise. Of all the ways in which her husband hurt and disappointed her, this had been the worst. She choked back a sob. Now was not the time to slip into that murky water.

Alice dozed in the opposite corner of the carriage. What a godsend she'd turned out to be! Eliza hadn't had a chance to ask her who it was she'd spotted outside the house. She wanted to wait until they got to the house before discussing details.

She glanced out the window as the countryside gave way to the city, ever so slowly. City houses. Businesses. Then the closer they drew to lower Manhattan, the more crowded the houses and streets became.

She and Hamilton had been in the thick of it until a few years ago. She had welcomed the change, but a part of her missed the excitement of the city.

The carriage bumped hard, waking Alice, who cackled with the abruptness of it all.

"Sorry, ladies," McNally called back to them.

"I used to love riding," Alice said.

It was an unexpected statement, another puzzle piece of Alice's background. Poor women didn't ride horses. They didn't have horses. In fact, Eliza might have to sell some of hers. It was unlike Alice to divulge anything personal about herself. Eliza kept her own counsel—but she wanted to ask more.

"Oh, me too!" Eliza said, recalling riding horses in Albany with her sisters and with the Iroquois children she played with. "I hated riding sidesaddle and disobeyed as soon as I was out of Mother's and Father's eyesight." She smiled.

Alice said no more. She simply nodded and looked out the carriage window, a winsome look on her face.

After she rested, Eliza planned to find Constable Schultz. It was time to get some help. He seemed open to her ideas, even before she received the warning note and the rock had been thrown through her window. Now with Jonathan Drake dead, it had to occur to more and more people that something strange was happening, that the murders were all linked, if not by the duel, then in some other way.

The sound of glass shattering was not pleasant. It shook her to her core when she reflected on it. She'd need to be careful. Her children needed her, but they also needed a role model. It was her Christian duty to help people, and she couldn't help but think others were in danger.

"Was he killed because of me?" Eliza thought out loud. "Was he killed because we were talking in the courtyard?" She gasped and her hands went to her mouth.

"Shhhhh," Alice wobbled over to Eliza's side of the carriage. "Nonsense. He was involved in something and it had nothing to do with you. Just take that right out of your mind."

"But the timing is . . . odd. If it didn't have to do with me, then most surely with Alexander. René saw the knife in Drake's house, then a few days later it surfaced on the riverbank?"

Alice's left eyebrow rose. "Aye, I admit that is interesting. But it's got nothing to do with you."

"He warned me."

"He did, did he? What did he say?"

"'Be careful, madam.' He whispered it to me."

Alice frowned. "Did you see anybody else nearby?"

"There were many people close by, unfortunately. It was embarrassing. We were just getting out of church and he approached me."

"You should try to remember exactly who was close enough to hear your conversation. The constable will want to know."

"Constable?" She'd made up her mind to talk with Constable Schultz, but she hadn't mentioned it to Alice.

"Angelica contacted Constable Schultz. He should be waiting for us at the house." A grin spread across Alice's face. "Your sister is quite formidable."

Eliza laughed. "I guess that's what you could call it."

CHAPTER 34

Constable Schultz met Eliza and Alice as they walked into the front room of the house on Pearl Street. They settled in with lemonade and ginger biscuits. Eliza and Alice recounted the past few days for him, ending with the rock thrown through Eliza's window.

"And you saw this man?" Constable Schultz focused on Alice.

"Aye, I did. But it was quick-like."

"What can you tell me about him?"

"He reminded me of Drake. He resembled a younger version of him. A brother? Son?"

"Drake was unmarried."

"Doesn't mean he didn't have a son." Alice's eyebrows went up.

The constable reddened and looked away. "True."

The room quieted before Eliza prodded, "What do you think, Constable?"

"Frankly, I don't know what to think. But I am very glad you have another place to stay. I will investigate the man who threw the rock. If I can find him, maybe he can tell us more."

Alice merely grunted.

"I've been giving this some thought," said Eliza. "He must have been familiar with the Grange and the neighborhood.

Familiar enough to know where my room is. And then he knew where to hide. For all we know he could still be there." Eliza pulled at her collar. She worried about her staff and Angelica.

"I'd say you're correct. He'd definitely been there before. But not to worry, he's probably long gone. He made his point. He wanted to scare you," the constable said, standing. "But I can see you're not so easily frightened. I must be going. I want to find this man. I'm going to need help."

"What will you do?"

"I will give a description to my colleagues and maybe someone will know something."

"But we need your discretion." Eliza wanted to be certain.

"I understand. We will just be seeking a man who threw a rock through your window. They don't need to know why we think he did it."

Eliza's nerves calmed and she remembered Paulette. "Constable, may I ask you a question?"

He stopped and turned. "Of course."

"Why would a constable ignore someone's testimony?"

"I have no idea. Is there a specific instance you can tell me about?"

She hesitated. She'd already thrown a great deal at Schultz. But this was important. "I know a woman who worked for the Peabodys."

He stiffened.

"She told the constable what she witnessed, and he ignored it."

"He must have considered her an unreliable witness."

Unreliable witness? Paulette? "I can guarantee that she's not."

Schultz's eyebrows gathered. "Perhaps I can talk with her?"

"I'd appreciate that, and I'm sure Mrs. Peabody would as well. Thank you."

He started to walk toward the door. "Oh! Any idea of who the constable was?"

"Andrews. She said his name was Andrews."

He nodded. "I know him." The tone of his voice led Eliza to think he was not fond of the man, but she didn't want to ask. That was not the important issue. Getting to the bottom of Peabody's death was the issue.

They reached the front door. He opened it and turned back to her. "I'm glad your sister called me, and I hope I can find the rock thrower."

Eliza smiled and nodded and shut the door after him.

"Well, let's hope he finds him and pries something from him," Alice said. "You must be tired. Would you like a nap?"

Eliza's mind was racing. She wasn't sure she could fall asleep. But her body craved a bed. A sofa. Anything to lie down on. The weight of the day was crushing her.

"I think I would like to lie down. Thank you, Alice."

Alice showed Eliza to her room, where her trunk stood on the floor and a few newspapers lay on the table. Eliza often read before sleeping, but she figured these newspapers would only add to her agitation and not allow her to sleep.

She set her trunk and the newspapers aside and lay down on the small bed. She didn't like being away from the Grange, though she was used to moving from home to home to home with Hamilton, his career taking them to many places. She'd only fully settled in recently in their new home. But she found this place welcoming. It reminded her of the simple beds and simple homes they'd had. Happier times, even with the children sleeping between them on small beds. Cocooned in love. She lay on the bed and remembered the love. She had to think of the good times, or she'd be swallowed by her grief and her worry.

Angel and her sweetness, Philip and his giggles, and Alexander and his moodiness. He'd always been an agitator. But he was no murderer, and he'd had countless friends and seemingly no enemies. He didn't have a bad reputation. Who would want to see her son imprisoned for murder? Besides Burr, who had anything against their family?

Surely Hamilton's political opponents would not stoop so low. Not even Jefferson.

Eliza closed her eyes and weariness swept through her. Each muscle gave way to the bed and she drifted off into dreams of apple trees and tulips.

When she awakened late in the afternoon, Eliza was not ready to emerge from her room. Instead, she took a moment to read the newspapers on the stand. The papers were still reporting about the duel, so she turned the pages quickly to the back where there were a few articles on the Lewis and Clark expedition and France's Napoleon Bonaparte. She flipped the newspaper over to the last page. She and Angelica often entertained themselves by reading the personal advertisements. She read the first one:

Louise, dear, I received your letter last Saturday, but not in time to meet you. Next Tuesday, Aug 1, I will meet you at the same time and place. East. Write to me again and give your address.

Your old acquaintance

She and Angelica would have made up a story about that couple. Were they courting? Were they having an affair?

Matrimony, the next ad read. *Widow, 44, Southerner, stranger, own home, West End, would like the hearthstone of her heart swept, and the cobwebs brushed away. Matrimony.*

A southern woman alone in New York City? Eliza could hardly believe it. Southern families were so protective of their women. Maybe overprotective, for it seems they didn't have the freedom and rights of their northern counterparts. There must be an interesting story there.

Her eyes skirted along the column to a group of letters and numbers.

Odd, as the letters made no sense. They were not words, just a jumble of letters. Perhaps it was a mistake made by the paper. Or maybe it was a code or cipher. She and Hamilton loved to invent codes. She'd helped him figure out some very important codes during the Revolution and after. She perched on the side of the bed and studied the letters.

A rapping at her door startled Eliza and she dropped the paper. She opened the door.

"I trust you've rested?" Alice said as she entered the room.

"Indeed." Eliza slicked back her hair.

"We'll be eating in about a quarter of an hour."

"Thank you." Eliza stooped to pick up the papers.

Alice turned to her. "I told René to take these papers out of here." She reached for them.

"It's quite alright," Eliza said.

"You don't need to worry about what the papers are saying," Alice said, reaching for the newspapers.

"I find the back page entertaining." Eliza folded the paper over and pointed to the ads she'd been reading.

Alice grinned. "René reads them to us sometimes."

"But look at this one." Eliza pointed at the nonsensical advertisement. "What do you think that means?" She unfolded the paper so they could see the whole thing. "I wonder if it's a code or a cipher?"

"I don't know anything about that . . . but did you notice?" Alice pointed next to the ad. It was an owl with two swords across its body. A more detailed version of the crude drawing on the rock that had been thrown through Eliza's window. Nausea waved in Eliza's stomach.

If this owl was the symbol of something, she needed to figure it out. It might lead her to the answers she sought. Had she seen the owl symbol before? Why was it so hard to recollect such things? Would she have even paid attention to it if she'd seen it? What did it mean, if anything?

Alice took the paper from her hand. "Mrs. General Hamilton, you are pale. Let us have our supper and relax this evening."

CHAPTER 35

Eliza wasn't sure she could ever relax again. After supper, she wanted to stroll along the East River. But Alice and René talked her out of it.

"You are in hiding," Alice said. "What would Angelica say if we went walking through the streets?" Alice's eyes lit.

"True enough." Eliza conceded that her idea to go for a walk along the river was not well planned on her part. But at the same time, she was beginning to feel a bit trapped. She wanted to know more about this owl drawing. And she wanted to find out more information about Drake himself. What had he been warning her about? "I'd love to attend Mr. Drake's funeral."

"It will be held at St. Paul's Church in the country," René said.

"Not a good idea for you to go. You are so easily recognized," Alice said, tapping her fingers on the table.

"Still . . . ," René said as she cleared away the dishes from the table. "It might be a good idea for us to see who attends."

"My thoughts exactly," Eliza said.

Jo spoke up. "We can disguise you."

"What? As a boy? Mrs. General Hamilton? I don't think so." Alice's tone was harsh.

"It might not need go that far. She's in widow's weeds already. We just need to give her a black veil. Nobody will see her face." Mary stood and helped to clear the table. "If she wants to go, we can join her. That way, if anyone even thinks it's her, they will think again. What would she be doing with the likes of us?"

"Yes, we could keep her in the center of us." René placed dishes in the dry sink and turned around. "What do you think?"

A black veil over her face. A group of women surrounding her. It sounded like a good plan. The funeral was tomorrow. The sooner the better. Eliza needed to find out more about Drake. What better way than to attend his funeral?

"I think it could work," Eliza said. "But I know you ladies are busy and I hate to take you away from your work."

"We can manage," René said. "We just delivered a good bit of lace and are ready to start a big embroidery job. It comes at a good time for us, right between projects."

Jo and Mary decided to stay behind, for neither one of them liked going anywhere near a church.

★ ★ ★

The next day the three women walked to St. Paul's, which was on Broadway just outside the busiest part of the city. It used to be in the country, but the city had grown up to its edge. But it still was often called "the country church." Eliza wore a black veil made of fine, tightly tatted lace. Her grandmother was right— lace was worn at every important life occasion. Birth. Marriage. Death.

It was odd that Drake's funeral was being held at St. Paul's as opposed to Trinity, but Trinity was so busy it sometimes had to reject funerals. That the minister there had attempted to reject

Eliza's husband's funeral due to the nature of his death still rankled her. They had been faithful congregants. And even though Hamilton sometimes took issue with the minister and he had refused to join the church, they still attended and Eliza persuaded him to keep his opinions to himself.

The pinkish-brown steeple of the country church came into view as the women walked quietly. A few people trickled into the chapel. But as the women walked toward the church, Eliza realized that there'd be few people here. Jonathan Drake was not a well-loved man, evidently.

Eliza and her friends walked into the chapel, which was filled with soft light, and sat in the back, as they had planned to do. There were about twenty people scattered in the pews, all in black, a stark contrast to the soft light and pink and golden-brown tones of the chapel. Eliza had always loved this chapel. It had survived the Great Fire of 1776, which many people considered a miracle of sorts. New Yorkers had taken great pride in their little country chapel.

The preacher's prayer struck into Eliza's heart. It was as if he was praying for her Hamilton. She could not attend Hamilton's funeral. She had been too distraught and out of her mind with grief. Tears flowed down Eliza's cheeks even though she'd barely known Drake.

Once the service had ended, Eliza, Alice, and René remained seated as the other attendees trickled out of the church. A young man who resembled Drake walked by them. Alice elbowed her gently. That must be the man she'd spotted hanging around the house when the rock was thrown into Eliza's room. She was right. He did resemble Drake. And he fit the description of the bejeweled man who Jinkins claimed had attempted to pay him off. Who was he?

Eliza was surprised to see Mr. Renquist, her own solicitor, walk by. Hadn't he claimed that Drake was a bad person? What was he doing here?

She recognized several of the other men who also walked by. Calvin Evans. Sidney Wingfield. Charles Greenwood.

A woman—alone, unveiled, with a swollen face and red eyes—walked by them. She was the only person to glance at them. Eliza panicked but then remembered that her face was covered with the black veil. The woman could not know who she was. And Eliza had never seen her before. Maybe Alice or René had.

Once everyone else had departed, Eliza and the other women walked out into the bright sunny day and slowly made their way over to where Drake's coffin stood, outside of an already dug grave. The preacher was speaking. Eliza wasn't paying attention, as she was too busy taking in the scene. A group of somber men, one woman, and the three of them stood around the open ground. Eliza wanted to remember these faces.

Mr. Renquist briefly regarded Eliza—or was it Alice?—and it startled her. But she assured herself that he could not see her face.

A small crowd of onlookers came up behind them and commented on the proceedings.

"Horrible way to die."

"Got what was coming to him, ask me."

"Couldn't pay his debt."

"You reap what you sow."

That had always been one of Eliza's favorite expressions from the Bible. She'd found it played out over and over again in her life. But sometimes it didn't, and she had to wonder about that. Would those who were lost burn in the next life, or would they get another chance?

She worried about Hamilton's soul. She had expressed this concern so many times. That he would not join a church or take communion bothered her—and he understood. She prayed that it hadn't been too late for him when he asked for last rites. The crowd continued to comment, interrupting her thoughts.

"A cad is what he was."

"A cad and a devil worshiper."

Eliza's heart nearly stopped.

A man shushed the woman who'd just spoken. "No, they don't worship the devil. They just don't believe in God."

Eliza's chest burned with fear. What was he talking about? Who didn't believe in God? Who were "they"? A chill moved through her as she remembered Drake's words: "Be careful, madam."

"He was a man, wasn't he? And he's lost his life," another voice said. "He's in the hands of God now."

"And there is a killer running our streets," a lower voice said.

Eliza didn't dare turn her head, but she made out sounds of scuffling feet and small chatter. She wanted to shrink away from the growing crowd. Fear traveled up and down her back, like a slippery cold snake.

The preacher, alarmed, looked up from his prayers. The young Drake lookalike stood straighter, his eyebrows gathered. A young man stepped closer to him, as if gathering defenses.

"There's a constable!" someone in the crowd cried out. "What are you going to do about the murder?"

Eliza turned to see a constable attempting to walk by. Another man, who Eliza didn't recognize, glared in their direction.

"There's a killer in our streets!" the man said. He wore a small cap on his head and punched the air with his fist.

"Yeah! And the constable does nothing!" the man's companion shouted.

The sound of someone spitting made Alice startle. "Let's go home. Follow me."

Eliza nodded, taking Alice's arm even as René took hers. Was there going to be a riot? She didn't know, but as she and the other two women ducked through a doorway into a dusty path of an alleyway, she whispered a prayer of thanks that she would not witness whatever was to come.

CHAPTER 36

Alice, René, and Eliza, all clad in black, made their way from the alley to the street. Eliza picked at her collar, sweat making it stick to her neck. Her heart raced. She lifted her eyes and forged ahead, led by Alice.

Walking from the country church to the city had always been a favorite walk of Eliza's. The harbor and the buildings clustered around it were now in sight, spreading out to the streets. Everything was crowded and snug as close to the harbor as it could get.

When they turned up Pearl Street, the smell of fresh oysters permeated as a line of women sat and shucked them along the street. They walked on, through the crowds, edging their way to the next corner, where a fiddler was playing some Irish tunes and a man next to him danced.

Eliza tore off her veil the minute they walked into the safety of the house. *Air!* She could breathe.

Alice shut the front door, her veil already off, eyes wide. "We almost got caught in a riot, I'd say."

Eliza's chest was still heaving. Was it from the heat? Or fear and excitement?

"Let's sit. I'll get some lemonade," René said and rushed into the kitchen.

Eliza and Alice sat in the parlor. Alice retrieved her crochet hooks and soon her fingers moved in slow, rhythmic measure. Suddenly her hand trembled slightly. Her eyes met Eliza's. "Well, that was quite an adventure."

"Indeed." Now that other New Yorkers were noticing the spate of murders, Eliza knew she was on the right path. If only she could discern which path that was.

René entered the room with a pitcher of lemonade. The women poured themselves glasses. "To say Drake was not a well-liked man would be an understatement."

Alice cackled. "'Tis true."

"Even so, the crowd seemed to be seeking justice." Eliza took a long drink from her glass.

"Pshaw! They just don't want a killer roaming the streets," Alice said, her fingers never missing a beat or a stitch.

Eliza laughed slightly. "Perhaps you're right." She remembered the lone woman at the funeral. "Do either of you know who the woman was that attended the funeral?"

"Her name is Joan," René said. "She's the daughter of Mary Higgans, the weaver who lives out near the bay. Her husband John is a trapper. They make a good living with beaver pelts and lovely blankets and shawls."

"Were they also at the funeral?" Eliza asked.

René shook her dark head. "I didn't see them if they were."

"Not many people were there. I reckon you'd have noticed them." Alice glanced at her, as her fingers continued their work.

"A young woman alone at a funeral . . . ," Eliza said.

"To me, whatever her interest is or was in Drake, her parents must not know of it," René said. "I will ask around about her. It can't hurt."

"And what was Renquist doing there?" Eliza was thinking out loud.

"Maybe he's Drake's solicitor," Alice suggested.

"But he spoke so poorly of him."

"Renquist is not a discreet man."

Eliza understood that. Yet Hamilton had kept him on as solicitor. She couldn't fathom it. She would find another one as soon as she could. Otherwise everyone in town would soon know of her financial circumstances. She couldn't let the widow of Alexander Hamilton become a charity.

"Maybe Drake owed him money and he wanted to see for sure that he was good and dead," Alice said.

"Very likely," René said.

Eliza had never liked Renquist, and this solidified her feelings. He was the Hamilton clan's solicitor, and yet he'd attended the funeral of one of Burr's men. A man, in fact, that he had warned Eliza about. "Who was the young man with the young man who looks like Drake?"

"Ah! That I know! He's Randall Ryman, son of Joshua Ryman. Drake's distant cousin. A remarkable resemblance. Do you know him?"

"I've heard his name." Eliza drank more from her lemonade as she searched the recesses of her mind. How did she know that name? He may have been a classmate of older son, Philip. She didn't want to think about that. Not now.

A knock at the front door startled all three women. René rushed to open it.

"Constable Schultz, please come in," she said.

Eliza and Alice started to rise from their chairs.

"No, please sit down. I'll be brief," the constable said as he entered the room. "I'm just checking to see if you are well." He studied Eliza.

"Yes, I am. But what—"

"There was an incident with a crowd not far from here and quite a few women were hurt in the scuffle."

Eliza and Alice tried not to look at one another, lest it might clue in the constable that they had been there earlier.

Their silence was met with an explanation. "Jonathan Drake's funeral."

"Why would there be a fight at a man's funeral?" Alice said.

"People are afraid. He was murdered and people want us to find his killer. That's why I can't stay long."

"I was sorry to learn of his death. Did he have a family?" Eliza wanted to know more about Drake and the young man who resembled him. After all, he was probably the same young man who was paying people off to act against her son.

"A younger brother," he said. "William."

"William Drake? I shall send him a condolence note. Where do I find him?" Eliza asked.

"On Wall Street, madam—769 Wall Street. Although the lad may soon be moving from there, as his brother paid the rent."

Alice tsked. "Maybe the landlord will take pity for a month or two until the lad finds his feet."

"He's a student, but clerks for Calvin Evans. Not much money to be made there, I'm afraid." Schultz stood awkwardly in the doorway of the room. "I'm glad to see you are staying in and unharmed. I must be going. I'll inform you about the investigation should I have anything to tell you."

"Thank you, Constable Schultz." Eliza rose to walk him to the door, with the intention of telling him to keep an eye on the younger Drake. She was certain he was the briber and may also have been the rock thrower. But as she walked, she lost confidence in these ideas. If she were to tell the constable now, and he then made it obvious that the police were searching for William Drake, their case against him might be lost. No, they needed more solid evidence before making accusations.

CHAPTER 37

The next morning, Eliza penned another note to Victoria Peabody asking her about the list that Rose Van Der Gloss had spoken to her about. Eliza handed the note off to René, who was delivering embroidered linens to the family that morning. It would take all day, as they now lived on Long Island. Delivery would require a long carriage ride to the East River, a ferry ride across, then another carriage ride, then all of it again in reverse.

As she was leaving the house, Eliza's carriage pulled up and Angelica popped out of it, dusting herself off from the ride.

"Angelica!" Eliza embraced her. "Please come out of the sun."

"I can only stay a bit." Angelica followed Eliza into the house. "We don't want to alert anybody who may be watching as to where you are."

"Are you being overly concerned about this?" Eliza asked.

"No," Alice interrupted. "She is not. Please come in, Mrs. Church. We have tea prepared."

"Thank you." She walked in and took in the home. "It's lovely."

And it was. Perhaps she too was remembering the smaller, cozy homes that Eliza and Hamilton had shared.

"Thank you," Alice said.

After they sat, Angelica handed Eliza a stack of letters. "I brought these to you, as I suspected there was something important here and that you may be looking for something to do." She'd also brought the box of Eliza's stationery so that she could write back.

"That's considerate. Thank you." Eliza set the mail aside. "Tell me—have you any news about the rock thrower?"

Angelica reached into her bag and pulled out a button and a piece of cloth. "McNally found these near the gum trees. Whoever threw the rock must have raced by them when Alice spotted him and tore his shirt."

"Aye," Alice said. "That was the direction he was moving in." She and Eliza exchanged glances.

"What is it?" Angelica said.

"We think we know who it was. Jonathan Drake's brother, William. We saw him yesterday at Drake's funeral and Alice recognized him." Eliza smoothed her black dress.

"And?" Angelica's eyes widened. "What have you done about it?"

"Nothing yet. We think we need to collect more evidence. If we turn him in and he runs, we may not get to the bottom of what's happening."

"Balderdash! You must turn him in immediately. Once the police have him, they will get to the bottom of it. You don't need to worry yourself with such matters."

"Angelica, I beg of you, please listen to me." Eliza hesitated. "There's more going on than someone hurling a rock through my window."

"I realize that."

Eliza turned to Alice. "He was heading in the direction of the gum trees. Did you see anything else? If he'd kept going in that direction, he'd have gone down the hill. Perhaps he had a horse waiting."

"I saw no horse, and neither did McNally," Alice said.

"Maybe he went through the forest. Maybe he hid there. Perhaps we should have McNally search around the forest." Eliza's mind's eye placed her on their front porch, gazing straight ahead, down the hill, the forest, and beyond it to the city and the harbor. He could have walked throughout the woods, come out on the other end, and headed into the thick of the city, with nobody none the wiser.

Alice set her teacup down on the table. "We went to Drake's funeral and there was a bit of a riot. We left before it escalated."

"Thank God for that," Angelica muttered and turned to Eliza. "What were you doing out in public?"

"I wore a veil."

"Clever."

Eliza recapped the experience for Angelica.

"So the Ryman boy and the Drake boy are friends?" Angelica said after Eliza had finished. "And the Drake boy is the one we think threw the rock through your window?"

Eliza nodded. "I know where William Drake lives. I wish I could sneak over there and see the comings and goings."

Alice raised her hand. "Leave that to me. One of the women here can surely move about unnoticed."

"Great idea, Alice!" Eliza said.

After a few moments of silence, Angelica said: "So maybe they are conspiring with one another. But why?"

"It's hard to piece together. But I know there's a link between all of the murders and the threats made against me."

"Excuse me, Mrs. Church. Do you remember who stood around you when Mrs. General Hamilton was talking with Drake outside of the church?" Alice asked.

"Unfortunately I did not look at anybody but Eliza. I was fearful she'd swoon at any moment. But maybe we can ask the ministers who signed the ledger that morning."

"Splendid idea!" Eliza said.

"I shall see to that immediately," said Angelica. "John wanted me to let you know that the blade they found was forged in Europe. Probably Prussia. That might provide a clue as to who owned it before Drake carved initials into it." She waved her hands. "What would Drake have against our Alexander?"

"He's Hamilton's oldest son now. I think that's enough for them." Eliza's voice was a whisper.

"But why? Hamilton is dead. What could they possibly be concerned about? Why can't they let him rest in peace and leave his family alone?" Angelica cried.

"Because there was something he and his friends knew that could implicate another person in a crime," Alice said matter-of-factly.

Eliza remembered the letter from Van Der Gloss, claiming they had proof that Hamilton was innocent of robbing the Treasury. "It may all lead back to the old rumor about Hamilton robbing the Treasury. They never found the culprit."

"Perhaps Hamilton did." Angelica stood and started pacing. "Of course it would be about money."

"It is much bigger than someone throwing a rock through my window." Eliza picked at her skirt. "People are getting killed over this. Someone wants to keep a secret buried."

"If we've figured this out, surely the authorities have as well," Angelica said, flopping back onto the settee.

"Pshaw." Alice slapped her hands on her lap. "They are busy trying to solve the murders of Drake and Van Der Gloss, alright, but I doubt they're searching in the right places."

"Alice, you are very pessimistic when it comes to the law," Angelica said.

She cackled. "That I am. That I am."

"Before I forget, here is what I found outside the Grange." Angelica reached her hand into her bag and placed a piece of torn fabric and a button on the table. "Add that to your other evidence, if you have any."

Eliza picked up the button and examined it. It was made of mother of pearl and had an owl carved into it. "Another owl . . ."

"What?" Angelica said.

"An owl was on the rock that was thrown into my room," Eliza stated.

"Yes." Angelica's face whitened. "It must be a symbol for something. I've seen it around town."

"The Bavarian Illuminati." Alice stood from her chair and brushed thread from her skirt.

Eliza's heart raced. "John mentioned them."

"What do they have to do with anything? Just a group of men who have nothing better to do than form some silly secret society." Angelica waved her hands as if to brush the idea of them away.

"Hamilton spoke of them. They are not Christian men." Eliza twisted at her skirt. "He went to a meeting and considered it folly. Never went back."

"Question is, if they are involved, why?" Alice said. "What would they have against your boy?"

Eliza considered this for a moment. "I guess the only way we'll know is to ask Alexander. He is almost finished with his exams."

"John will see him tonight. They are meeting for dinner. I will speak with him." Angelica stood. "I must leave. I've probably stayed too long."

"Must you go?" Eliza rose to embrace her.

Angelica nodded. "And you must stay here until we know that you're safe."

★   ★   ★

After Angelica left, the house quieted. As always, after Angelica left a room it took Eliza a few moments to adjust. It was as if the air and light had momentarily vanished. Eliza tried to settle her longing for the Grange, her sister, and her children. They were all scattered and it didn't sit well with her. But for now, that's how it must be.

She sat down on the settee and stared at nothing.

"Mrs. General Hamilton, can I get you anything?" Alice asked.

"No, I'm fine." Eliza lifted a newspaper off the table and scanned it. There was nothing of interest on the first page. She turned the page and a headline grabbed at her: *City's Murdered Cry for Justice*. She read further:

> *A riot broke out at the funeral of Johnathan Drake. The citizens of New York demanded justice for his murder and the murder of John Van Der Gloss. There have been two murders within a week of one another—plus the suspicious death of Floyd Peabody. It all adds up to a conspiracy of murder. Is it one man committing these heinous acts? Or a group of men?*
>
> *One must ask what the three victims had in common.*

Eliza was no longer the only person in town to put all of this together. But now that these allegations were being made public, would the culprit run? She read further:

> *Were they friends? Did they even know one another? The answer is yes. Two of the men were great friends with the beloved Alexander Hamilton and one was Aaron Burr's man. I'll leave you, dear reader, to imagine the entanglements.*

Eliza dropped the paper and gasped.

Alice ran over to her. "What is it?"

She pointed at the paper. Alice picked it up and read over it. She then sat down next to Eliza and wrapped her arm around her. The two women sat in silence.

"It could be a good thing," Alice finally said, moving her arm away. "Now that I've got my thoughts together about this."

"How?" Eliza could barely manage to speak with the weight pressing on her chest.

"What we want is justice. We don't have to be the ones who deliver it. We can help, if they need it."

Eliza drew in some air. "Yes, but if the killer has seen this article, they will surely escape town."

"Ach, we have no way of knowing how a killer's mind works. That's what I'd surely do. But then again, I also would not kill a person."

The fluttering in Eliza's stomach calmed. "Yes, I suppose I shouldn't attempt to apply logic to an utterly mad situation."

"Indeed. That's not to say we should have no concern in the matter, knowing how they tried to blame your boy. Let's hope the newspapers don't find out about that."

Eliza's worry spun into anger. She would not allow her family name to be besmirched. She had worked so hard to tell the true story of Alexander Hamilton. Before his death, she'd already begun traveling and interviewing Revolutionary War soldiers about him. Gathering materials for a biography. Other Founders had their biographies. Where was her husband's? Now this. Their second son may drag the family name into the mud through no fault of his own. No. This would not do. Not at all. She longed to get Alexander out of town as soon as his exams were over.

She'd think about how to do that. There had been a group of Hamilton's friends who'd said they'd help Alexander find a position. She balled her hands in her lap. She usually cleared her mind with a walk. But she could not go out unless she wore that hot veil.

Alice handed Eliza some dainty crochet hooks. "Did you say you know how to make lace?" She had a gleam in her eye. "'Tis the thing that sets my nerves right."

Eliza shrugged. It was worth a try. "It's been a few years." As she held the hooks in her hand, the weight of them soothed her—a bit. She remembered her grandmother knitting furiously one night, angry at something her grandfather had done.

"Mother, you will kill that scarf if you're not careful," Eliza's mother had said with a grin.

"Better it than your father," Eliza's grandmother had muttered.

CHAPTER 38

By the end of the day, the familiar rhythm of needle and linen thread had calmed Eliza's mind. And she had a lovely collar to show for her efforts. As a young lady she could make ten or more in the same amount of time. But now she was just finding her way back, her fingers not quite as nimble as her formerly practiced hands had once been.

She set her crochet hooks on the newspaper and her eyes caught the advertisement featuring the owl and the strange letters next to it. The more she contemplated it, the more she surmised it had to be a code. Looking at every three letters by crossing out the other two out did not lead her anywhere, nor did substituting letters with numbers. It was the oddest configuration of letters.

Hamilton's words rang in her head: "Betsey has an eye for ciphers. If she can't figure it out, I don't think any man, woman, or child can. She even learned to read messages that the Iroquois wove into their wampum belts. She helped Lafayette when he went to speak with them at a meeting with the Iroquois Confederacy. Before she even knew me."

I was someone before I became Mrs. General Hamilton. And I will be someone now, after him. But forever changed because of him.

She warmed, remembering how he'd boast about her, even though her face would heat every time he did so.

She scanned the letters again, but nothing came to her.

René opened the front door of the house and ambled in. "Mrs. General Hamilton!"

"Yes, René?"

"I have a note for you from Mrs. Peabody." She handed it to her, and Eliza's attention diverted from the puzzle in the paper. She opened the note carefully and read:

My Dearest Eliza,

What I have to say cannot be written. Meet me tomorrow at Hoboken Ferry #123 at ten in the morning.

May God keep you safe.

Victoria Peabody

Eliza's heart thudded against her ribs. This might be the very thing she had been seeking. If anybody had a list of men who were connected to this treacherous plot, it would be Victoria.

"I have taken the liberty, Mrs. General Hamilton, of securing a ride for you tomorrow morning." René clasped her hands together. "I shall ride with you."

"To where?" Alice said.

Eliza handed her the letter with a trembling hand, excitement coursing through her. She'd finally see Victoria one-on-one and they could speak their hearts and minds.

"What if it's a trap?" Alice asked.

"What?" Eliza said.

"'Tis no trap," René said. "I saw her write the note myself."

"Did anybody else witness it?" Alice asked.

René looked confused. 'No, it was just the two of us in her private room."

"It appears too easy to me." Alice squinted. "Something is awry."

Eliza was at a loss for words. High hopes one moment and the next they were dashed. "I have nothing to lose by showing up."

"Except your life!" Alice said. "I don't like it. Why Hoboken?"

Eliza was taken aback by this show of emotion. "I understand your concern. Would you feel better if you came with me?"

"No. What's an old lady like me going to do to save you? You need to take a man with you."

"Shall I send for Davey McNally?" René asked.

Alice pursed her lips. "I'm not sure he can make it in time."

The women sat in silence for a moment.

"What if we send a woman who resembles a man?" René smiled. "She just needs to have the appearance of having a man with her."

Alice cackled. "It may be the best choice."

Eliza's stomach settled. It was a plan, then. She, René, Alice, and Josephine, dressed as Joe, would take the hired carriage to the docks in the morning to meet Victoria.

★ ★ ★

The next morning was a steamy brew of heat and stink throughout the city. As Eliza, Alice, René, and Josephine climbed into the carriage, a herd of pigs made its way across the street, a woman trailing behind and swooshing them with her broom.

"Pigs are getting to be more of a problem," René said.

Eliza had read about them but had barely witnessed them herself since she'd been spending most of the time at their country home, where the pigs were enclosed and bred for slaughter. Wild pigs were a different matter altogether.

The carriage was small and the four women, one dressed as a man, were squashed together. Eliza, already a sweaty mess, longed for the cool river breezes of Harlem. But today she'd be at the river, further north, and she hoped for a little reprieve from the city heat.

The carriage rattled more than any other she'd ever been in, and they bounced to and fro in a most uncomfortable manner. Finally they reached the ferry to New Jersey and disembarked from the crowded carriage.

"Please wait here for us, as we discussed," Jo said to the driver.

The four women, only three of whom wore dresses, boarded the ferry. A slight breeze blew over Eliza's skin. Hoboken was a bit too close to where Hamilton had dueled Burr, but Eliza had no choice if she were to find answers.

The ferry dipped and swayed as it started off for the Jersey shore. Eliza watched as the city faded into the distance. She turned toward Hoboken, a less civilized outpost, to be sure. She hoped that she would find Victoria Peabody exactly where she said she'd be.

The ferry moved slowly to the dock. Soon after it stopped, the plank was attached to shore. Eliza could barely contain herself. She glanced around and glimpsed nobody resembling the Victoria Peabody she had once known. She stepped from the plank onto the dock, flanked by her companions, and searched for the numbers she sought.

"There!" René said. "There's the correct place."

Eliza squinted her eyes against the sun. A woman dressed in black with a white bonnet stood and faced the other direction.

"Wait here," Eliza said. "I don't think there's any need for you to come further."

"But—" Jo started to say.

"Look," Eliza gestured. "She's alone."

Alice, Jo, and René walked a little farther with her, then broke off. Eliza walked alone down the long pier to where the woman waited. As the woman turned to meet her gaze, shock moved through Eliza. For yes, it was Victoria standing before her—but a much diminished version of her former self. The word "pale" did not capture her ghostly hue, nor did the word "skeletal" capture the lack of weight. Eliza bit her lip to refrain from gasping. Just how long had it been since she'd seen her? A year? Six months? She and Hamilton had the Peabodys to dinner shortly after Christmas of last year . . . Could a woman have changed in appearance so drastically within that short a time?

Victoria walked toward Eliza with the same gait she'd always had, which alleviated some of Eliza's fears. As Victoria drew closer, Eliza discerned she had changed in other ways. Her friend's hair was now completely silver, including her eyebrows and eyelashes. She was a pale shadow of a woman. The way the sun lit her skin gave her a translucent glow. She was but one step away from the angels.

CHAPTER 39

When they embraced, Eliza sensed no life force within Victoria. Pulses of fear shot through the center of her.

"Oh, my dear." Victoria held Eliza's shoulders and took her in. "Are you well?"

Not for the first time, Eliza wondered about her own countenance and what others might think—but she did not have the time to dwell on that.

"I am." Eliza's eyes locked with hers. "And you?"

Victoria shook her head. "Not at all." Her voice cracked.

Eliza glanced around. They were alone on the pier, but the sensation of being watched was palpable.

"Thank you for coming." Victoria slipped her arm through Eliza's and pulled her along toward the end of the pier, facing the city. "I cannot spend long with you, dear. But I felt the need to explain some things."

Finally. Could she be getting answers? "Yes. I appreciate that. It's been confusing."

"I'm certain my husband was murdered." It was a plain enough statement, but it sent Eliza's heart racing. "As surely as yours was." She lingered, as if searching for the right words. "They were close to making an arrest. The man who had framed

Hamilton for stealing money from the Treasury. You remember that incident."

"Of course." This fit with the letters she had seen. "Do you know who this man is?"

They were almost at the end of the pier. Victoria stopped. "I do not. But I figure the man knows that our husbands recognized him. He's behind the deaths of my husband, Mr. Drake, and Mr. Van Der Gloss."

Eliza's mind raced. "Who else knows this man's identity? I've been trying to deduce that because someone else may be in danger."

Changing the subject, Victoria said, "Eliza, you are flushed with perspiration." She took out a handkerchief and gently wiped Eliza's brow. "Please take this handkerchief. It's special to me."

Confused, Eliza obliged. It was a warm day, but was she really perspiring that much? Eliza slipped the handkerchief into her bag.

"Whoever the guilty man is, he is powerful," Victoria said, not answering Eliza's question. "Please take care of that handkerchief. It holds some answers for you," Victoria whispered, then pulled away.

Eliza had surmised that there was someone powerful pulling the strings of the situation, like a puppeteer. But what answers could a handkerchief hold?

"You must stop questioning people. You must back away from this line of inquiry. They will kill you without a second thought." The words were sharp and crisp, and Victoria's tone was pleading. "Please."

Chills traveled through Eliza, even in the humid, hot air.

"Consider your children." Victoria pleaded with the one last tool she had—Eliza's role as a mother.

Eliza *had* considered her children. But she also had a duty to her husband and his memory, and if she could save another person's life, she must.

"May I ask you—" Eliza began.

"We are being watched. I am always being watched, except when I am at my parents' farm," Victoria interrupted.

Eliza looked around but didn't see anybody. She was starting to suspect that Victoria was even more unwell than she appeared. Victoria turned in the other direction, toward Hoboken, and led Eliza back toward solid ground.

"Where was your husband on the day of my husband's duel?" Eliza finally asked.

"My darling Eliza, both my husband and Rose Van Der Gloss's husband were the men who rowed your husband ashore."

Eliza's stomach waved. She swallowed hard. They were the boatmen. Now both were dead. "But what of Drake?"

"Drake? I don't know anything about him. These men are powerful and cruel. What they did to my husband to protect themselves was . . . unfathomable. I know not what they might do to you, the widow of Alexander Hamilton. You must take care." The breeze picked up and Victoria adjusted the ribbon holding her hat on her head, looking back and forth as if she were certain they were being watched.

"Who are these men?" Fear and anger stormed inside of Eliza. She swallowed the bile she felt creeping into her throat. "Is Aaron Burr behind this?"

Victoria stopped walking, the sound of the water coming from behind her. "Burr? I don't know. But I don't think he was. He was probably nothing more than a pawn in someone's sick game."

Eliza swallowed again.

What had she learned from this meeting? Was Victoria going to be able to help? She had just discovered that all of her instincts had been correct, but it seemed that Victoria didn't have a list of names for her.

"René said that a group of men visited your husband the night he was killed." Eliza reached out and held Victoria's shoulder.

Victoria's gaze fell downward as she nodded.

Eliza didn't want to ask, for she could see the pain on Victoria's face. But she had to. "Who were they?"

"I wish I knew."

"Why didn't the lawmen believe Paulette's statement?"

"That is a good question. Maybe because she couldn't understand them. Prussian is hard on the ear. They may have assumed she was exaggerating."

Eliza stopped walking. "Did you say Prussian?"

"My husband's mother was a Prussian and he spoke it fluently. So did the men who visited with him that night. That much I know."

Why did this strike such a chord of fear in Eliza? There were many fine Prussian immigrants in the city.

They'd reached the other side of the pier. A bird swooped down in front of them and walked back and forth.

"I must bid you farewell," Victoria said. "I've already taken too much time. My father is waiting for me and I'm certain others are watching."

Eliza nodded, certain that nobody was watching, but she wanted to be respectful. "Will you come back to your home in the city?"

"My home is to be sold soon and I hope to never return."

Eliza reached for her hands. "May God be with you, my friend."

CHAPTER 40

Eliza, with a heaviness in her heart, returned to the dock where her friends were waiting. Her son was accused of murdering men who had been friends of his late father. These men had unearthed a secret—the name of the person who stole money that Hamilton was accused of stealing. It all made a sordid sense. But why Alexander? Why not someone else? Why did it have to be Hamilton's son?

She, Alice, Jo, and René boarded the ferry back to Manhattan.

"Did you get the list?" Alice asked.

Eliza shook her head. "She would not answer me when I asked who the men were."

Alice grunted. "I thought that's why we came." She glared at René accusingly. René merely shrugged. Jo looked out toward Manhattan.

"In that regard, our mission was a failure. But I see clearly what has happened. My intuition has been accurate. Mr. Peabody was murdered as surely as Drake and Van Der Gloss." Eliza peered out toward Hoboken and watched as it faded into the distance. Blues and greens and grays.

Alice crossed her arms.

The sun beat down on them with a ferocity that made Eliza wish she hadn't come, though she was glad to see Victoria. She reached into her bag for the handkerchief Victoria had given her and patted her face with it.

René's expression changed from somber to happy. She reached for the handkerchief, snatching it out of Eliza's hand. "You mustn't use this one. Do you have another?"

"What are you doing, daft girl?" Alice scolded.

Empty-handed, Eliza reached for another handkerchief. René laid out the handkerchief she held over her lap. There in embroidery stitches were the names of five men. Only one of whom was still living.

Jo lean over her lap. "What the—"

Eliza squinted. "Does that say Renquist?"

Alice grabbed the handkerchief and placed it in her bag. "Let's talk about this later." There were others milling about on the ferry. Alice's prudence was measured. Renquist? Was his life in jeopardy? What could she do about that?

She didn't like the man, but she certainly didn't wish him dead. She needed to speak with Constable Schultz.

"I did learn one curious thing today," Eliza said in a low voice. "The men who visited Mr. Peabody spoke Prussian with him that night."

Alice frowned; René pursed her lips. "That's why Paulette couldn't understand them!" René said.

"Let's discuss this at home." Alice folded her arms. She looked as if she were about to burst.

Jo nodded and sat back down. "Yes, good suggestion."

Eliza wished she could read her thoughts, for there was surely something brewing in her mind.

A man passed by them.

"I can't stand this heat," René said, maybe a bit too loudly.

"We'll be home soon enough," Alice said.

★   ★   ★

Eliza's thoughts turned and twisted from the woman she'd left behind—distraught, prematurely gray, and aging—to the nervous, twittering Renquist. She reflected back over his visit, then when she'd observed him in town. He understood more than he let on, but did he know his life was in jeopardy? Would he heed her warning? He'd already considered her nothing more than a widow whose mind was in decline.

He had tried to warn her about Drake. Drake had tried to warn her as well.

Poor Drake. She whispered a little prayer for him as the ferry docked. Her body jolted with the movement.

★   ★   ★

The women rushed into the house on Pearl Street just as a storm started. Wind whipped trees and plants and rain pelted the windows. The sky was almost as dark as night.

Eliza sat in the parlor with Alice and René as they worked on their embroidery. She picked up a hook and started the rhythm her hands remembered. "I need to think."

Alice nodded. "We all do."

Eliza's fingers found their way into making a delicate start to scalloped lace. "I don't know who to turn to next. Renquist? Schultz?"

René flopped a newspaper down on the table. "Schultz is quite busy." She pointed at the headline: *Angry Mob Demands Justice for Murders*. Eliza read on:

It is sometimes difficult to solve a murder, but we've had two recent killings. Are the constables and justices helping the cause?

Both of the murders of Van Der Gloss and Jonathan Drake were particularly hideous in nature. Rumor has it the law has a suspect, but he is being hidden by his influential, rich family. We demand protection from this man.

Eliza's heart quickened. Fear was escalating. What would happen if people found out her own son was the suspect? The son of the great Alexander Hamilton a murderer? Even if he were proven innocent, just his name being brought up in such a manner would cause great trouble to her family. Even more trouble. Another false accusation against a member of her family. Would it never end?

She hoped that John would be able to continue to keep Alexander's name out of the newspapers. Otherwise, if an angry mob found out he was the suspect—innocent or not— her own son could be killed. And she had had enough loss to last a lifetime.

If he wasn't killed, his name would still be dragged through the streets—the name of her husband, her family. After everything the whole family had sacrificed and worked for, there was the possibility of even more scandal. Eliza's skin prickled. She continued to work on the piece of lace in an effort to distract herself. "I suppose I'll need to talk with Renquist."

"We'd be wise to warn him." Alice's fingers worked and worked. "But will he give us the information we need?"

"I simply don't know," Eliza said. "But it's a start." Weariness overcame her. She set the hooks down and rubbed her eyes. A good storm always made her sleepy. She glanced at the newspaper again, turning to the back page advertisements. There, next to an ad for stays, was another owl with swords. The same image from the previous newspaper and the rock thrown into her room. Another owl. She shivered.

As she lifted the paper to study the cipher closer, it was as if a fog lifted from her mind. "Prussian!"

"What?" Alice exclaimed.

"The reason I've unable to figure out this cipher. Do you have a pencil?"

René handed her one. Eliza crossed out some letters and circled some numbers. She didn't speak Prussian, but Dutch was similar enough that she was able to calculate exactly what the cipher said. "It's an address and a time."

"But for what?" Alice said.

"A meeting of some kind," René guessed.

Eliza drew in closer to the other women. "It's a meeting we must attend."

Silence filled the room.

"Why?" Alice finally asked. "Why do we need to attend?"

"The rock thrown in my window bore that sign . . . they must know something. I must have rattled them when I was asking questions around town," Eliza said.

"What are you going to do? Storm in there asking questions? What questions will you even ask?" Alice's hands continue to twist and pull. She tsked. "You are not thinking clearly."

Wasn't she? The symbol and the fact that it was in Prussian meant something. Prussian was spoken by the men who'd killed Victoria Peabody's husband.

"When and where is it?" René asked, ignoring Alice and her concerns, her eyes lit.

Eliza gave her the address and time.

"Ach, we can't do it. The Tam's Arms. Women are not allowed in that establishment," René said.

Alice harrumphed in victory.

"Can we send someone else?" René asked.

"I don't think there's anyone we can send that wouldn't be noticeable. Maybe John Church or Davey McNally." Eliza's mind raced. How could they manage to attend this meeting? What was it about? Why did these people have to keep meeting locations and times so secretive? Hamilton used to laugh about these secret societies. "A bunch of rich men with nothing better to do," he would scoff. But he was a member of a few of them himself, though not of the same nature. But still.

"Maybe this is a job for Jo?" Alice said. "We know some servers at the Tam's Arms. Why can't Jo go in and see what this is about? It'll settle this owl business once and for all."

"Excellent idea!" René said.

But Eliza had an even better one. She couldn't send someone alone to do her work. She needed to be there herself. But could she get away with it? Could she dress as a man and carry it off?

CHAPTER 41

Alice tsked. "I don't think it's a good idea. You are Mrs. General Hamilton. You mustn't demean yourself." Her jaw twitched.

"Alice, this is for my son. For my family. It may be the first step in making certain my husband's story is told—the correct story, that is. Dressing as a man is nothing in the face of all that." Eliza had never been so certain of anything before. She could dress as a man. How difficult could it be?

"But surely Jo can do it and report back to you," Alice persisted.

"I considered that." Eliza held up the trousers René had given her. "But if I can do a task myself, I'd rather do it. You know me, Alice."

"Aye." Alice coughed. "We will need more male clothing, I'm afraid. But I know a shop."

"Everybody knows her face," René said. "We can't take her to the shop."

"We shall dress her in old clothes and keep her head covered," Alice said. "What do you think, Mrs. General Hamilton?"

"If I can demean myself as a man, I surely can as a woman," she said in a jesting manner, and the women laughed.

Clad in her baggy old dress and with a scarf wrapped around her head, Eliza walked arm in arm with Alice, snaking through the dusty, dry streets of the city. The stench of pigs prompted Eliza to lift her handkerchief to her nose. She stepped over a pile of pig manure and continued walking. She and Alice mingled with the crowd, the sound of carriages and horse hooves pounding the dirt road. They turned onto a cobblestone street with ropes of colorful triangular flags streaming across the street from windows above them.

They were now in the shopping district. Eliza recognized it well. She and Angelica used to love to frequent the shops when Eliza and her family lived in the city. This was one of the many things she missed while living in the country. Her heart sped up as the Grange popped into her mind's eye. She remembered the first moment she stood on the front porch of their new home and gazed out over the city, straight down to the harbor. She could still do so when the day was clear. She missed that view. She missed her home. Would she be able to keep it?

Alice pulled Eliza's arm and led her into a tailor's shop. A bell rang as they entered the shop. They were met with stifling air as they entered. Three men scurried around the small shop, each with cloth in their arms. They wore the same head covering as Jewish men Eliza had met through Hamilton. He had worked to secure many Jewish families when they entered the country. He'd attended a Jewish school when a boy. But she'd never been in a shop owned by a Jewish man. Clean and orderly, the fabrics stood in piles arranged by color, then by weave. Wool. Muslin. Silk.

An older man approached them. Alice took down her scarf and showed her face.

"Madame Vin—" he began to address Alice.

"Sir," Alice interrupted him. "Might we speak with you in private?"

His eyebrows gathered as confusion played over his face. Then he gathered himself. "Of course. Please follow me."

He walked with a slight limp as he led them to a small room in the back of the shop. Huge spools of thread hung on hooks and a man-sized sewing form stood in the corner. "How may I help you?"

"I know that you keep men's clothing for emergencies. I need them." Alice pointed at Eliza. "Her brother is about the same size as her. He has recently come upon bad times, sir, and has need of some clothing."

His hand went to his chin. "Unfortunately, I do not have much to select from. Let me see. I will return momentarily."

Eliza and Alice stood in silence and waited.

"Alice, what did the man call you?" Eliza asked.

Alice lowered her eyes. "You were a great help to me once and to other women like me. I hope to help you in every way that I can." She grabbed Eliza by the shoulders. "I will tell you if you insist. But you must believe me. You are better off not knowing."

A pang of disappointment stabbed at Eliza. More secrets. But she, of course, would respect her friend's preference. "Alice, I will abide by your wishes. I only hope that someday—"

But the tailor entered the room, interrupting Eliza. "Here we are. I apologize. They are not the best of material. We've had these for a while. But they are quite small. Perfect for a smaller man."

Alice inspected the trousers and shirt. "This is indeed perfect for our needs." She beamed. "I knew we could count on you."

A smile cracked his face, creating dimples on either side and creases of age around his eyes. "I'm very pleased to hear this. We shall wrap it for you."

"I am most grateful." Alice reached into her bag and pulled out money. She slipped him a few bills.

"Madam, I cannot take money from you."

"You will," she said with a firmness in her voice that chilled Eliza. Alice was a woman of many aspects.

But maybe all, if not most, women were. After all, here was Eliza Hamilton herself, hiding in the city, investigating killers. Procuring clothing to disguise herself as man. She couldn't help but contemplate her situation. Oh, how life could turn. Especially for women.

"Might I ask you a question?" Alice patted the tailor's shoulder gently. "I know you are well learned."

"Of course. You may ask me anything."

Alice reached into her bag and pulled out a slip of paper with the owl drawn on it. "Do you know what this is?"

His jaw twitched. "Where did you get this?"

"I drew it myself," she answered. "But we've been seeing it in the papers and a few other places."

"Does this have something to do with your brother's hard luck?" he asked Eliza, who nodded. "Then you must tell your brother to take heed. This is a group of men who will step on anybody in order to succeed."

"How dangerous are they?" Alice asked.

"I don't know. But to me and my people, they have not been kind. One of the members attacked a rabbi."

"Attacked?" Alice said, her voice lowered.

"The man almost died over some . . . misunderstanding."

"Misunderstanding?" Alice grunted. "Prejudice, no doubt."

He shrugged and looked at the floor. His stance spoke a million words.

Eliza felt embarrassed for him, but more embarrassed for the ignorance of the men who committed this act of violence.

"They are a powerful group of men with eyes everywhere. I'd steer clear of them, if you can," the tailor said.

"I understand," Alice said. "We must be going. Thank you."

Package in hand, Alice led Eliza to the door.

"I hope God keeps you in his bosom," the tailor said.

Alice turned to face him. "I wish the same for you and your family, Daniel."

"Come back any time," Daniel said as the two women walked through the door. His words held an air of desperation that Eliza could not shake during the walk back to Alice's home.

CHAPTER 42

"It will be fine," René said as she handed Eliza a shirt. "We've sent a message to the Lander boys, who are serving at the Tam's Arms. They are expecting us."

"We'll need to bind your breasts with this. No way around it, I'm afraid." Jo held up reams of fabric. "It all starts from what's underneath. It's like constructing a doll."

Alice cackled.

"We need to get rid of as many womanly curves as possible," René said. "And you definitely have a woman's body."

Eliza was unaccustomed to this kind of conversation. She did not know what to say.

Eliza didn't have her sisters' curves. She was leaner and sinewy, which may turn out to be a good thing in this case. And she was no stranger to binding her breasts, which she'd had to do a few times when she wanted to stop nursing her babies. But she appreciated that she needed to do what Jo instructed.

"So we bind and then you'll wear a shirt that's slightly large." Jo lifted the shirt up to demonstrate.

"Let's do it." Eliza slipped her shoulder out of her dress. René unfastened the stays from Eliza's corset and removed it from her body. Eliza slipped her chemise over her head and they wrapped her chest up, tight. It reminded her of the days when stays and corsets were tight beyond measure. Fashion had recently changed, and she far preferred the new looser-fitting dresses and corsets.

"Is that alright?" René asked. "Too tight?"

"Not too tight." Eliza reached for the shirt and pulled it over her head.

She stepped into the pair of men's trousers. As she pulled them over her legs and hips, the fabric hung against her skin in the oddest of ways. She didn't like the way it clung to the inside of her thighs. She shook her legs. "Quite uncomfortable."

Jo laughed. "That's what I thought at first, but soon you'll find it more comfortable than your skirts and dresses. It allows for so much more freedom of movement."

Alice looked away. "I still don't like this."

"Many women have done this. I remember Hamilton talking about several soldiers in the Revolution who were women dressed as men. He admired them so, but often they got in trouble for pretending to be someone they weren't." Eliza ran her hands over her shirt. "I'm going into a different kind of battle. For my son and family."

She glanced over at her black dress hanging in the corner, feeling a prick of loss again as she took it in. Just because she didn't wear her mourning dress did not mean she wasn't still in mourning. She would ever be mourning her dear Hamilton.

"Let's see you walk across the room," Jo commanded.

"No. It won't do," René said after observing Eliza. "Watch how Jo walks. It's much more of a flop, flop, flop movement."

Eliza watched Jo make her way around the room. First she walked in her normal manner. "Now then, this is how a man walks. It's not just about flopping. It's also about confidence. Of course, we'll be serving boys, so we won't do much in the way of preening."

Jo strutted across the floor with a walk that did not appear womanly at all. She clomped her feet, puffed out her chest, and stiffened her hips.

"I shall try now." Eliza tried to bear down and stomp with each step.

René, Jo, and Alice all laughed. Eliza flushed but then found herself laughing as well.

"You are going to do fine," René finally said.

Next, they coached her on her speech. First, she was told not to talk much at all, then they practiced lowering her voice and also not speaking in proper English.

"Oh, my poor mother struggled for years to get us to speak properly," Eliza remembered and laughed. "Here I am trying to unlearn it all!"

Then the gathering sat at the kitchen table and strategized.

"What are we seeking?" René asked.

"I'm not sure." Eliza tapped her fingers on the table. "We know the symbol for this group is an owl, which was painted on a rock and thrown through my window. What we don't know is why."

"You've gotten too close to someone's secret," Alice said.

"That is true," Eliza responded. "I think we're looking for anything in their conversation that could link them more closely with the rock incident and the murders. And with my husband and son."

"We need to learn what they are all about," Alice said. "Why the secret meetings? What are they doing?"

"There are so many secret societies these days. I sometimes think it's just another way for men to get away from their women," René said.

"Hamilton said something similar to me once." Eliza's stomach tightened as she said her husband's name. *If only you knew, my love, what I'm about to do.* Infiltrate a secret meeting of men, dressed as a man, with two other women doing the same. *What would you think?* She smiled to herself. She liked to think he wouldn't be too surprised. He'd seemed to love her even nature, but loved it even more when her youthful enthusiasm prodded her into doing something a little out of the ordinary.

"One more thing. I hesitate to bring it up, but if we are found out, we'll need to run. We need to determine a place to meet, should that happen," René said.

Eliza tamped down the fear creeping into her center. René's words were an appropriate reminder that this exercise was not folly. If they were found out, who knew what would happen? It would be worse for her family than she wanted to imagine. She envisioned the headline: *The Widow Hamilton Caught Dressing as a Man in a Local Pub.*

No. That couldn't happen. She would not be found out.

CHAPTER 43

Jo, René, and Eliza met the Lander brothers behind the Tam's Arms. The two brothers were short and waif-like, both with icy blue eyes.

"You've done this before?" one of them asked Jo.

She nodded.

"You know how to serve? Keep the pitchers of ale coming?" the other asked.

René tsked. "Come on, boys—we've been serving our whole lives, one way or the other."

"Right," said Peter, and slapped his hands together. "We'll show you where things are kept and then be on our way."

Eliza's heart raced as they entered the establishment. She'd never been in a pub or tavern before. It was not allowed for women of her station. She'd never cared to go to one, either, though she'd been a bit curious as to what went on in them since women weren't allowed in. She blinked her eyes to adjust to the dim light as they were led through the kitchen, where several pitchers were already filled with ale. The place smelled of sour hops.

"When you're not serving, you stand in the corner or behind the door and listen and watch. Be there *before* their glass is empty. We have a reputation for keeping the glasses full," Peter said.

Eliza heard the pride in his voice and nodded reassuringly.

Thirty minutes later the men began to enter the room, and René reached for Eliza's hand. "It will be fine."

Eliza lifted her chin. "We need to do this."

"And we can," Jo said.

As Eliza entered the room, her heart thudded so hard in her chest that she worried the others could hear it. Her legs trembled. *Stop. Stop. You are here for your family. You can do this. It's just like playing make-believe when you were a child.* She took one step forward and then another. With each new step her trembling subsided.

As she poured the drinks, she kept her head down. But René was correct in her observation that the men wouldn't even take notice of the serving "boys."

Joshua Ryman sat at the head of the long table and briefly glanced at her. Though Eliza's heart raced, she pretended not to notice. Several candles lit the dark hall and shadows played across the table and throughout the room. Eliza poured Ryman's drink and watched as he lifted the cup with his meaty hand. His brass buckles caught the light. She squinted to study what she thought she saw. For on his button was the very owl symbol she'd been seeing everywhere.

"Let us get right to it," Ryman said. "Does anybody have anything to report?"

A man raised his hand. Eliza recognized him. Calvin Evans. She had been to tea with his wife, Dove. "I've made inroads at Trinity."

"How so?" asked Ryman.

"I've been named a deacon," Calvin Evans said.

A rotund redhead laughed. "You? A deacon?" The other men joined in the laughter.

"That's right." Evans grinned. "And I'll get a turn at the pulpit soon enough."

Eliza wondered what Trinity had to do with these men and why they were laughing.

"That's good. We needed a man at Trinity," said Ryman.

For what? Eliza wondered what they were going on about.

"Speaking of Trinity . . . a constable came to see me," one of the younger men said and stood up. "They said they had a witness that I was at the riot at the country church. I said I was there, but not a part of the mob. But they are watching me."

"Daft man! You should've been more careful!" Ryan exclaimed.

The young man nodded. "Yes. I was just caught up in the moment. People wanted justice for Drake's death."

Silence in the room. Eliza poured more ale into an empty cup. The pouring liquid was the only sound in the room.

"God rest his soul," a soft-spoken man said.

Eliza wiped her palm on her shirt and switched the pitcher to her dryer hand. She glanced at Jo across the room. They made eye contact and then looked away.

"He was an enemy of this club," another man said.

Eliza's heart skipped a beat. Just the kind of words she wanted to hear.

"Yes, but still a man. What a horrible death," another man said.

"Indeed. Jonathan Drake's body draped over a tombstone at Trinity is not the kind of church news I'm seeking. We need to make further inroads. These church leaders are trying to take over the city." Ryman gazed out at the group over his spectacles.

Eliza had never heard anything so ridiculous in her life. What utter nonsense!

"I'm in place at the country church," said a man. "I think they trust me."

"Good. Maybe it's time to make a move, then," Evans said.

The other man nodded. "Soon."

Move? What kind of a move? Why did they want to take over churches?

Another man spoke with a thick Prussian accent. "Did you read the article in the paper that suggested the person who killed Drake also killed Van Der Gloss?"

"We aren't here to discuss the recent murders, Burgess."

"I just think it's interesting," Burgess continued. "Both men had a good deal in common."

Ryman wiped his brow. He lifted a glass to his mouth with his sweaty hand.

"Aye, they did," another man said. "They were both Hamilton's men."

Eliza's heart pounded in her chest at the sound of her husband's name.

"What are you suggesting?" Ryman asked, a vein throbbing on the side of his forehead.

Burgess shrugged. "Nothing, really. Except it seems to be convenient for—"

Ryman slammed his fist on the table. "For nobody! Their deaths are convenient for nobody!"

Eliza jumped slightly when he hit his hand on the table. The redhead across the table stared at Ryman. The tension in the room escalated. Was the man accusing Ryman of murder? What was the convenience he spoke of?

"I'm about the enlightenment of the people. Business. Education. We don't want them crushed by a strong church. I am not about murder. Swear to me, Joshua Ryman, that you had nothing to do with those deaths." Evans crossed his arms.

"Me?" Ryman's hands went to his chest. "Absolutely not. Those men had their hands in a lot of mischief and politics, not just that old business with Hamilton."

Eliza stood in the corner now, holding a pitcher of ale, which reeked of sour mash. But she nearly jumped at the sound of the word "Hamilton." What business with Hamilton?

"Can we get to the reason we are gathered for, instead of harping on the Hamilton thing?" another man said.

So there was a link to her dear Hamilton. What exactly was it? What was she supposed to do with this information? Would the constable believe her? Eliza bit the inside of her lip. Obviously, the redhead believed Ryman had something to do with the murders. But why? One must be either daft or brave to accuse a man of murder. She shivered, even as sweat dripped down her back. This wasn't the first time she'd been in a room with killers, but it was the first since her Hamilton had died. That she knew of. She suddenly longed to be with her father and children.

"What is the Hamilton thing anyway?" another man spoke up.

"It's no concern of this group," a red-faced Ryman said. "Let's get back to the matter at hand."

René came out of the kitchen with a fresh pitcher.

The redhead cleared his throat. "We are in a war, gentlemen. A war against the vagaries of religion. The clergy want nothing more than to make us all their sheep. But we are men of the mind."

Eliza wanted to cry. As if you couldn't be both a person of God and of the mind? Eliza bit the inside of her other cheek. They wanted to take over churches? To what end? She couldn't imagine anything good coming from that. But what was the link to her husband and family? Was one of the men here the guilty party that stole money from the Treasury all those years ago?

A gentleman in front of her drained his glass. She stepped forward to fill it. She filled the glass, hoping nobody spotted the tremor in her hand.

"We are also at war on our very streets. Two men murdered!" Evans said.

"And one suspicious hanging," the redhead said. "Do we really think it has nothing to do with us?"

Ryman coughed. "Of course it has nothing to do with us."

The redhead slammed his hand down and rolled his eyes. As he did so, Eliza spotted his owl button—the same as Ryman's.

There were only six or so men. But the room was small, and the men overpowered it. The room smelled of sour body odor and ale. Eliza tried not to allow it to distract her from soaking in every detail. The owl buttons. Ryman's huge hands. The younger man's odd little mustache. Each freckle on the redhead's face.

Ryman opened a satchel and lifted out a fine piece of linen to the light. Eliza tried not to stare as letters and numbers came into view on the linen. It was a list.

"This goes deeper than Hamilton's men." Ryman squinted. "Who knows how deep it goes? He had more friends and enemies than most." He held up the linen paper. "This is from the Master. He's concerned about the murders as well, but instructs us to carry on. He's given us a list of people who may know more about the killings."

Eliza clutched her stomach with one arm. She stood, planted, watching the door she yearned to walk through. It took everything in her to stand firm.

"I'll tell you who knows more. The oldest Hamilton boy. That's who knows. Is he on that list?" one man said as he stood.

Ryman handed the list to him. "See for yourself."

Eliza swallowed. *The oldest boy.* Their oldest was dead. They must be talking about Alexander. Why would he be a threat to them? Unless he knew who stole the money? Why would he keep that information to himself when he was being set up for murder?

Her jaw tightened. There was only one reason she could think of—to protect her, his father, and his family.

Chapter 44

Alice was not much for pacing. The walking back and forth did no good. And yet here she was, pacing. It was long past the time Eliza, Jo, and René should be back from the tavern.

She stopped pacing. If harm came to any of them, she'd never forgive herself for allowing any of this to go on. She should've put a stop to it. Yes, she should've. Alice lit a candle and watched its flame flicker. Its light spread across the table, then the room.

Would any of them have listened to her?

She grunted.

Jo with her wide-eyed enthusiasm would never believe anything could go wrong, René was seeking adventure and didn't seem to care if it placed her life in jeopardy, and Eliza . . . Eliza was driven to find answers.

What was Eliza hoping for?

She wanted to clear her son's name. That made sense. But to risk her own life? Alice surmised that there was more to it. A sense of duty. Of honor. Of decency or Christian duty?

Alice grimaced. She was not a religious woman. Her religion was one of needle and thread and weft and weave. Of creating things and family. Taking in those who needed it and giving them work to do. She had no time for church and prayers.

They would be home soon. They had to be.

Alice stood and grabbed a plate from the cupboard and filled it with leftover biscuits. She found an apple and sliced it.

They would be home soon. She just knew it.

She arranged the biscuits and sliced apples on the plate.

They would be home any minute.

Alice's heart raced. What if they were not? What would she do?

She bit her lip. The kettle. She'd heat the water. They'd need tea when they arrived, wouldn't they?

Alice sat back down at the table and tapped her fingers on it as she waited.

CHAPTER 45

Jo, René, and Eliza walked along the streets, lit only with the occasional torch. They steered clear of taverns, which were well lit.

"I'd have loved to get my hands on that list," René said after they passed a clutch of men walking together.

"Me too," Eliza said. "But did you notice that several of the men wore buttons with owls on them?"

"No, I didn't notice that," René said, glancing behind them.

"I did," Jo said.

"I don't understand why they want to take over the churches," René said. "Seems a ridiculous goal for an organization."

A carriage slowly rolled by them. There were not many people out at this time of night. The city was quieter, though not entirely put to bed.

"Aye, I think they are just like little boys playing some silly game, as they often do," Jo said.

"But they did bring up my husband and son. So whatever they are up to, we need to take them seriously," said Eliza.

Jo yanked the other two women into an alley. "Someone is following us," she whispered. "I'm sure of it."

"What? How did you—" asked Eliza.

"Let's just say I've been followed before." Her eyes were lit with excitement.

"Let's lead them on a merry good chase then," René said. "We can't go back to the house, surely."

"Wait. Why would they be following us?" Eliza asked. "Were we discovered at the meeting?"

Jo shrugged. "We need to be careful."

"Let's try to get a look at 'em," René suggested.

They stepped back out on the street and stood on the corner. Eliza reminded herself that she was dressed as a man, so passersby wouldn't notice that there were three women out after dark. She'd never been on the streets after dark without her husband or another male escort. Wisps of excitement and fear tangled in her.

Jo led them in the opposite direction from the house. Eliza glimpsed a man from the corner of her eye as they crossed the street. He was a young man. It wasn't any of the men from the meeting. They were getting farther and farther from their destination. Light gave way to mostly dark, where anybody could be hiding.

The man still followed them.

Eliza was being followed by a strange man at night. What had her life come to? What would Hamilton think of this predicament? What was she thinking? Had her senses completely vanished when she put on a man's clothes? She just wanted to be at home, with her children, in her garden.

"There's only one thing left to do," Jo said in a low voice. "We split up. It will confuse him."

"You hope," René said. "See you at home." She then ducked into an alley and Jo took off running. Eliza quickly crossed the next street and almost ran onto a street she recognized as one leading to the house on Pearl Street. The man pursuing them was nowhere to be seen.

She was alone in the dark city.

She should be more frightened. But after the kind of evening she'd just had, she wasn't sure what she was feeling. Her heart raced. The night air pulsed around her. Dark trees shivered as she walked by. The little house on Pearl Street waited for her. She kept it in her mind's eye as she edged forward.

She walked along a little farther and stepped around a corner. The rushing sound of the river was close. She looked in all directions. No person—female or male—was walking nearby. She shivered. She took a strong breath, calming her racing heart. *Just one step at a time.* And she stepped forward. As she approached the house, Eliza recognized two figures also on their way to the house. All three of them reached the home within moments of one another.

Alice met them at the door. "Get in out of the dark, ye daft women! I've got some refreshment for you."

The three of them followed Alice to the kitchen table, where she'd laid out some biscuits, fruit, and cheese.

"Thank you, Alice, but I don't think I can eat anything." Eliza sat down at the table, still wearing men's clothing.

"You must keep your energy up," Alice responded. "Just a bite or two of the biscuit."

Eliza reached for a biscuit and spread butter on it. Jo sat down next to her. "You did wonderful tonight. You're a quick study."

Eliza smiled. Oh, she was so tired. "Thank you."

"It must've been hard for you to hear all that." René reached for an apple and bit into it.

"What did she hear?" Alice asked as she stirred sugar into her tea.

"They mentioned my Hamilton several times. And Drake. And from what I could gather, the redhead thinks Joshua Ryman may have had something to do with it," Eliza said.

"He pretty much accused him of murder," Jo said. "I don't think this group has anything to do with the murders, officially. But Ryman? Who knows? There must be a reason the redhead was so adamant."

Eliza frowned. She bit the biscuit, which was so light that it almost melted in her mouth. "And they mentioned my son Alexander."

"Oh, surely he has nothing to do with it," Alice said.

"There's only one way to find out," Eliza replied. "I'll ask him about it as soon as I can. He's a good boy. I don't think he'd intentionally get into mischief. But then again, our children sometimes surprise us. You raised them the same way, yet they all come out different."

"Isn't that the truth?" Jo said. "I had a son who fought for the Tories. I'll never get over that."

Had a son. Jo had lost a son, just like Eliza had. Eliza reached out for Jo's hand. "I'm sorry."

"So what do we do with this information?" Alice asked after a moment of silence.

"We go to the constable." Eliza was certain they needed to get to someone who could put these pieces together and do something about it.

"The only proof we have is hearsay," Alice said.

"We have more proof than that. We have the rock. The letter I received. Newspaper clippings with the owl and the code about the meetings." Some of those things were at home at the Grange. "Constable Schultz will help us. Of that I'm sure. But what I'm not sure about is Renquist. He's the only one left on the list. If we reveal that we know he's in trouble, who knows what he will do."

Alice grunted. "He's a highly unlikable man."

"Jeremiah Renquist?" Jo asked.

Eliza nodded.

"I'm delivering linens to him in the morning. He's to marry soon and ordered fine embroidered linens for his new bride. I finished the last touches yesterday."

"Keep your eyes open and let us know what you see. Let us talk with Schultz before we approach Renquist," Eliza said.

"I can do that," Jo said. "He is a bit of an odd bird. A very sour disposition."

"Maybe a wife will help with that," Alice said and cackled. "Many men become softer with marriage."

"And many don't," René said with a tone that sent shivers along Eliza's spine. Her work with widows had been enlightening in that regard. She'd never seen a woman who had been hit by a man before then. She'd heard whispers at tea parties and balls but had never seen the evidence.

"If his life is in danger, we should get word to him quickly," Alice said.

Eliza nodded. "I fear his reaction will not help. I think we should go to the constable first and allow him to determine how to handle it."

Alice tsked. She stood and cleared away the dishes.

"Well, I'm off to bed. I've an early day." Jo stood. "Good night, ladies."

They said their good nights and soon enough Eliza was in her small bed in the simple room, where she lay on top of the quilt thinking about all she'd seen that night. Ripples of anxiety and fear waved through her. She'd gotten at least a dribble of the information she was after. But would the constable and authorities take her seriously?

She rolled over onto her side. Tomorrow she'd send for Angelica. She needed to know if John had found out anything more about the knife. She needed to know if Angelica herself had been digging around, as she said she would.

Eliza needed to know that Alexander was safe. She'd contact her son tomorrow and arrange to meet him. If he knew anything about any of this, now was the time for him to divulge it. No need for secret-keeping. Not anymore.

CHAPTER 46

The next morning Eliza awakened to the clacking of the loom downstairs. The sunlight streamed in through her window, and she tried to blink away the light. She untangled herself from her quilt and made her bed, pressing her hands over the linens to get rid of any wrinkles.

There was a slight rapping at her door.

"Please come in," she said.

Alice opened the door. "There's some food for you on the table and some tea. Are you well?"

Eliza flushed, realizing she'd done nothing but sleep that morning, which was unlike her. "I am. We were up late last night."

"Indeed. I've some deliveries to make and will return after that. René is here. Please make yourself at home." Alice turned to go.

Eliza made her way into the kitchen, where René was standing, holding a long cloth.

"Good morning," Eliza said. "What do you have there?"

René turned it over for Eliza to get a better view. Eliza's mouth dropped and she gasped. The cloth was covered with embroidered flowers. It was full of colorful threads and made with a precise delicacy. "What is it?"

"It's for a baby's bed. Decoration. It was a special commissioned piece," René said, beaming.

"Did you fashion this?" Eliza ran her finger over the flowers softly.

"Yes, I did." She smiled.

"You have a very fine hand, indeed, René."

"I was trained at a school in France." She folded the crib piece and tucked it in a box. Eliza poured herself some tea as René went on. "We didn't just learn to make lace. We came to the New World with the hope of starting our own business, but my husband died soon after we arrived. I had two small children then. Thank the Lord for the Widow Society and Alice. It was her idea for us to gather forces. It's worked out well."

"It sounds like it." Eliza wondered if she would have been so resourceful. She hadn't even imagined ever having to make money for her household until recently. And here there were women like René who had been doing it all along. And she wasn't a servant.

Eliza noted the pride on René's face. Gratification at having done a job well. She drank her tea, buttered a biscuit, and gathered her thoughts on her plan for the day. "Speaking of children . . . I need to get word to Alexander today."

"We can make that happen."

"Thank you," Eliza said. She bit into the airy biscuit, chewed, and swallowed. "I'm impressed by the way your group here gets things accomplished. You seem to be well connected."

René laughed. "Indeed we are. We have connections in most of the big households. If we are not providing our services, then we at least know someone who works for them. Alice knows many of the business owners and that has served us well too." She placed her box on the table. "She works hard at maintaining those relationships. Well, I suppose we all do, to some extent. But for some of us, it's better just to work and not worry about the relationship part, yes?"

Eliza nodded. She'd never considered the vast web of servants, enslaved laborers, and other household staff before—or at least not in this manner. A rush of shame moved through her. Once again, her station in life gave her much to be grateful for, but every so often she glimpsed other ways of living. And sometimes it felt like an opening to a new way of understanding.

As she ate her breakfast, she thought about Alexander. She was excited and anxious to see him. What did he know about the missing money from the Treasury? And how did it relate to this new, wicked situation?

★   ★   ★

"Mother? What are you doing here? What is going on?" Alexander said when Eliza opened the front door of the Pearl Street house.

"I'll explain it all. Please come in."

He followed her into the parlor, where she had tea set up.

"Are you well?" he asked, leaning forward.

"I'm fine. I'm here because your Aunt Angelica thinks I'm in danger. She may be right. A rock was thrown through my window at the Grange." Eliza folded her hands on her lap, not quite ready for tea.

"What?" Alexander stood. "Why wasn't I informed?"

She gestured to his chair. "Sit down, please."

He reluctantly sat.

Eliza was not a good disciplinarian. She had a soft spot for all children. But she girded her loins, for her son was no longer a child and she needed information from him. This was not the time to be soft with him.

She drew in a breath then released it. "Alexander, I need information from you."

He nodded.

"Your uncle is working hard to keep your troubles out of the paper, and I've been doing a little investigating on my own, trying to figure out who killed Van Der Gloss as a way to help you."

"Mother—"

She held up her hand. "Let me finish before you speak. I've also been trying to figure out why *you*. Why are you the person who is being set up? Were you just in the wrong place at the right time? Or was the whole thing a trap created for you?"

He shrugged and gestured with his hands, as if to say he had no idea.

She poured tea and handed him a cup full of the brew. "Do you remember when your father was accused of taking money from the Treasury?"

He took the cup from her. He liked his tea with no cream or sugar, so he sipped before answering. "Yes, very well."

"The money was never found. Nor, of course, has the true culprit been found." Eliza poured another cup of the tea and stirred in cream. She watched the clouds form in the tea.

Alexander frowned. "Mother, I fear for your health. What does any of this have to do with me? And why are you troubling yourself with it?"

"I think you've been caught up in some intrigue. The men who've been murdered all had a few things in common. They were with your father at the duel. And they'd discovered who stole that money." She said it with as flat a tone as she could muster. No need for hysteria, even though it sat at the bottom of her spine ready to erupt at any moment.

Alexander batted his eyes several times before saying, "Who?"

She sipped her tea and placed the cup back into the saucer. "You tell me."

He shook his head. "Don't you think if I knew I'd tell you?"

"Think, Alexander. You may know something that you don't realize. That has to be why someone is trying to get you sent away for a murder you didn't commit." She refreshed his tea, noticing it was already empty. He lifted it from the table with a slight tremor in his hands. "Had your father talked with you about any of this?"

"Mother, I—"

"Please don't. I was in a room last night with men who spoke your name, as if you knew something."

His blue eyes flashed with concern. "What? What men? Mother, what are you doing? I beg of you to return to the Grange and stay home until you're feeling better."

"I am fine. Except that I have a son who is accused of murder and does not seem to be taking it seriously," she quipped. *Return to the Grange and stay home. As if she could just do that.*

He sighed. "I am. Believe me."

"What do you know?" she said through her clenched jaw.

"Only what you already know. That Father and his friends had found evidence of who actually stole the money. I told Uncle John that and I stand by it. I know nothing else."

Eliza's heart lifted. If she could find out the identity of the thief, then her husband's reputation and story would be absolved—and Alexander could be cleared of the murder charge.

"I don't understand what this has to do with me," Alexander added.

"The men who were killed were all men who would recognize the thief. The thief must think you do as well. Sending you off to prison would keep your mouth shut and, of course, add another strike against your family honor. A thing that was important to your father."

He lowered his head.

"What is it?"

"I know honor was important to him, but I can't help but remember when the accusations started. That's when everything about his . . . indiscretions . . . also came out. Which was highly dishonorable, Mother."

Eliza's face heated. "Your father had his reasons for crafting that story. Maria Reynolds was nothing more than a way to distract the public's attention away from the much more dishonorable reality of him being investigated for taking money from the government he loved and worked hard to set up."

Alexander finished drinking his tea and set down the cup in its saucer. "If that's how you choose to remember things . . . then so be it."

The door knocker clanged and René answered the door. She led Constable Schultz into the room. Eliza divulged all of the information she'd gathered.

"May I ask how you've gotten this information?" the constable asked.

"Is it important?" Eliza responded.

"It might be further along," he replied.

Eliza didn't want to implicate any other women who'd helped her, in case things went sour. "I've been making inquiries among the widows of the victims, and, to tell you the truth, I have been eavesdropping."

"Eavesdropping?" Alexander's face reddened. "Where have you been? Who have you been eavesdropping on?"

Constable Schultz held up his hand as if to calm Alexander down. "Mrs. General Hamilton, I trust that you will give me that information should I need it."

"Of course." She hoped it wouldn't come to that. She glanced away from him to her son, whose face was still red, even as he cradled his head in his hand. "Now, will you tell me what you know about these men?"

"The group of men you're talking about is a group of businessmen who have designs on more power. They were a part of the Bavarian Illuminati but branched off to start their own group." The constable's annoyed tone bothered Eliza.

"Mother! You must take care. Who knows what these men are up to?" Alexander's voice cracked. "I fear I've not been a good son, allowing you to run about town like this."

"They just want to take over churches," Eliza responded. She ignored the fact that her son felt authority over her. She'd deal with that later. "But they have other mischief they are involved in, like with your father."

"I don't know what the link between them and the missing money would be. They are all quite well established. When they mentioned Hamilton, did they mention the money?" Constable Schultz asked.

Her husband's name on Schultz's lips rankled her. *Hamilton, what have you done? What kind of treachery did you leave behind for me to untangle?* "Not precisely, no."

"In any case, we can't blame innocent men. We need proof." Alexander stood and paced the room.

Schultz eyed Alexander as he walked. "You, sir, will make a fine attorney."

"If I don't go to prison for murder."

"Here's a piece of my proof that Renquist is in trouble." Eliza pulled out the handkerchief Victoria Peabody had given her. Both men examined it. "Renquist is the only man alive on the list. He knows something that the others deem worth killing for. Gentlemen, what do we do about it?"

Schultz's mouth hung open. Alexander's eyebrows hitched. "Where did you get this list, Mother?"

"A very reliable source." She was not amused by the situation, but she was amused by the fact that these two men seemed shocked that she should have such a list. "I will not give up the name to you for fear she'd come to harm. But believe me, this list is accurate."

"It is accurate in that all the men on the list are dead except for Renquist. That much is true," Schultz said.

Alexander cleared his throat. "Should we warn the man?"

One of Schultz's wiry eyebrows lifted. "On the basis of a handkerchief with his name sewn into it? I have my hands full trying to find who killed the others."

All of them sat in silence for a moment.

Eliza's heart sank. Names sewn into a handkerchief were just as important as names on a piece of paper. Why was Schultz being so condescending? "If Renquist knows who stole the money my husband was once accused of stealing, then his life is in danger."

"His son is to be married at noon tomorrow," Alexander said.

"Son?" queried Constable Schultz.

"Yes, Jeremiah Junior," said Alexander.

Jeremiah Junior was the one ordering the linens, not the solicitor, Eliza realized. He had the same name as his father! Of course!

"I am to attend the wedding." Alexander's jaw twitched.

"Are you friends with this man?" Eliza asked.

Alexander nodded. "Not close friends, but we attended school together. He graduated last year. I believe he and William Drake, Jonathan's younger brother, are going into practice together."

Eliza's heart skipped around in her chest. The younger Drake must be the man who threw the rock at her house. Yet he hadn't been at the meeting. Neither were the Renquists. She hadn't told anybody that Jonathon Drake was involved, and she wasn't sure she should. Not now. William and Jeremiah were acquainted with Alexander. There was the connection she needed. Eliza struggled not to scream and to keep her voice calm. "I don't think it's a good idea for you to go to the wedding."

"Why ever not?"

"Yes, why, madam?" Schultz chimed in.

"I believe those young men are dangerous."

"Mother! You are talking in riddles." Alexander's face was flushed.

Schultz nodded. "I quite agree."

She stood. "In order to keep Alexander safe, I will tell you what I know. But you must not act on it. I fear if one thread unravels, the whole of it will come undone before we have a chance for justice. Do I have your word?"

"Of course, Mother."

"Mrs. General Hamilton, I am an officer of the law. I cannot make such a promise." Schultz looked at Alexander and then back at her.

"I understand. Then you must leave so I can talk with my son."

Constable Schultz's eyes shifted back and forth again and he sighed. "Fine. I promise not to act on what you tell me."

"The younger Drake is the man who threw a rock into my home."

"How do you know?" Schultz asked.

"Alice saw him and then we saw him again at Jonathan Drake's funeral. She pointed him out. I also believe he was the man who bribed others into lying about Alexander. He fits the description that Paul Jinkins gave me."

Alexander balled his hands into fists. "I'll kill the bastard!"

"Alexander!"

"Sorry, Mother."

"You will not raise a hand to him." Eliza eyed Schultz. "You will not arrest him yet."

"Mrs. Gene—"

"It you arrest him, it will alert whoever else is involved in these murders and they will run. Have you caught the killer yet?"

Schultz shook his head.

"That is because the killer is right under our noses. He is from a good family and knows you well, Alexander, and doesn't like you. He wants to see you rot in prison. Think, son—why?" Eliza raised her voice to a level she didn't recognize, and she didn't like.

"I will think about it," Alexander promised. "But why don't you want him arrested, Mother?"

Schultz spoke up. "Because he probably is not the killer. He is probably working with him."

Eliza smiled. "You see my logic."

"But then we can't do anything!" Alexander said.

"No, son. We can't." Eliza said. "Go back to your studies. Do not attend the wedding. For surely another incident is planned for which you may be blamed. If not at the wedding, then on the way there or back. Surely."

Alexander looked at Schultz.

"Your mother should have been a lawyer. No—a judge." The constable rolled his eyes. "I will grant you your request. But I will be circling the perimeter of that wedding, even without the attendance of your son."

Eliza had no intention of studying the law. Ever. All she wanted was to keep her son safe and her husband's honor intact. Which may be harder to do than she at first imagined.

CHAPTER 47

After her son and the constable left, Eliza paced the small room. On the one hand, she herself wanted to run to Renquist to warn him. But she recognized that he would never take her seriously. Better that Constable Schultz handle the matter. She hoped and prayed that Alexander would not attend that wedding. Something was amiss with those young men.

Alice opened the front door and walked into the room. "Mrs. General Hamilton."

"Hello, Alice."

She hobbled into the room. "I just sold more of your lace. And I sold René's lace. There is a new milliner on Maiden Lane." Alice's eyes were ablaze with excitement. "I think he will keep us in business for quite some time."

"That's wonderful!"

"I'll be going there again tomorrow with other samples for him of the work we do. He may be interested in linens and weavings. It might be quite fortuitous." Alice sat down. She wiped her forehead with her sleeve.

"Let me get you some water. Or lemonade," Eliza said.

"Ach, ordinarily I don't want to be waited on, especially by a lady such as yourself, but I admit I'm a bit overwrought." She smacked her lips. "A cool glass of lemonade sounds delightful."

When Eliza returned, Alice was gazing out the window with a look of satisfaction on her face. Her dealings with the shop-keeper seemed to have lifted her spirits. "Thank you," Alice said as she accepted the cool glass from Eliza.

"I'm so happy that this is working out for you. For us." Eliza sat next to Alice on the settee. Her chest of lace at the Grange came into her mind's eye.

"Aye. It's been difficult to get shops to carry our goods. Many of them import from England, Belgium, and Italy. They stopped doing that during the war. That was good for us. But they went right back to their usual suppliers after." Alice took a long drink of the sweet yellow brew.

Eliza remembered how difficult it had been to find fabric, let alone a luxury like lace, during the war. Of course, for her, she dared not wear anything but the simplest of garb for she and Hamilton had little money and also did not want to appear as if they had more. They were all for the cause of freedom, with little concern for fashion.

"But I warrant that will change. There are weaving facto-ries being built. Warehouses filled with American fabric." Alice sighed. "Does my heart good. I'm a Christian woman, but I do despise the English."

"Alice!" Eliza jested with her.

"I cannot lie." She grinned. "Ah, but I will take their money. Theirs is as good as any."

Once again, Eliza wondered about Alice's past. She was so smart, wily even, and she had such a fine hand with lace. Only women of a certain status learned such things. But she didn't want to pry.

"What about your day? Did you see Alexander?" Alice cra-dled her glass in her hands.

"I did." Eliza recounted what she'd learned from her son and what Schultz had agreed to do.

"Better that he deal with Renquist," Alice cackled.

"Indeed."

René came bounding into the house with a newspaper in her arms. She threw it on the table.

"What are you doing, woman?" Alice scolded.

"Look at this!" René held out the paper, displaying a new cipher. Letters and numbers were circled in black ink. "Looks like a smaller group may be meeting tonight, beneath the torches at the corner of Pearl and Maiden."

Eliza's thoughts raced. "They just met. If there is a smaller group meeting, there must be a break in the group."

"The redhead bore no love for Ryman. I think he suspects he's involved in the murders," René speculated.

"Nay, surely," Alice said. "He's an old man. 'Twas a young man who did the killings."

"I see your point, Alice." Eliza folded her hands in her lap. "But I think he knows something about them. There were subtle allegations being made the whole evening."

"Yes!" René said. "He is old and soft. I see the point. And the murderer must have been fit."

"So what of this meeting?" Alice asked.

Eliza didn't know. What of it? If it was a small meeting between just two or three men, then she and René would surely be spotted. And they couldn't disguise themselves as servers if they were meeting on the street corner. But perhaps they could lodge themselves nearby to watch and listen to the proceedings. The question was whether they could hide themselves well enough to be able to gather information.

René cleared her throat. "I'm happy to spy on them."

"Spy? Hush, woman!" Alice said. "We've got a business to run. Our reputations to consider."

René shrugged. "I will disguise myself."

Alice waved her off. "Not again. You do put yourself in danger!"

"I fear she's right." Eliza nodded. "It is dangerous. But I will go with you. We should find a place to hide so we can watch and listen, then we can go directly to Constable Schultz with any information we discover."

Alice's eyes widened. "Where do you come up with such ideas?"

"I am plagued with ideas. My parents often had their hands full with me and my ideas. And let's not even speak of my husband."

"I dare say he would not have been the man he was without those ideas," René said in a low voice. "Mrs. General Hamilton, great women are always behind great men."

Eliza swallowed. For that surely was not the case. Her Hamilton was born great. For a man to overcome the circumstances that he had been born into was nearly a miracle. Orphaned and alone, living on the island of Nevis, he'd survived a hurricane and written about it. His talent stood out to the local leaders, who sent him to New York City to study when he was about twenty. All of the stars had aligned for him, but he had not been without his own hard work and keen mind.

She, on the other hand, had been born into a wealthy family. She, her sisters, and her brothers lacked for nothing. Eliza had been blessed from birth, and for this she was grateful. She had a keen mind and was of decent intelligence, as her parents had seen to her education. But great? No. Great people were born. Not made. There was a spark within them that allowed them to make themselves greater, like her Hamilton. Her touch with greatness came from her father and her husband.

But Eliza held her counsel as René's remarks played in her mind in delightful ways.

CHAPTER 48

"You two resemble the sweetest of lads." Alice teased. "Please be careful."

"We will, Alice," Eliza said and then exited the house with René.

Once Eliza had figured out the latest cipher, she was relieved that the proposed meeting time was closer to the dinner hour than after sunset. The memory of being followed through the dark streets was still fresh on her mind. She tamped down the thread of fear in her and focused on the mission at hand: to find out more about these men, what they were meeting about, and whether it had anything to do with the murders. The ultimate goal, of course, was to keep her son's reputation in good stead and to keep him out of prison.

They walked by the tailor shop Eliza and Alice had visited earlier. The shop was dark now, as were most shops at this hour. The streets were not busy, as most people were dining. Wasn't it an odd hour for two men to meet on a street corner? As Eliza mulled it over, she realized that recently life had been nothing if not odd these past few weeks.

"There's our corner," René whispered.

Eliza scrutinized the area in search of a hiding place from which they could observe.

"There!" René said, pointing to a shop near the corner. The door was set back from the rest of the street. "If we stand there, we might not be seen."

"Yes, but what if the shopkeeper sees us?" There were no lights on in the shop, but a window on the top floor was dimly lit. "Perhaps that's where the shopkeeper lives," Eliza said, pointing.

"I suppose we take our chances. I can't see any other spot."

She was right. Everywhere else was in the open, where they didn't want to be. As they crossed the street, Eliza took in her surroundings. A few women passed them as they walked. Three men then approached the corner, laughing, perhaps drunk. Eliza didn't recognize them, and they continued to walk on.

Eliza and René kept watch as a couple approached the corner, and then another group of men. They all crossed the street together. One man, dressed in a suit, approached the corner and then stopped. Eliza's heart pounded in her chest. She didn't recognize him. He stood for a few moments and appeared to be searching for something—or someone. Then he crossed the street and walked off into the distance.

"I thought . . . ," René whispered.

"Me too." Eliza began to wonder if this was a good idea.

Two women walked closely by them, fanning themselves. They smelled of flowers. One woman made eye contact with Eliza and nodded as if to say hello. Eliza lifted her chin in response. The women kept walking down the street until they were out of view.

Two men approached the corner and stood for a moment chatting about the weather. One took his watch out of his pocket and scanned the area, then moved. The other man walked away in the opposite direction. Neither of their faces looked familiar to Eliza.

Eliza glanced at René. "Did we misread the cipher?"

"Maybe. Surely it's past time."

Eliza went over the message again in her mind. Had she made a mistake? She didn't think so. Her interpretation was correct. What was going on here? Her heart raced. Tingles of fear traveled along her spine. She'd learned from her Iroquois friends to pay attention to such feelings. "We need to go."

"But maybe we should wait a little longer. Maybe they were delayed."

Eliza's tingle of intuition grew stronger. "No. We need to go home."

René nodded. "As you wish."

As they walked back, Eliza could not shake her sense of foreboding. Yet nobody followed them. Not that she detected. Each shadow grew longer and full of danger as they moved along. A pig scampered in front of Eliza and almost knocked her over. She gasped, feeling as if her heart had jumped into her throat.

René wrapped her arm around Eliza. "It's fine. Just another one of those pigs."

"They really need to do something about them," Eliza said.

"Indeed." René dropped her arm. "We are almost home. Are you feeling better?"

Eliza nodded. "I believe I am. But I'll feel even better when we are inside the house."

Soon enough, Eliza spotted the house where Alice and her group of crafty women lived.

When they approached the front door, Alice opened it. Had she been standing there the whole time they were gone? "What happened? Who did you see?" Alice badgered.

"Nothing happened," René said. "Nobody showed up."

"I fear it was a ploy," Eliza said.

"Ploy?" Alice asked.

"Yes. I don't think I made a mistake interpreting the text." She'd gone over it again and again. Was she missing something?

"Do you think someone is suspicious of us?" René took off her cap and her long brown hair fell around her shoulders, softening her face while the rest of her remained boyish-looking.

"It's either that or it was simply canceled. How can we be sure?" Eliza said. "All we know is that they didn't show up."

"Let's go into the kitchen. I've made us tea and biscuits." Alice led them into the kitchen.

Eliza sat at the table, her mind rattling with different scenarios. If someone suspected them of spying, then they likely also had detected that they had been at the meeting. Would they be next on the murder list? What had she been thinking? She needed to be more careful.

"Perhaps the meeting was canceled or postponed." Alice handed Eliza a cup of steaming tea. Eliza drew in the scent of the chamomile, the perfect tea to soothe nerves.

"Let us assume that," René said. "Otherwise there could be a turncoat among us."

"Here? Surely not. We are bonded together in this house. All of us widows. The trust is thick and deep. Nay. I won't believe that." Alice held a cup to her lips. "I won't believe that of one of us."

"We were followed that night, remember." Eliza's mind raced. "If they succeeded in figuring out who we are, then tonight makes perfect sense. They meant to trap us."

"But nothing happened," René said. "We just stood there. Nobody approached us."

"They wouldn't need to. They just wanted to make certain. And we fell for it." Eliza's head ached. Every muscle and sinew in her neck tightened.

"We've no way of knowing. Let us not jump to conclusions." Alice tapped her fingers on the table, a sign that she wasn't as calm as her voice or words suggested.

Eliza drank her tea. She may have placed these women in danger. Hard-working, open-hearted woman who had opened their door to her. Shame rolled through her. This was her problem. She should never have involved them. Perhaps she should have returned home, no matter what Angelica said.

"If not one of the women here, who else even knows about any of this?" René asked.

"That would be the constable, Angelica, and my son," Eliza replied.

"Don't forget Mrs. Peabody," Alice said.

"She knows of the situation, but not about our disguising ourselves. She'd have no way of knowing that," Eliza said. But what if someone had spied her and Victoria together that day? Which is what Victoria had been afraid of. "Victoria was certain we were being watched, though I saw nobody." She chilled. That would mean someone knew she was staying at the house on Pearl Street and was just waiting for . . . what? She didn't know.

"Surely not!" Alice said, eyes wide. "I'm a watchful sort. I would have noticed prying eyes."

"That's true," René said. "We've learned to be watchful. A certain kind of man likes nothing more than a group of widows to harass."

"And another certain kind of man does not like the competition we provide, nor the freedom we have. A group of independent widows? Some can't fathom it and it bothers them. Sometimes resulting in harassment." Alice's voice rose as she emphasized the word "harassment."

As Alexander Hamilton's wife, Eliza knew harassment. But it was of another kind. She'd always had Hamilton and her family to protect her. Gratitude swept through her for those years. But now she was alone. She was a widow, like these women, and didn't know if she would survive this scandal as she had all the others.

CHAPTER 49

The Churches visited the morning after Eliza's failed attempt at surveillance. John got right to the point.

"The knife that was used to kill Van Der Gloss was forged in Europe, probably Prussia or Bavaria," John said.

Eliza frowned, uncertain if she should tell her brother-in-law about the ciphers and the meeting she had gone to. "What meaning does that have? Many in New York could have purchased it from anywhere. So many ships come every day with all sorts of goods."

He started to say something, then stopped. "I understand your reasoning. But I have reason to believe that this knife is associated with the Bavarian Illuminati."

"We've discussed them before," Angelica said as she fanned herself.

"They can be very dangerous," John said.

If they were correct, Eliza had been followed by a couple of members of the Illuminati—and had outwitted and outrun them. But she could not tell John that. Were they dangerous? Were they killers? They certainly had discussed the murders, but there was no solid thread to pull on linking them to the killings.

"How dangerous?" Angelica asked.

"They seem to have fingers everywhere—in business, in churches, and they practice unethical measures," he said, lifting an eyebrow.

"Then it's not too much of a stretch to think that they may know something about the theft Hamilton was accused of?" Eliza asked.

The room quieted.

"My dear, that happened so long ago," John said finally in a soothing tone.

"Yes, but it is the one thing that ties everything together. All of the men killed must have known the thief's identity." There, she had finally said it.

"What? Where did you come up with that?" John asked.

"We've put some pieces together," Eliza replied. "You don't need to know the particulars. I've been working with Constable Schultz. I'm in no danger."

That wasn't exactly true, but she placed her hand on Angelica's hand as she viewed the panic in her eyes. She needed to change the subject. "What do you know about the Ryman family?" Because John had been involved with Hamilton and his bank, along with his own business dealings, he was familiar with many New Yorkers' finances.

John grimaced. "I'm no fan of them. I find their manner crude."

"She's not asking about that," Angelica said. "What about their family finances? Are they involved in politics?"

"They were absolutely destitute a few years ago. They came to the bank for a loan." His chin waddled when he spoke.

"Did they make good on it?" Eliza asked.

"Yes, but in as slow a manner as possible. In fact, I thought they'd never pay off their debt. But they did." He pursed his lips.

Eliza was trying to piece a time line together in her mind. "When was this?"

"It was before the theft at the Treasury."

"So, before the theft they were destitute and after the theft they paid off their debts?" said Angelica. "Why hasn't anybody investigated this further?"

"Because, my dear, on the face of things, they've done nothing wrong. Many good families suffer setbacks." John gingerly placed his hand on Angelica's thigh. She removed it and then continued to fan herself.

Eliza realized John was right. Hamilton had never gone into detail about it, but he had said she'd be surprised by how many of New York's finest families were not what they seemed. "What can you tell me about Calvin Evans?"

"Not much." John shrugged. "The Evans family has not been here long. They are from Philadelphia, I think."

"I've met his wife and son," Angelica said. "He's about Alexander's age."

Eliza's heart raced. All of the players seemed to be about the same age, with children of similar age.

Angelica went on. "They seem like a fine family, but they are not interested in society. I only met them briefly at church one day."

"Is the son in school?" Eliza asked.

"I imagine he is," said Angelica.

"I believe he clerks for Joshua Ryman," John said.

"I thought the younger Drake clerked for him," Eliza said.

John nodded. "They both do, along with his son."

The younger Drake and Evans both clerked for Ryman.

"How many clerks does one man need?" Angelica asked.

John shrugged. "It's none of my concern."

Eliza was trying to keep track of it all. The web of possibilities expanded. All of these young men knew one another and were linked to men who understood the true nature of the theft of which Hamilton was accused.

Alice had been out that morning but returned at that moment. She poked her head in the room to say hello and then headed for the kitchen. Eliza imagined she needed something to drink as the day was even warmer than yesterday.

"What do you think about coming back to the Grange?" Angelica asked. "We've hired a man to watch the place. A guard, if you will. Between him and McNally, you should be safe."

Eliza's heart sped up. "Of course, I'd love to return home. When can I do that?"

"Tomorrow." Angelica beamed, still fanning herself. "This dreadful heat!"

"I assure you that there will be no more problems," John said. "We've hired the best for you."

Eliza hadn't even considered a guard. Instead, she'd been chasing shadows in the city and not getting very far. The notion of returning to the Grange brightened her spirits.

At the same time, leaving Alice and the women she'd come to respect and like gave her pause. It was a house of women. A house of possibility. Perhaps it was a glimpse into a future where women would have opportunities to work doing what they loved and live with a kind of freedom.

Eliza appreciated that freedom was hard-earned. They were all widows. All down on their luck. But they'd come together and created a life for themselves through their handwork. And they were happy to give Eliza a glimpse into it. Her thoughts tumbled. Their lives—and everything they represented—had given her a kind of hope bigger than herself.

At the Grange, she would not be so close to the action of the city—or the danger. She might walk about unworried about a stranger recognizing her. Ah, yes, she'd go for a long walk in her garden, down as far as the forest, maybe. The idea of it warmed her.

And also at the Grange she had gathered pieces of evidence. Now, with everything she'd learned, she wanted to sit among the evidence, pull it all together with her new knowledge, and see if she could find answers.

"I will be with you like a fly on honey, my dear. Nobody will bother you," Angelica said, reaching out and placing her hand over Eliza's.

Just like that, Eliza's visions of walks alone in the garden evaporated.

CHAPTER 50

After Angelica and John departed, Eliza's head was swimming. Keeping all of this straight was a challenge.

The younger Ryman, Drake, and Evans were all friends, and they all knew her Alexander.

Ryman and Drake were also members of a secret society that wanted to take over churches and the city. Maybe even the country.

Many of these men must know who had stolen money from the Treasury. A secret worth dying for? She confessed to herself she'd never understand the ways of men. Where did Alexander fit into all of this? If anywhere? It might just be that he was the perfect scapegoat, being the son of Hamilton and not knowing the true identity of the thief.

She felt the urge to walk. She did her best thinking while walking. She'd been in hiding for days, not allowed to go out unless covered or in disguise. Why should she disguise herself now? She'd been summoned home. It wouldn't matter if she was seen one night on the streets. Besides, she'd search for the quiet streets. Maybe she'd walk by the river, as she and Hamilton used to do.

Alice and the others had already retired for the evening, so Eliza would not disturb them. She slipped out the front door and drew in the fresh air. She would not be gone long, as the heat would prevent it. She walked to the end of the street and turned left, toward the river. Maybe it would be a tad cooler there. A river breeze would suit her. She craved it.

Eliza continued to walk, recalling recent events and all of the evidence she'd gathered since being in the city. It was leading her to someone. Perhaps she didn't need to find the guilty person; perhaps all she needed to do was gather enough evidence to prove her son was not the guilty party.

A stab of guilt pricked at her. It was her Christian duty to see this through. Renquist could be in danger, and who knew who else? She thanked God for Schultz taking over with Renquist. There was no way Renquist would ever believe Eliza.

But then again, could she blame him? It was a fantastical tale. She imagined her father's reaction to all of this, and then Hamilton's. A fantastical tale indeed, but unfortunately one filled with death and sorrow.

The sound of a carriage coming closer intruded upon Eliza's contemplation. The rhythmic sound of horse and carriage was always background noise in the city, but this was nearby and coming closer. Then the noise stopped, and the evening was quiet for a moment. She stopped in her tracks.

Suddenly arms appeared from behind Eliza and a hand holding a rag covered her mouth and nose before she could scream. It smelled medicinal and strange. She struggled to free herself from the arms around her, but the stranger pulled her into the waiting carriage. She struggled for air as the rag was held over her nose and mouth even tighter. The sight of the carriage ceiling blurred, its swirling patterns dancing before her eyes, as her body was held fast against a man's.

Why had she gone for a walk alone?

Stupid woman . . .

Her mind was not her own. She had no control of her body. The man held her firm, but she couldn't move if she wanted to. She had no choice but to breathe in whatever the rag was soaked in. She could hold her eyes open no longer and finally closed them.

★   ★   ★

She opened her eyes to darkness. She struggled to sit up and failed. Where was she?

She felt pain. A longing to move her legs. Her arms. Her legs were bound together, as were her hands. She struggled unsuccessfully to free herself.

Who would do such a thing to her? What were they going to do with her? Would she ever see her children again?

Oh, Eliza, you've certainly gotten into trouble this time. This was no girlhood adventure. This was real. She wasn't dreaming. Her head pounded. Heart raced. And she could not loosen her bonds.

It wasn't just that she was bound. It was also that her head was swimming. She was dizzy and light-headed, and her thoughts came in bits and bobs. She found it hard to form a sentence in her mind.

The creak of an opening door and light coming through the crack of the opening prompted her to close her eyes. The sound of footsteps and hushed voices filled the small room.

"Eliza Hamilton, for God's sake," a voice said with a sting.

"Calm down. She was getting too close," stated a smoother voice.

Too close to what?

"We don't know that," the first voice said.

"Yes, we do. I told you when you tried to use her son as a scapegoat there'd be repercussions. She's no fool."

"He was there and I thought it a grand opportunity to finally besmirch the Hamilton name once and for all. Well, now what?"

The voice was familiar to Eliza. She tried to place it through her muddled mind, but it remained hard to focus.

"When she wakes up, we'll question her and see what she knows."

"She will see us and then she will know quite a bit, if she doesn't already. Are you mad?" the familiar-sounding voice said. How did she know this voice so well? Prickles ran up and down her spine.

"We will blindfold her, of course."

"She'll be out all night. Someone will come looking for her soon," the familiar voice said.

"Then we need to work quickly. We'll wake her first thing in the morning and question her."

"Then what, Ryman, you idiot? You didn't think this through. You cannot harm her. I won't allow it."

The sound of scuffling ensued. "Allow it, Renquist? You are not in a position to tell me anything. We will take her and dump her in the river. Her body to wash up in the harbor, just like Van Der Gloss. I don't care if she's Eliza Hamilton or some whore off the street."

Eliza couldn't believe her ears. Renquist!

"We must keep my father's name clean. The best way to ensure we are alright is to continue with the plan," the smooth voice said. He must be Ryman the younger.

Oh, she had completely misread that list. She'd judged that Renquist was in danger, that he was next to die. But no—he was conspiring with them. Eliza's heart pounded so fiercely in her chest she was afraid the men would hear it and realize she was no longer asleep. She needed to get out of this room before morning. She would not answer any questions and she would not allow them to dump her lifeless body in the river. No. Not Eliza Hamilton.

CHAPTER 51

Alice awakened with a start, then reminded herself that it was René's day to prepare breakfast. She sat up slowly and rubbed the sleep from her eyes. Her room was just beginning to lighten as the sun streamed through the window. She stood, hobbled over to the wash basin, and splashed water on her face.

Today, Eliza's family would be fetching her. Alice hated to see her go home. Eliza seemed almost happy with them in their little home. How could it be? Such a grand lady!

But appearances only spoke of what one wanted you to see. Alice herself had escaped a different life as a young woman. A life of pampering and excess. But she'd fallen in love with a Jewish man of considerable wealth that her Catholic family could not abide. Her father had forbidden their marriage.

Most young women in Belgium followed their orders to marry whoever their parents had chosen. A few did not and were ostracized. For Alice, it was traitorous for her to even consider marrying anybody who was not within the huge family of royals.

The night she left her country with Benjamin and headed for the New World, she understood she'd never return, that she would be labeled a traitor. But still she'd never been as happy as she was with him by her side, starting their new business and family. Happy times.

She swallowed down the creeping lump in her throat. She dressed and readied herself for the day. No point in dwelling in the past. She had her friends, her daughter, who would soon make her a grandmother, and her business. She had much to be grateful for. She opened her bedroom door to find a pale and frightened René.

Alice's heart quickened. "What is it?"

"I can't find Mrs. General Hamilton." René's lips quivered.

"What? What do you mean?"

"I mean she's gone. I can't find her," she sobbed.

Alice wanted to shake her but instead she patted her shoulder. "Let's stay calm. Surely there is an explanation." Alice's ankle cracked as they descended the stairs. "Maybe her sister arrived early."

"All of her things are still in the bedroom. All of them." René's voice notched up to an almost hysteric level.

"When is the last time you saw her?" Alice's mind raced with a thousand thoughts, including wondering if someone had stolen Eliza in the night.

"Last night before I went to bed."

"Me as well. Have you told the others? Someone must have seen something!" Alice walked to the kitchen table. She needed tea to help her think through this. She poured with a shaky hand. "I went to bed early last night myself. I'm such a sound sleeper. I heard nothing. Let's get everybody together. Ring the bell."

René rang the kitchen bell and women came from all corners of the house. Jo was not among them.

"Where's Josephine?" Alice snapped.

"She had a delivery to make this morning," Mary, another lacemaker, said.

Alice frowned.

"What's going on?" Mary asked.

"Mrs. General Hamilton is not here." Alice regarded the group of women, hoping they had answers. "Did any of you see her last night? This morning?" She brought the tea to her lips and swallowed, tasting every bitter element, drawing it in slowly as if it were an elixir that held answers.

"I did!" Mary said. "After her sister left, she soon departed. I supposed she were going with her."

"She was not!" Alice hissed.

"Where was she going, then?"

"I don't know! Think, woman—which direction did she go?"

Mary's face wrinkled as she tried to recall. "I'm sorry. I just don't know. As I said, I noticed her leave the house, but I didn't watch her after that."

In one direction lay the city, in the other the river. Knowing Eliza, it was the river she wanted. "Listen, ladies. Not a word of this to anybody." If word got out that Eliza Hamilton was missing, who knew what would happen? "We will find her," said Alice.

"How?" René said. "Where do we even begin to look?"

"We search in the houses of the men she was investigating, first of all. We know the servants. We need to scatter today and find out if any of them have her in their homes. Barns. Whatever." *Oh, it was too early in the morning to have to strategize!*

"Should we get a constable involved?" Mary asked.

"Not yet," Alice answered, but she was already thinking about finding Constable Schultz. She could trust him to not leak this to the papers or the rest of the city. He'd appreciate the gravity of the situation.

Yes, she'd go find him now.

CHAPTER 52

Waking and sleeping. Waking and sleeping.

Eliza dreamed. Or was she awake?

Hands cupped her mouth and she drifted into a haze. Another hand brushed her hair gently back of her face. "My love," a voice said.

Was that . . . Hamilton?

"My Betsey."

She struggled to open her eyes, lift her head, but there was nobody there. She wanted to cry, but the blindfold made it difficult. For a moment, she felt him next to her, that this was all a bad dream. That her Hamilton was still alive.

She drifted off again.

"You must run, Betsey. You must get out of here." His voice came to her again. She shivered.

"How?" she wanted to say but couldn't. *Think, think, think.*

She needed to free her hands, Yes, that's what she needed to do. She began to twist them and pull at the rope that was wrapped around them. But she soon tired and could no longer hold her eyes open.

Her burning wrists awakened her once more. Had she been twisting them in her sleep? The burning pain didn't prevent her from trying to free herself. She felt a loosening of the ropes and dampness. Was it sweat?

She brushed her hand against something sharp in the floor. As she explored, she realized it was a nail. She needed to twist her hands just so and move the ropes to the nail.

The muscles in her arms screamed at her, but she kept sliding the rope over the nail. Finally, the rope gave way!

She worked quietly, as she didn't know if anybody was in the room with her. She suspected she was alone. But couldn't be certain, since she was blindfolded. She listened and heard nothing. No breathing. No shuffling about. She must be alone.

She reached for the gag and took it from her mouth, allowing air to flow in her mouth and nose more freely. She took long, deep gulps of air. She was parched. Her lips were dry as dirt.

Her hands found the blindfold and she slipped it off. The dark room held no comfort. She batted her eyelids, trying to adjust her eyes. Where was she?

She didn't care where she was. She just needed to get out of here. Get out of this building! She was certain she could find her way to someone who'd help. She worked off the rope binding her legs.

Please, God, help me to get out of this place. I know we haven't been on the best of terms, but I'm trying. I'm trying to do good. To be a good mother. To be a good citizen. To honor my husband.

As her eyes adjusted to the darkness, objects took form. A barrel sat in the corner. A pile of ropes. A couple of bottles and rags. She stood, her legs a bit wobbly. But she found her balance and strength. Breathed in and out.

Now she knew that Renquist was as guilty as the others. But she still didn't know who had actually killed the men. Who had sliced Van Der Gloss's throat and blamed her son. Or who killed Drake and Peabody.

But she knew, beyond anything else, that she would not be next.

Her broken heart reached out for more strength, reached to the only thing that had sustained her through her life, throughout the troubles with her marriage, throughout the long nights during the Revolution. It was God. It was always God. She realized now that she'd lost her faith. But now, she dug deep to find it. *God, you are there, I know it. Please help.* She took a step forward, trying to be quiet, as surely they would have a guard somewhere. Outside the door?

She picked up one of the bottles. She might need it. Eliza hated striking another person. But she would. Oh yes, she would.

Eliza crept forward, ignoring the fear in her belly. The door was just ahead. Did it open to the outdoors? Or to another room? She tamped down the fear creeping from her stomach into her throat.

Eliza, you must do this. For your husband's memory and legacy. For your children.

She slowly opened the door. Just a crack.

It opened to the outside. A place she didn't recognize. No matter. She needed to move quickly and find her bearings. She searched for a road. A road she could follow. She walked ahead with only the glow of the moonlight to guide her way. There was nothing there . . . just woods. She turned and walked in the opposite direction, spotting a road. She followed the moon, having no idea if that was the correct choice. As she did so, a man came out of nowhere and lunged at her. The bottle slipped from her hands and she tumbled forward. She quickly turned herself onto her back as the man came forward.

It was Randall Ryman. She shoved her feet beneath his hips and pushed him hard enough that he fell backward. She found her bottle and hit him over the head with it as hard as she could. He groaned like a stuck boar as his eyes rolled back in his head. He fell down like an axed tree. Randall was soft and fat and could not match wiry Eliza.

She left him lying there in the road and continued to walk, following the moon. Up ahead she spotted the river. She must be only a few miles from Alice's home. They must be mad with worry. She didn't know why she'd done such a foolish thing as going for a walk alone at night. She just hadn't been thinking.

The sound of the river rushed through her ears. It wasn't over yet. How to get to safety? She longed to find the constable and tell him of their gaffe. They had supposed Renquist would be the next victim, and in warning him, Schultz had given him a reason to come after her. Maybe Schultz would be next. Would they be so foolish as to go after a constable?

She was alone in the expanse of the dark night, stepping one foot after the other, walking toward the sound of the river. She jumped at every sound she heard—the scattering footfall of rats or beavers, the sound of leaves rustling in the breeze, and in the distance, a growl.

CHAPTER 53

Night had fallen and the women of the little house on Pearl Street had yet to find Eliza. So Alice took herself to the constable's office.

When Alice and her Benjamin had left the old country—she didn't even like to even think the name, let alone say it—it hadn't been easy. Constables, guards, spies. She spat. They were all easily paid off. They'd take your money then deceive you anyway. The familiar fear crept up her spine.

She took a deep breath. She was safe now. She was better than she probably had a right to be. But the fear still haunted her.

Would Schultz help? Or turn against them? Turn against Eliza Hamilton?

Alice stood at the opposite side of the street from the constabulary. She'd given up praying a long time ago. She wanted no part of a God that had taken her Benjamin away after everything they'd been through. But if she still prayed, this would be the moment for it.

She placed one foot in front of the other and crossed the crowded street, dodging carriages, pedestrians, and horses. She walked up to the door and opened it.

"Can I help you?" a constable walking toward her asked.

"I'm looking for Constable Schultz." *This wasn't so hard.* He seemed pleasant enough. He had kind eyes.

"Schultz?" the constable yelled out. The next moment Constable Schultz stood in front of Alice.

"Miss Rhodes?"

She nodded. "Is there someplace we can talk?"

"Follow me." He led her down a long hallway into a gray room with a table and a few chairs. He waved at her to take a seat. She did so and he sat down as well. "What is happening?" he queried.

Finding the words was harder than she had imagined. She'd never had this problem before.

"Alice? I don't have much time."

"It's our Mrs. General Hamilton. She's missing."

"What?" He stood quickly and shut the door. He pointed his meaty finger toward her. "Tell me everything. And start at the beginning."

Alice harrumphed. "We don't have time for that. But my friends have been to several of the homes of the men Eliza was investigating. *We* were investigating. And there is nothing untoward at any of them. No trace of Eliza anywhere. We woke up this morning and she was gone, which means she's probably been gone since last night."

Schultz eyes widened. "We should get a search party going for her."

"I beg of you—this needs to be kept secret!"

"Why? Her life is in jeopardy. We can't laze about."

"Everything will come crashing down. The killers will find out and escape before you have a chance to apprehend them." Alice lowered her voice. "We need to go about this in as subtle a way as possible. We need to get her to safety, but we also need to keep it out of the papers."

Schultz smacked his head. "You're right, of course." His eyes darted back and forth, as if considering their options. "Here's what I'll do. I have a few friends, some of whom are constables. We will look for her. I give you my word there will be nothing in the papers. None of these men will utter a word. I'd trust them with my mother's life."

"Bring your men to my place in an hour." Alice stood. "My house on Pearl Street is nondescript. My friends and housemates are waiting. We can work together."

He raised his eyebrows. "All women?"

She nodded.

"I fear for their safety."

"Fear for your own. Fear for Eliza. Don't fear for the women of Pearl House. We will see you in an hour."

CHAPTER 54

Eliza found her way to the constabulary. Her feet felt as if they were bleeding, but she set that pain aside in her mind.

She had no idea what time it was. It was dark and the moon was high. But constables worked all hours. She knocked on the door. A constable opened it. His eyes widened at the sight of her. "Madam?"

"My name is Eliza Hamilton and I'd like to see Constable Schultz." Her lips were dry as a bone.

"Please come in. Can I bring you some water?" His eyes were wide with concern and wonder.

"Yes, please." She entered the office. A few men sitting in a group lifted their faces to her. She must look dirty? Dry? How did he know she thirsted more than she ever had before? She licked her cracking lips.

"Please have a seat. I'll be right with you," the constable said.

Eliza sat down, against her will, as she wanted to run free, breathe more fresh air, and walk in her gardens. She wanted to dip into the river and feel the cool water embrace her, as she and Hamilton had done so many times before.

"Madam," the man said when he came back into the room with a glass of water. "Constable Schultz is not here. This is not his shift."

He handed her the glass of water and she drank it, trying not to gulp it down. Was there ever water that was more delicious than this? She didn't think so. She drained the glass. "His life is in danger. Is there a way to reach him?"

"What?"

Eliza knew where the Ryman family lived. By process of deduction, she ruled out their home as the place she had been held. She was certain it was Renquist's house because she remembered Hamilton speaking about his home along the river.

"I've just come from what I think is Solicitor Renquist's home, where I was held captive. It's a very long story, but we have no time to waste. You see, we assumed we could trust him. It turns out that he's behind it all."

"Jeremiah Renquist?" The constable's eyebrow lifted. He faced the other men. "Fetch Schultz immediately." He then turned his attention back to Eliza. "We need to get you home." His voice softened. "We need to have your wrist examined by a physician, and I warrant you need your bed."

"Bed? I couldn't sleep if I tried." Her wrists burned and bled. She hadn't noticed the trickling blood until now.

"I know you feel like that now." His demeanor was fatherly and kind. "Was it Renquist who held you against your will?"

"He was there. I don't know who snatched me from the road. I think it was Randall Ryman." Her stomach roiled. Perhaps she had drunk the water too fast. She held up the wobbly glass. But it wasn't the glass that wobbled. She was shaking.

"Mrs. General Hamilton, please follow me into the back. Can you do that?"

She stood slowly on her quivering legs. "Yes, of course I can."

He helped her into a room with a bed. "Lie down. We have a doctor coming to examine your wounds. I'll get you more water."

She eased down onto the edge of the bed. "You must move quickly. When they see I'm gone, they will run and hide."

He nodded. "I already have men on the way. Please do not worry yourself. You've found your way here and now you can take care."

The bed felt soft. Softer than what she remembered of any other bed. The quilt pulled over it had familiar stitching and patterns. She pulled back the edge. "René."

"Who?"

"She is a quilter."

"Oh yes, we've got several blankets and such from the women at Pearl House."

The women at Pearl House. Eliza smiled as warmth spread through her. "Can you get word to them as to my whereabouts? And to my sister, Angelica Church?"

She lay back on the bed. She closed her eyes and unraveled like a spool of thread.

"We will do our best, madam," were the last words Eliza made out before she drifted into darkness.

★ ★ ★

When Eliza awakened, still wrapped in the quilt at the constabulary, Alice's face came into view.

"What were you thinking?" Alice said, brow furrowed. "To go off like that . . ."

"I went for a walk."

Alice nodded. "I know that, but you were gone so long. We started scouring the streets looking for you. Why did you leave?"

A sharp pain jabbed at Eliza's temple. "I just needed air and since I was going home, I didn't think it mattered if I was seen."

Alice caressed Eliza's forehead with a trembling, cool hand. "I was sick with worry."

The shame of Eliza's decision swept through her. She hadn't meant for any of this to happen. "I'm sorry."

"It's fine now, so long as you are alright. I'd ask you to promise not to do that again, but I warrant such circumstances will never occur again."

"True enough." Eliza tried to sit up.

Alice pushed her gently back down. "Stay there. I'll fetch you some water. Please don't get up yet."

Alice left the tiny room. Eliza lifted her hand to scratch her head. The bandages on her wrists made the movement awkward. When was she bandaged? She had a dreamy recollection of a man examining her wrists.

"Have they gotten Renquist and the others?" Eliza asked when Alice entered the room with water and set it down on a table. She then came over to the bed and helped Eliza sit up.

"Nice and slow," Alice instructed. Once Eliza was upright, Alice brought the water over to her.

"They have both Rymans and Renquist. I hear he denies it all. Claims you are out of your mind with grief." Alice handed her the water.

Eliza harrumphed. "I'm sure he does."

"Drink slowly," Alice said. She sighed. "He is well connected. But you are Mrs. General Hamilton."

Eliza swallowed her water. "And I have proof that there's much more going on here. I have the handkerchief with the list of names. I have a note someone wrote to me. The rock that was thrown through my window. And for heaven's sake, why would I make any of this up?"

"Yes, and it was a good thing that you involved the constable. He's on our side. He's in a room with a judge and several constables and marshals as of this moment. I warrant they are putting it all together."

Eliza held that vision in her mind's eye. Men gathered, trying to figure out a path to justice. It was the measure of things—the men gathered forces, but it was Eliza and the women at Pearl House who showed them the path forward. As Eliza contemplated, it was also the way of things.

"When can I leave?" Eliza grunted.

Alice held out her arm. "Now is as good as any time, I reckon."

Eliza Hamilton clung to Alice as they walked down the constabulary hallway. The old wood floors creaked as they moved. Gratitude swept through Alice, for she had an unspoken pact with the dead Alexander Hamilton. The day she saw him half dead. The day they locked eyes. She swore then to help Eliza anyway she could. And besides, Eliza was dear to her. Here she was, next to her, clinging to her.

"Miss? Miss?" A voice came from behind them. "Where are you taking her? She's a witness."

"And a victim." Alice glared at the young constable. "Constable Schultz knows where to find her. She needs to go home."

Eliza nodded. "I quite agree. But thank you for your concern."

The women turned and walked out of the office.

"Fresh air!" Eliza said. She sounded better than she looked. Her clothes were rumpled and hair mussed. And then there were her wrists—red and swollen.

"Aye, 'tis good to be out of that dark, dank office. But let's take it slow, shall we?" Alice didn't want to alarm Eliza in any way, for she appeared as if she'd keel over any minute.

"My feet are bruised and cut. I have no choice." Eliza grimaced.

They only had a few blocks to travel, but Alice knew what it was like to walk while in pain. They stood at a corner and waited until a carriage passed by and then crossed. Eliza's gait was that of an old woman's.

Alice sought to lighten the mood. "I fear I must warn you about something."

Eliza's dark eyes widened. "What, Alice? What now?"

"Angelica is at the house waiting for you." Alice grinned.

Eliza laughed. "I'm not surprised."

A woman turned and glanced at Eliza, failing to mask her interest. Eliza lowered her face.

"She didn't think it would be a good idea to visit at the constable's office," Alice continued as they walked past a fishmonger. The scent of fresh seafood followed them.

Eliza laughed more. "No, indeed."

Alice loved to hear her laugh. It had been twenty hours of wondering if she'd ever see her friend again. Wondering where she'd gone. Who she was with. If they were hurting her. She held on a little tighter to Eliza. Here she was, Alice Rhodes, walking Mrs. General Hamilton toward her little house on Pearl Street. Life certainly was curious.

CHAPTER 55

When Eliza returned to Pearl House, Angelica was indeed waiting for her. Angelica nearly knocked her over with her embrace.

"What on earth happened? Where were you? Are you alright?" Angelica's eyes were wide with excitement and concern.

"Calm down and I shall answer each question." Eliza held her sister's hand as they walked into the parlor, which was already set for tea. Eliza nearly swooned. How long had it been since she had tea or biscuits? She had had something they called tea at the constable's office, but she could barely get it down.

After all of the women of Pearl House were situated with tea in hand and biscuits on plates, Eliza recounted her experience.

"I can't believe you hit him over the head!" Alice said after Eliza had told them the story.

"I can," Angelica said. "Eliza has always been a bit . . . scrappy. She wrestled our brothers to the ground on more than one occasion. But the question remains—will they be brought to justice? Will Alexander's good name be kept intact?"

"Let us hope so," Eliza said and sipped her tea. Good tea could never be appreciated enough.

"I don't understand," René spoke up. "What does this have to do with the men we spied on? The secret society?"

Eliza shrugged. "Nothing. Renquist isn't even a member. But Ryman is. And that's where we were distracted. He's the one who stole the money years ago. The money my Hamilton was blamed for stealing." Eliza swallowed the tea, along with her rage. When she reflected on the rumor that her husband was a thief and all it had set into motion, she wanted to scream.

"Is he truly the killer of all these men?" Angelica asked. "Hard to believe. He's fat and old and I just can't see it."

"You're right. I believe it was Ryman's son, working on his father's behalf. At least that's what I overheard when I was captured."

"But why Alexander?" Josephine asked.

"That's what I want to know as well," Paulette said.

Alice sat quietly, observing.

"I heard them say it was happenstance. He happened to be there. And they also thought besmirching the Hamilton name would be fun. But the important thing is they have both of the Rymans—father and son—and Renquist. Let's hope they keep them in custody."

The room was quiet for a few moments, marked only by the sound of cups hitting saucers and spoons stirring sugar into tea.

"You need some rest," Angelica said as she reached over to Eliza and patted her hand.

Eliza placed her other hand over Angelica's. "I quite agree."

"McNally is waiting for us." Angelica stood.

Eliza surveyed the room, at the faces looking at her—René's deep brown eyes, Jo's winsome smile, and Paulette's dimpled chin turned up. Alice stood next to them.

"Ladies, how could I begin to thank you? I could not have managed without each and every one of you." Eliza's voice cracked. "Beyond what you've done for me, you've helped deliver justice. Victoria Peabody and Rose Van Der Gloss will rest easier." She glanced around the circle of women. "Thank you, from the bottom of my heart."

A muffled sob escaped from René.

"Now, now, there'll be none of that," Alice shushed her. "It's been an honor, Mrs. General Hamilton."

"Please call me Eliza. All of you. We are now friends, surely. Almost family."

CHAPTER 56

"I'm not certain I understand any of this at all." Angelica fanned herself in the carriage as she and Eliza made their way to the Grange.

"What part don't you understand?" Eliza smoothed her black dress in a nervous gesture. Sad to be leaving the women of Pearl House. Happy to be returning home. Hopeful that justice would indeed be served.

"I suppose the biggest question is why they targeted you with their threats and rock throwing . . . and kidnapped you!" Angelica's eyes widened.

"I wouldn't stop asking questions. I knew too much, I suppose. I think they must've assumed I'd be too distracted by Hamilton's death to help my son after he was falsely accused of murder." Eliza couldn't wait to get into a freshly laundered mourning dress. Nor could she wait for a bath.

Angelica grunted. "I suppose none of them really know you. You are, without a doubt, the strongest woman I know."

Eliza doubted that. She didn't feel strong at all. If she had to describe herself with one word it would be "protective." All a woman had was the reputation of her husband and family. Once those were gone, life could be devastating. A knot formed in her throat. "Thank you. But it takes one to know one."

She spoke the truth. Angelica was as strong as a woman could be. One could be misled by her busyness and manner into thinking she was a fragile flower, but that was not the case. Eliza swallowed, trying to will herself to relax, to not be so on edge.

She needed to see her son. She needed to lay her eyes on Alexander to calm herself. She also certainly needed to see her other children. She longed to join them in Albany at The Pastures. She pictured them there, rambling in the fields and woods as she had as a child. It seemed fitting.

The carriage made a sharp turn onto Bloomingdale Road. Eliza glanced out the windows as the crowded city gave way to woods and gardens. Homes here were set much farther apart, between rolling green hills.

Angelica sighed. "Could it be that Hamilton's reputation has been saved at last? That people will no longer think he robbed the Treasury? Poor man. They never had proof of it, but his name was entangled with that crime for years. I hope Ryman burns for this."

"I wish it was Burr in prison," Eliza said. "He seems to be long gone. And although I once thought him the culprit, he's clear of this treachery."

"Of course you did, through no fault of your own. He killed our Hamilton."

Eliza shivered, even though she was sweating in the heat of the carriage and the summer day. She placed her hands firmly on her lap to stop them from trembling. "We shall see to it that the robbery of the Treasury is no longer connected with Hamilton's name. Nor will there be any murders connected to his son's name."

"Let's not forget the murders. Ryman shall surely burn in hell for the killing of those innocent men." Angelica's voice cracked. "Their poor families."

"I believe that it is the younger Ryman who will burn for those." Eliza's God was a just God. She'd lost him many times in her life, then found him again. But she always believed that the ultimate justice was in his hands. Didn't she? Mostly. She'd never understand Hamilton's death. There was no justice in that. Unless it was to expose and ruin Burr. Still, that didn't seem just. But then again, who was she to think she could understand the ways of God?

Her mother's voice rang in her head: "You must have faith, Eliza."

I'm trying, Mama, she thought.

"Indeed," Eliza said aloud to her sister. "For many widows, their lives are never the same after the patriarch is gone. It takes the children down bad roads as well."

"You never have to worry about that," Angelica said. "I hope you know that. We have enough money for everything and what good is money if you can't use it to help your family?"

Eliza's heart exploded. It was a sweet thing to say. Why was she so stubborn about accepting help? Why did she not want to be aided by her sister's wealth? An overabundance of pride? "I know that, sister. If I need help, I promise I'll ask for it."

In the meantime, she'd continue to do what she could. Alice and her group had given Eliza hope that she could fend for her family—and herself.

"Please do."

Eliza could see how important it was to Angelica to be needed. Eliza could relate to the feeling. It was good to be needed. It was also good to be in a position to help.

She drew in some air. It was too hot to relax. She sensed something lingering—or perhaps she was simply still too keyed up from her adventure.

The carriage slowed down, inching forward. Maybe there was a hole in the road or McNally spotted something up ahead, thought Eliza. Her stomach churned when the carriage came to a halt. "McNally?" she called out.

There was no answer.

"McNally?"

Her eyes met her sister's in a panic.

A gunshot rang out and a thud sounded across the carriage. *McNally! Had he been shot?*

"Get down!" Eliza said to Angelica.

Eliza and Angelica crouched on the small floor of the carriage. The sound of scuffling ensued. Yelling. Women's voices. Men's voice's. Grunts. Groans. Smacking.

A woman's piercing, shrill scream stabbed into Eliza's head.

A woman? What on earth was happening? Eliza had assumed they were being robbed. But a woman robber?

Eliza's heart throbbed in her ears. Angelica was as white as a sheet. Her eyes watered. "What is happening?" she mouthed.

Eliza held her finger to her mouth, attempting to quiet Angelica, to stop her from screaming. She hoped whoever stood just outside would move along and not open the door.

CHAPTER 57

The carriage door flew open. A woman stood with a pistol pointed at Eliza and Angelica.

Eliza recognized the woman. But from where?

Angelica screamed so loudly that the woman lurched back a bit. "Get out of the carriage!" she ordered. "Now!"

Eliza struggled to stand, as her whole body trembled. She stumbled out of the carriage with Angelica behind her. They stood with their arms wrapped around one another.

"What do you want?" Angelica said. "Take whatever you want and leave us alone. I beg you!"

"You stole my life from me!" The woman glared at Eliza.

Suddenly Eliza realized their assailant's identity. It was Joan Higgans, the woman who had attended Jonathan Drake's funeral. She had been the only other woman there and stood out because of it.

She opened her mouth to speak.

"Don't be ridiculous. Eliza would never harm a fly," Angelica said in a trembling voice.

The pistol wavered as the woman pointed it at them. Eliza wondered where McNally was. She couldn't see him anywhere and hoped that he was unhurt.

"I'm sorry," Eliza said. "You must have confused me with someone else."

"No!" Joan's eyes darted between Eliza and down the road, as if she were watching for someone. "I know you. Everybody does. The high and mighty Eliza Hamilton, going around town asking questions as if the world owes her anything. Who do you think you are?"

Eliza glanced around quickly; she didn't want to take her eyes off the woman. She was unhinged. Was she alone? Eliza could not see anybody else. "Joan," Eliza said. "I am most sorry if I offended you." Eliza didn't recognize her own voice, which was low and trembling. Why couldn't she control her voice?

Joan harrumphed. "I bet you are . . . now that I have a pistol in your face."

"What do you want from us?" Angelica asked again.

"Nothing! I mean to kill you. Both of you," Joan said. Sweat dripped off her face.

Then why hadn't she done it? Pulled that trigger? And where was McNally?

"You've taken it all away. My future. My fiancé's future. All of it. We were to be married next week. Now there is nothing. He will go to prison. And I have no future!"

"Oh my dear," Angelica said. "If your fiancé is going to jail, you are better off."

Joan screamed. "No! Joshua is a good man. His father forced his hand! Please, you must believe me!"

"Please put the gun down and let us talk about it," Eliza said, lifting her open hand. "We can forget this ever happened. Please drop the gun."

This woman—enraged, frightened—bore the consequences of her fiancé's actions. Eliza's thoughts spun around as she considered her own actions. While she was trying to do good by so many people, she had unintentionally hurt this woman.

"Are you mad?" Joan yelled. "I have you right where I want you!" She held the gun up and aimed. Her eyes were flecked with hostility, like a creature from a fairytale.

Was this Eliza's ending? Would she be joining her son, mother, and husband at the pearly gates? Would she ever see her children again? She lowered her eyes and prayed, as her chest pounded, like the Iroquois drums of her youth.

The sound of rustling footfalls and leaves forced them all to turn. Alice, René, and Jo emerged from the woods with a man who held a pistol. They all rushed at Joan, pinned her to the ground, and grabbed the gun out of her hand.

Angelica fell to the ground, swooning. Eliza crouched down beside her, patting her face.

Alice stood in front of them. "Is she unwell?"

"She just fainted." Eliza continued patting her sister's face.

Angelica began to waken. "Eliza? Alice?" she murmured as she tried to stand.

"Easy!" Eliza said as she and Alice helped Angelica to her feet. They walked her over to the carriage so she could lean up against it.

René and the man with her held Joan still.

"What are you doing here?" Eliza asked them.

"We noticed her lurking, then following you. René recognized her, and said she was a ne'er-do-well. We figured she was up to no good. But to try to kill you?" Alice's voice shook.

"Oh, Alice." Eliza perceived the heart of her friend once again. She embraced her. "Thank you."

Suddenly a groaning erupted from the other side of the carriage. "What now?" Angelica asked.

A very rumpled McNally came around the side of the carriage rubbing his head. His face was bruised and swollen. He looked about him and regarded the unknown man and René holding an upset Joan. Angelica was pale and leaning against the carriage, and Eliza and Alice were arm and arm.

"Who hit me?" McNally asked. "What did I miss?"

CHAPTER 58

Eliza and Angelica finished the rest of the carriage ride home in silence, listening to the sound of the horse's hooves on the ground and the jangle of the harness.

What was there to say? A desperate woman was going to jail tonight after holding a pistol on them and hitting McNally across the face with it. A woman with parents who loved her. Joan's parents were good people who worked hard. What had happened to her? How did she get involved with such a bad lot?

The closer the carriage drew to the Grange, the cooler it grew in the carriage. But not cool enough. Eliza yanked at her collar, damp with sweat and scratchy against her neck. She wiped her face with her handkerchief.

The carriage turned up the long hill to the Grange, and Eliza's first glimpse of her home made her want to cry. There were moments a few days back when she didn't think she'd ever see her home again. The home Hamilton had worked so hard for. That they had both worked so hard for.

As if Angelica had read Eliza's mind, she reached over and clasped her hand and smiled. "We're home."

★ ★ ★

Before Eliza opened the front door to the Grange, she turned around to take in the view. It was a clear day, and she gazed out over the city and beyond that the harbor. She loved the city. Gratitude welled up in her. She was here. She was alive. She would make the rest of her days count. She wanted to matter.

"What are you waiting for?" Angelica said and opened the door to Mrs. Cole, who had lemonade and sandwiches waiting for them.

"Thank God," Angelica said. "I'm famished."

Eliza took a drink of lemonade before saying, "Mrs. Cole, I'd like a bath."

"Your water is just drawn, mum." Mrs. Cole turned to Angelica. "Yours too, mum."

"Thank you," Angelica said.

Eliza bit into a sandwich, made with strawberry jam created with the plants she and her Hamilton had planted together. The jars of jam were lined up on the shelf in the pantry. She hoped they'd last through the fall. If she was even here for the fall. No— she would not lose her home.

"Well," Angelica said. "John would never believe any of what we've just been through."

"Then I suggest we don't tell him," Eliza said and finished her lemonade.

Angelica cracked an impish grin, peeling back the years on her face with one expression. "I suppose you're right."

★ ★ ★

"What will you do now?" Angelica asked later over a light supper of salad and fish cakes.

"What do you mean?" Eliza set her fork down next to her plate.

Angelica swallowed her bite of fish before answering. "Now that everything is solved."

"I plan to join the children in Albany, of course." A winsome pang swept through Eliza. She hadn't allowed herself to think of the children, but now that this treacherous business was over, she ached for them.

"Wonderful. I shall join you for a while. But John wants to get back to London."

Eliza's heart dropped. "What? No. Not yet."

"I'm holding him off as long as possible."

"I for one don't want to think about that. I don't know what I would've done without you."

Angelica cracked a smile. "I'm sure you'd have figured something out."

Eliza pondered how Angelica had swooped in and taken care of myriad mourning details and then whisked her off to stay with Alice. Not to mention the emotional boost Eliza received from having her close. "I may have. But I wouldn't have wanted to."

John Church entered the room. "Ladies, I'm sorry to interrupt your supper."

"Darling." Angelica stood as he walked over to her and embraced her.

"Can I get you a plate, sir?" Mrs. Cole asked.

"That won't be necessary, but thank you." He turned back to Eliza and Angelica. "I have news."

"Please sit down," Eliza said, pushing away her plate.

"Three men have been arrested," said John.

"Get on with it, John!" Angelica urged.

"Your solicitor Renquist has been arrested. He'll never practice law again, even when he gets out of prison. They are still trying to figure out how much he understood about the murders. He claims to not know anything."

"He's lying. I heard him speaking about it," Eliza said.

He nodded. "Thought as much. The judge will want to speak with you. Be prepared for your summons."

"I almost can't wait," Eliza said—and it was true. More than anything she wanted justice, but she also wanted to put everything behind her.

"As you requested, the kidnapping case will disappear," John stated.

"What? Oh heavens no! Those men should burn!" Angelica protested.

Eliza cleared her throat. "That is up to God. As for me, I will not be remembered as a victim."

Angelica opened her mouth, then closed it, shaking her head.

"As to the murders of Drake and Van Der Gloss, both Ryman men will face trial and I suspect will be found guilty, for the evidence is overwhelming." John stood and walked over to the sideboard where a decanter of whiskey sat and poured himself a glass. He held it up toward Eliza. "Your son, dear sister, has passed his exams, despite everything. He will return home tomorrow an innocent man. In the eyes of the law, of course." He cocked an eyebrow. Then he lifted his glass and drank.

Eliza's eyes burned with stinging tears. She tried to bat them away.

Angelica reached for her sister's hand. "It's over."

Eliza sensed things were never really over. Things had a way of appearing to be done and buried, then one day popping back up onto the surface. People loved to dig up the past and find some dark mischief. She didn't know how any of this would come back to haunt her or her children. But for now, she supposed Angelica was right. Justice had been served on many levels. But she had a feeling that Joan's attempt to kill them was just the first of many repercussions they would face. But her

Hamilton's name would be cleared, and that mattered. To be wrongfully accused of such a thing and to have it hanging over your head for all of your life . . . and then to have the proof you needed, only to be shot in a duel and never see justice. Eliza bit her lip, trying not to cry.

CHAPTER 59

The next day, Eliza received her summons. In consideration of all she'd been through, the judge allowed her to write her testimony instead of going into the city. It took her several hours of writing. When she was finished, she sent the document with McNally to the courthouse.

The rest of the staff and Angelica were preparing to go to Albany the next day. Finally—days after Eliza had told her father she'd be there. And even though he would be upset to learn what had happened, he'd definitely understand.

But then again, he didn't need to know *everything*. Eliza was set for a couple of months, and then would need to sell more lace. She'd make more and have Angel make more as well. They'd manage. For now.

Eliza opened the door of her armoire, where dresses hung and trunks were piled. The more colorful the dress the more memories assaulted her. She ran her hands over the silky blue dress Hamilton had loved so much.

"Betsey, you are a fine woman," he'd say. "And that dress suits you so well."

She'd smile coquettishly at her husband and say, "Thank you, kind sir."

It was not a dress she wore often, only for special occasions. And she admitted that it made her feel good when she wore it. Hamilton had the dress made for her when they had nothing. Which was most of their marriage, if she were being honest.

She'd save the blue dress for Angel. The rest? The rest she'd send to the Widow Society. She had no need of the dresses anymore. She was the Widow Hamilton and would be for the rest of her days. And she would make those days count, donning her weeds everywhere she went to remind people of her dear husband. Perhaps planting seeds with her black dress of what a great man Alexander Hamilton was.

She took the dresses and piled them on her bed. Each one held a memory of its own. President Washington's inauguration. The day Independence was claimed. The winter ball.

She stood back and examined all of her dresses spread across the bed. She took them in. Some were in better shape than others. Her everyday dresses might need some patching before giving them away. She'd ask Paulette to work on them while she was in Albany and when she returned the Widow Society would be her first stop.

Eliza would be fine without these dresses. Maybe someone else could use them.

That night, when she slept, she dreamt of her children running through the fields of her home, splashing in the streams and chasing one another through the huge house. She awakened to sunlight streaming through her fixed bedroom window, a smile on her face.

Eliza met Angelica in the dining room for breakfast.

"Good morning," Angelica said. "Look at this feast Mrs. Cole prepared."

Eggs, biscuits, a blackberry cobbler, and strips of bacon sat on the table.

"Smells wonderful." Eliza sat down and poured herself some tea. Tea first. She was so excited that she wasn't certain she could eat. Soon she would have her arms around her children and her father.

"I spoke with Paulette yesterday. She said you've given her a project. You want her to repair your dresses so that you can give them away?" Angelica buttered her biscuit. "I said there must be some mistake."

"No mistake. I don't need them."

"Oh." Angelica lifted an eyebrow. "You may need them in the future."

"No, I won't."

"Do you plan on—"

"Yes. I plan on wearing widow's weeds for the rest of my days."

"But—"

"Let's not talk about this anymore. Can't we eat and enjoy the lovely food?"

Angelica quieted and spooned some blackberry cobbler into her bowl.

"Mother!" Alexander said as he walked into the room. He kissed her on the cheek.

"Aren't you looking fine? I didn't know that you'd arrived," Eliza said.

"I just got here."

"Sit down and eat," Angelica said.

"You won't have to ask me twice." Alexander pulled up a chair, but first he set a small package on the table.

"What's that?" Angelica asked.

"It's a gift for my mother."

Eliza set her cup down. "Whatever for?"

"Do you think I don't know what you've done for me?" He poured himself tea.

Eliza was startled into silence.

"You put yourself in harm's way. I don't want you to ever do that again for me—or for anyone else."

Eliza blinked away the threatening tears. "Nothing that any other mother would not do."

"I doubt that," he said.

"I do as well." Angelica said.

"Well, open it," Alexander said with a grin that belonged to his father. Eliza's heart nearly stopped at the resemblance.

Alexander slid the package over closer to her.

"What a lovely ribbon," she said, pulling on it. The silky pink ribbon loosened, and she lifted the lid off the box.

Inside, couched in a bed of cotton, was her grandmother's black lace collar. She gasped and clutched her breast.

"I found it in a shop on Eighth Avenue. They had a lot of lace. Even some gold lace, which I'd never seen before. But I knew you'd like this collar. It reminded me of the one you already have."

He had no way of knowing this was her grandmother's, the one she'd sold to pay for the house staff. But Angelica would know.

"It's lovely!" Eliza said and closed the box. "Thank you so much, son. It wasn't necessary." She needed to talk about something other than the lace. "What is the weather like this morning?"

Angelica reached for the box before Eliza could stop her. She opened it and pulled out the black lace collar. She examined it as if it were a diamond. Finally, she leveled a stare across the table. "A fine hand made this lace."

Eliza ignored her sister's glare. "A fine hand, indeed, sister."

Chapter 60

The Schuyler home was the first thing one saw when sailing into Albany. Its red brick and white columns sat on a bluff facing the Hudson River. It drew the attention, and perhaps awe, of all travelers, but to Eliza and Angelica it was home. Angelica grabbed onto Eliza in excitement as the house came into view. Eliza refrained from jumping up and down. She was a grown woman, yet it was what she wanted to do.

She and her sister cut ominous figures on the boat, both dressed in black, with two somber gentlemen accompanying them. John Church stood next to his wife and Alexander next to Eliza.

There had been moments over the past few weeks when Eliza longed to reach out to her father and could not. There had been many more times when she longed to hold her children and could not. Now she drew in the river breeze. She looked to her childhood home, where the rest of her family was gathered, and resolved to put it all behind her. For good.

Angelica pointed and laughed. For there were all of the Hamilton children standing at the pier awaiting them.

Eliza's heart melted. She squinted against the harsh rays of the sun. Who was holding little Philip? A new maid?

Alexander reached for his mother's hand. "I forgot to mention—grandfather hired someone to help with the children."

"Hired a nurse? That's not like him." Her father had always been an active father and grandfather. Fear suddenly coursed through her.

"He's advancing in age. His gout sometimes gets the best of him. I think it speaks highly of him that he realizes his limitations," Alexander said with a soft tone.

The ferry pulled in to the shore. The passengers formed a line and disembarked from the boat. John helped Angelica down the ramp and Alexander helped his mother, or at least made an effort to. Eliza was distracted by the children racing toward her. She wrapped her arms around them, tears splashing. Finally. They could be together safely. To heal.

Eliza moved toward Angel, whose arm was around the woman holding little Philip. Eliza's heart almost stopped. Her baby! Her children! All here—looking well.

The woman turned. "There's your mama," she said and the child lifted his arms out.

The nurse placed him into his mother's arms. Little Philip clung to Eliza.

"I'm Greta. I've been delighted to get to know your children." The young woman spoke with a strong voice.

Eliza started to thank her but was interrupted.

"Where is he?" Angel chimed in. "Why isn't my father on the ferry?"

Greta's face fell. "She's getting worse," she whispered to Eliza.

"Angel, my love, your father died. Remember?" Eliza said. Eliza hated that she had to remind her daughter of Hamilton's death. Each time she did so, she could almost see a piece of her daughter's soul chipping away. And she felt her own doing the same as well.

Angel's eyes locked with Eliza, as if she were trying to see some truth there. Her eyes filled with tears and she nodded, gazing away into the distance.

"Can we go fishing?" William said and pulled on Alexander. "I want to catch some fish!"

Alexander grinned as they walked along toward the house. "Calm down! Give me a chance to rest from the journey." Alexander ruffled William's hair.

Eliza couldn't help but smile, holding her little one with one arm and holding the hand of little Eliza with the other, surrounded by her children, walking toward her home. They passed the chicken yard, where one of her father's enslaved laborers worked. He looked up and smiled at Eliza. She smiled back, feeling a lump in her stomach. She didn't like that her father kept these laborers—neither had Hamilton. They had tried to gently talk him out of it many times to no avail. And now, with her father's age and health problems, Eliza thought to save her words. But she prayed that all of the laborers here would find freedom soon.

They walked around to the front of the house and entered the great hall with its marble floors. Floors Eliza had grown up running on, dancing on, and even once getting sick on after eating a bad berry. The home's natural light had been thwarted by the black crepe hanging over the front-facing windows. Light and shadow played across the black and white floors.

"Betsey."

Eliza turned toward the voice. Philip Schuyler stood there, frailer and smaller than she remembered, giving her a start. But when she fell into her father's arms it was as if no time had passed. He was still the great Philip Schuyler, the war hero and great statesmen. More than all of that, he was a father who always had the time for his Betsey. As she reveled in the embrace of her father, Eliza's emotions spun. She unraveled in his arms.

"Dear, dear, Betsey," he said over and over again.

★   ★   ★

After supper, the adults, along with Alexander, retired to the drawing room, where Eliza and Angelica told them about their adventure.

"I hate to think of you putting yourselves in danger," her father said when they were done. "But what else could you do?"

"Exactly, Father," Eliza said.

John Church harrumphed. "What does any of it matter now? The Treasury and all that business?"

Philip Schuyler glanced at his daughter and then back at John Church. "It matters to his memory. And now that's all we have left." His voice cracked.

"Indeed," Angelica said.

Eliza's ruminations tumbled out of her mouth. "I will live the rest of my life fighting for his memory, making sure his name and all he stood for are remembered well." She gazed at her children. "One of the most important causes to his heart were children with no parents. If we could, we would've adopted all of them." She smiled to herself as a way forward opened up in her mind and heart. "I want to give orphans a home."

"What do you mean?" Angelica said. "As in invite them into your home?"

"I've just started thinking about this, so I don't have all the details. But I warrant I'll work with the Widow Society to figure it all out. But no, I mean a building, an orphanage."

Everyone in the room was still.

Angelica sobbed and held her handkerchief to her breast. "How perfect."

Starting an orphanage would honor her Hamilton, himself an orphan who had taken in a few over the years. But it was merely one way for Eliza to move her story further. Now, she was the Widow Hamilton. But she was also more than that.

"You know I will help you all that I can," Philip said, lifting a glass to her. "To my wonderful daughter, with a heart of gold, and a mind to match. Always a dreamer."

Is that what she was? Eliza soaked in the warmth of her family around the table, holding their glasses up and toasting her. She was a dreamer, yes, but she worked those dreams into reality. She resolved to provide for her children, to be there for them in every way possible, and create her own legacy, separate from the long shadow of Alexander Hamilton. Finally, she saw a way forward. A swirl of emotions whipped though her—longing for her husband, love of her family, anger, regret, and, finally, pride.

Author's Note

Some writers of historical women are accused of giving their female characters a modern outlook. Eliza Hamilton, however, gave me the gift of being just that. From everything I've read about her, she was definitely a woman grounded in her time, but also a woman who was exposed to much more than most women. She soaked it all in, from the time she was a child to her death. It invariably affected her. When I read about her visiting people days after her husband's death, her character took root for me. So while she's gifted me with a modern sense of being slightly rebellious, her reasoning all goes back to the love of her husband and her family. She does not rebel for her own sake.

It's risky for a writer to take on such a beloved American character and take her in directions that are not quite historically accurate. But once the story took root in my mind, I had to write it.

History tells us that Eliza left town a few weeks after Hamilton's death. I needed to keep her there for the sake of the story. Of course, none of the events in the mystery part of my story are true. So I wanted to keep everything else as historically accurate as possible, including, as much as I could, Eliza's character.

It's true that when researching women's lives you have to research their husbands' lives as well to get a good picture. I know more about Alexander Hamilton than I wanted to. Recent research suggests he owned slaves, but my sources say he could never afford a slave. Yet, even as he was active in the anti-slave Manumission Society, and outspoken against the practice of slavery, he helped his wealthy relatives with brokering slaves. With those acts, he was certainly complicit.

But, for the purposes of my story, I touch on the issue briefly, though Eliza's eyes in 1804.

In regard to keeping the fabricated story as historically accurate as I could, once I took a tour of Hamilton's New York City, my story had to change a bit. The Grange is quite far from the city. So I had to figure out ways to get Eliza to stay in town, where she could investigate. Hence her stay with Alice and the women of Pearl Street House. Pearl Street is still thriving in the city, though now it's not as close to the shore, nor is Trinity, which also was on the bank of the North River, now known as the Hudson.

As far as we know, the Bavarian Illuminati was active in the U.S. briefly. There's not much information about it, so I fabricated the offshoot group included in this story.

All of the secondary characters are also fabricated. The only characters based on real people are Eliza and her family. It's been an honor to get to know them. History gives us hindsight, as we know that Eliza Hamilton did go on to make a difference, most especially in helping to start the Graham Windham Orphanage, which still functions today.

I think many modern women can relate to Eliza Hamilton in so many ways. I can't tell you how many fellow *Hamilton* the musical fans have said they wanted more of Eliza's story. I hope I have done her justice, though I know there's so much more to her.

—Mollie

ACKNOWLEDGMENTS

Oddly enough, the first person I want to thank is some-one who will probably never read this book: Lin-Manuel Miranda. His genius in writing *Hamilton*, the musical, inspired me in so many ways. Oh my goodness, what I wouldn't give to have coffee with him and pick his brain!

I found myself needing a realistic compass when it came to New York City. I'm familiar with today's city but was having a difficult time with historical NYC. Books and YouTube can only get you so far. I reached out to Jimmy Napoli of "Hamilton's New York" tours. We had a long conversation while he was on his way to St. Croix. I also spoke with Eva, his lovely and knowl-edgeable wife. Ultimately, I was given a private tour by the astute guide George. Thank you from the bottom of my heart. Learn-ing how small the city was then and seeing it with my own eyes made a huge difference to the story. As did realizing how far away the Grange was—but that they could still see the harbor from high on their hill in Harlem!

I'm very grateful to my friend Jen Brecht for a wonderful beta read of the manuscript. Also grateful to historical romance author and friend Joanna Bourne for helping me with the first few chap-ters. I'm also grateful for my friend India McIntire, who offered to give the book one last read before sending it off to my fabulous editor, Terri Bischoff. Another favorite editor, Martin Biro, gave this manuscript an expert read. As always, Martin, you challenge me and make me a better writer, for which I am grateful.

My agent, Jill Marsal, was unyielding in her belief in this book. Thanks so much, Jill, for not giving up while trying to sell the book during the worst of the Covid-19 pandemic.

Sometimes I think it takes a village for a writer to sit in front of the computer and tune out the world in order to write. I'm grateful to my understanding daughters, Emma and Tess, who have both become so independent and cool. I'd hang out with them, even if they weren't my daughters. I love you both very much.

—Mollie